Dear Reader,

We were excited when Guideposts asked us to write *Forgotten History* and *Hidden Treasures*, the two books that make up Chesapeake Antiques Mysteries. As a daughter-mother writing team (Pam is the daughter; Barbara is the mother), we have been happily collaborating for more than twenty years and continue to find it gratifying.

As a subject, the antiques world is a shared passion of ours. Barbara is an avid collector of stamps and postcards, and she has written about postcards for antiques publications and conducted a postcard auction for charity. Pam cherishes books passed down by her grandmother, who was a voracious reader. Our love of antiques made writing these two books a whole lot of fun! Both stories involve mysteries with elements from the past, which center around an antique. We enjoyed getting to use our knowledge to create page-turning plots.

We also both relished spending time with the inhabitants of Maple Landing: Miriam Maxwell, who moves back to the Chesapeake Bay village; Bess Watkins, her best friend from high school; retired admiral Samuel Bentley, Miriam's high school sweetheart; and Phoebe Watkins, Bess's slightly clumsy but computer-savvy granddaughter.

Take a trip to the bay area and make some new friends!

All the best,
Pam Hanson & Barbara Andrews

CHESAPEAKE ANTIQUES MYSTERIES

Forgotten History

PAM HANSON &
BARBARA ANDREWS

New York

Chesapeake Antiques Mysteries is a trademark of Guideposts.

Published by Guideposts Books & Inspirational Media
110 William Street
New York, New York 10038
Guideposts.org

Acknowledgments

Every attempt has been made to credit the sources of copyrighted material used in this book. If any such acknowledgment has been inadvertently omitted or miscredited, receipt of such information would be appreciated.

Cover and interior design by Müllerhaus
Cover by Bob Kayganich represented by Deborah Wolfe, Ltd.
Typeset by Aptara, Inc.

Printed and bound in the United States of America
10 9 8 7 6 5 4 3

Forgotten History

Chapter One

W hat on earth is this?" Miriam Maxwell asked herself as
she dusted a bizarre little figurine in her late sister's antiques shop. It was sitting between a Roseville water lily vase, easily
identified because their grandmother had had one similar to it—or
could it actually be the same one?—and a brightly colored teapot
by a famous English potter.

The little statue was made of garishly painted wood with seashell
eyes and feathers for hair. It had to have some value because Ruth
had priced it at six hundred dollar, but Miriam had no idea what it
was. She was beginning to feel that way about the entire store. The
deeper she delved into the stock, the more mystified she was by her
sister's reasons for buying what she did.

After a hard morning of trying to organize the shop she'd inherited in picturesque Maple Landing, Maryland, on the Chesapeake
Bay, Miriam was entertaining serious doubts about whether
she could run her sister's business. It had long been a dream of
hers to have a shop of her own, but it was a puzzle to her how

1

Ruth had made a success of the disorganized jumble in the old building.

For several weeks Miriam had been trying to ready the store for a mid-June reopening, but she was still at a loss to figure out her sister's business systems. The stock was a hodgepodge of anything and everything, and the second floor and the cellar were loaded with unsorted boxes and items not in the store inventory—not that Miriam could read many of her sister's scribbles in the ledger.

Their phone conversations in recent years hadn't been very informative, especially not where the antiques shop was concerned, and Ruth had always seemed too busy for the long heart-to-heart conversations of earlier times. One of Miriam's reasons for returning to her hometown was to regain the feeling of closeness she'd once had with her sister, but so far she was only bogged down by dust and confusion.

"At least I'm good at dusting," Miriam said out loud to bolster her resolve.

She moved her stepladder so she could reach the items on top of a display cabinet. A cobweb dangling from the ceiling brushed against her cheek, but she made short work of it with her feather duster. Thankfully she was wearing old jeans and an oversized plaid shirt with her hair covered by a red bandana. If the students who'd been in her high school business classes back in Indiana could see her now, they might not recognize her.

As she reached over to dust an old weather vane mounted on a wooden base, she was startled by the tinkle of a bell over the front door. Turning on the top step to look toward the door, she hoped it was someone interested in a job. She'd advertised in the local paper and put a large sign in the window, but so far no one had applied to be her shop assistant.

The man who entered had carefully styled white hair and was dressed in a finely tailored blazer, not what she'd expect to see on a candidate for her job.

"I'm sorry, we're not open yet," she said, brushing a silver lock of hair out of her eyes.

"Miriam? Miriam Davis?"

She looked into the pleasant face of a man with a neatly trimmed snowy-white beard, and could hardly believe her eyes.

"Samuel Bentley?"

"It's been a long time, Miriam, but I'd recognize you anywhere. What are you doing here?"

"Attempting to reopen my sister's antiques shop. She passed away this winter and left it to me, but I'm not sure I'm up to it."

"The girl I knew in high school could handle almost anything," he said.

Except your going away to the naval academy, she thought, remembering how they'd dated during their junior and senior years. Their separation became permanent when she went off to a teachers' college, but now the happy memories flooded back.

"Everything but seventh-hour biology," she said with a laugh. "It still creeps me out to remember the snake Mr. Van Hoff made us touch."

He laughed with her. "You must have washed your hands twenty times that day."

"It's been a long time," she said, starting to climb down but forgetting how dirty her feather duster had become. A big puff of dust caught her unaware, and she sneezed violently, nearly losing her balance on the ladder.

Samuel rushed over and steadied the ladder, saving her from a fall, and extended his hand to help her down. Grateful for his help but a tad embarrassed, she thanked him and brushed her hands off on the sides of her jeans.

"How long has it been?" he asked thoughtfully.

"More than forty years." She remembered he was only a few months older than she was. He'd turned sixty in March.

"I'm guessing your name isn't Davis anymore," he said, glancing at the wedding ring she still wore. "Have you and your husband lived here long?"

"It's Maxwell. Ray passed away nearly five years ago, but I just moved here."

"I'm sorry to hear about your husband," he said. "Do you have children?"

"A daughter and son-in-law in Indiana. They have two lovely twins, Becky and Abby. I debated with myself a long time whether to leave Terre Haute to take over Ruth's antiques shop."

"Are they planning to join you in Maple Landing?" Samuel leaned against the old country store counter that held the shop's cash register. His shoulders under his navy blazer were broader than she remembered, but he was still trim and fit.

"No, afraid not. In fact, my son-in-law's job will be taking them all to California soon."

"How long did you live in Indiana?" Samuel asked. It reminded her of the way he'd always shown interest in others.

"We settled in Terre Haute after our marriage. I taught high school business courses for more than thirty years, but I'm retired now—retired from teaching, anyway. I may have bitten off more than I can handle with this shop." She suddenly felt a little self-conscious telling him more than he'd asked. "What brings you to Maple Landing? Last I knew you were going to make a career in the navy."

"Admiral Samuel Bentley, USN, retired," he said with a self-deprecating grin. "I decided to leave the service when they assigned me to a desk in Norfolk. I'm on my own now—my wife passed away suddenly six years ago from an aneurysm, and my two sons are both in the military."

"You live in Maple Landing now?"

"I just moved here. In fact, I'm furnishing a house near the water. That's why I came to your shop. I'm in need of a desk."

"Any particular style?" Miriam asked, realizing Samuel was her first customer. Did she know enough about Ruth's furniture inventory to sell him what he wanted?

"My dad used to have a late-nineteenth-century oak rolltop. I sort of have that in mind, but I'm open to any good piece."

"I don't have a rolltop, but my sister must have liked desks. There are quite a few back here."

She led the way to the rear of the store where the furniture was on display, along with a collection of eccentric items like an ox yoke, an old dentist's sign, and a hand-woven Native American rug. They had to step over a child's wooden wagon and a rusty scooter to reach the desks, reminding Miriam of how badly she needed to hire someone to help organize everything.

One good thing Ruth had done was rewire the old building. Modern fluorescent light fixtures hung from the metal tiled ceiling, illuminating a large but somewhat jumbled selection of antique furniture.

Samuel followed her, squeezing past a Victorian love seat and a mid-nineteenth-century cherry dresser with handkerchief drawers on either side of the top. Miriam made a mental note to apply some beeswax to it before opening the store.

Obviously he wouldn't be interested in an early student's desk with a hole to hold an inkwell, and he passed by a mid-twentieth-century Danish teakwood piece. Her sister's stock was nothing if not eclectic.

"Now, this is nice," Samuel said, peering under and around a Queen Anne desk with inlaid mahogany. It was more table than desk, with only three small drawers across the front, but it was easily the most beautiful piece of furniture on display.

"I like the pad feet," Miriam said, admiring the characteristic legs, almost modern-looking in spite of being antique.

She wished she had the language to describe some of the beautiful things in the shop, but hopefully that would come as she continued to consult the many books in her sister's library at home. In addition to her shop, Ruth had also left her the post-Victorian home where they'd grown up, but Miriam had been too overwhelmed with settling the estate and her new responsibilities to do much studying. Like the shop, the old house was a storehouse of items her sister must have intended to sell eventually. Miriam had been hard-pressed to find room for her own possessions in the family home.

"It isn't what I had in mind, but this should work better than a rolltop. I work on a laptop computer, but I need a lot of room to spread out my research materials," Samuel said, pulling out one of the three drawers along the top. "Ah, I like the pullout trays on either side. More space to pile things," he said. He opened another drawer, taking it out to examine it. "Dovetail construction. I don't have any doubts about its authenticity."

Miriam worried she wasn't much of a salesperson. She didn't have a clue what to say to close the deal, but the way he was examining it, he seemed to be selling himself on the lovely old desk.

She watched as he tried to open a third drawer, but it wouldn't budge.

"*Hmm*. Odd, the other two worked fine," he said, bending to examine the stuck drawer.

"I should have a carpenter look at it," Miriam said, concerned. Most of the items on display were in good condition.

"I don't think it's a major problem. How long would you say the top is?" Samuel didn't wait for an answer as he used his hands to gauge the length. "Fifty-two, maybe fifty-four inches."

"You must plan to do a lot of work," Miriam said for lack of anything else to say.

Turning toward her, he smiled broadly. "Would you believe the guy who struggled in a high school lit class is planning to write a book?"

"Struggled and got an A minus, the only class where you didn't get a straight A," she teased, remembering what an outstanding student he'd been. "What kind of book?"

"A history of America's navy," he said. "It's something I've always wanted to do, and now's my chance. That's part of the reason I retired, although it was time to try something different."

"That's wonderful!" she said, genuinely enthused. "I can't imagine such a big undertaking."

Or maybe she could. Her life would be much easier now if organizing objects was as uncomplicated as organizing thoughts. She was beginning to realize what an overwhelming jumble her sister had created. Although Miriam loved Ruth and missed her, she knew Ruth was much better at finding odd and unusual things than she was at arranging them to sell.

"It's in great shape except for the drawer and the scratch on this side," Samuel said, still examining the desk from all angles. "I would say it's the original finish."

"Oh my!" Miriam bent to see the defect he'd noticed. "I recognize this scratch. This desk was in my family for generations. We always thought some naughty child tried to scratch an initial on the side. I can't believe I forgot about it."

"Maybe it's not something you want to sell," Samuel said. "I don't want to deprive you of a family heirloom."

"No, it's definitely for sale. The house is so crowded with all my furnishings and everything Ruth left that I can't possibly find a spot for the desk."

Glancing at the price tag neatly tied to one drawer handle, she wondered if it was really worth as much as Ruth had been asking. If there was one thing Miriam had learned about the antiques business from her sister, it was that everything was negotiable.

She was debating what kind of discount to give Samuel to compensate for the stuck drawer and the scratch when he took the initiative.

"I'll take it. How do you want me to make out the check?"

"To Ruthie's Antiques. I'm keeping her name on the shop as a way to honor her memory. But I can do a little better on the price since there is some damage."

He waved a hand. "It's minor. The price is more than fair." He followed her to the counter and wrote out the check. "I was so taken aback by seeing you again, I didn't even ask about your sister. I'm really sorry you lost her. She was considerably older than you, wasn't she?"

"Ten years older. In fact, she was almost a substitute mother for me after our mother died. She was on a buying trip in Pennsylvania when she suffered a fatal heart attack—although I'm not sure why she needed to find more stock. You wouldn't believe how jammed full the cellar and second floor are here. But she died doing what she loved best: picking for antiques."

"I take it she didn't have children since she left the shop to you," he said.

"Sadly, no. After her husband died, she put all her energy into finding and selling antiques. I gave a lot of thought to auctioning all her stock and the contents of the house and selling the buildings, but I couldn't bring myself to do it. I feel closer to her surrounded by the old things she loved. I just have to figure out if I'm up to running the shop. So far, I haven't made a very good start."

"If I know you, you'll have everything in tip-top shape in no time," he said. "You always were a great organizer."

"There's a big difference between being chairperson of the senior prom and this chaos," she said, gesturing at the large but overcrowded space around her. "But I haven't asked about your family. Do you have grandchildren?"

"Yes, my son Colin has two, Katie and Kevin. Scott is the maverick in the family—he joined the marines instead of following in his father's footsteps. Unfortunately I don't see them as much as I'd like, but now I have the freedom to travel and visit them." His voice reflected his pride in his offspring.

Although Samuel didn't seem in any hurry, Miriam took his check and tried to be professional about the sale.

"I don't have any employees yet, so I'll arrange for a moving company to deliver your desk," she said. "If you'll just give me your address—oh, I guess it's here on the check."

"You don't need to bother. My cousin still lives in Maple Landing, and he owns a trailer to haul his motorcycle. I'm sure he won't mind helping me with the desk."

"That's very nice of you. I haven't worked out delivery details yet. Ruth owned a big van, but I haven't had enough nerve to try driving it yet. It's about three times as long as my car, and I can't imagine parallel parking with it."

"Fortunately, parking isn't a big problem in Maple Landing," Samuel chuckled. He took her hand between both of his. "Miriam. It's nice to have you here. I hope we'll see more of each other."

"That would be nice," she said a bit awkwardly, not sure how she felt about seeing her high school boyfriend as a retired admiral. "Thank you for buying the desk. I'm glad it's going to a good home."

"I'll certainly appreciate having it," he said sincerely. "Good luck with getting everything shipshape in your shop. If there's anything I can do, let me know."

"Not unless you're looking for a job," she teased. "I haven't had any success finding a sales assistant yet."

"I'll ask my cousin whether he knows anyone, although his kids have left the nest. I'll see you again."

Miriam watched him leave, feeling nostalgic about the times they'd shared when they were young.

Could she make a go of living in Maple Landing and running her sister's business? Maybe she was too old to start a new life. She could retire and enjoy her family, but would she be satisfied with her garden, her bridge friends, and her church work? As fulfilling as her life had been, she still faced long days alone in Terre Haute now that her daughter's family was planning to move to California. Was this a second chance, or a bad mistake? Only time would tell.

First she had to solve the puzzle of Ruth's jumbled way of doing business.

Chapter Two

Dusting had seemed like a good way to learn the stock in the shop, but Miriam tossed aside the feather duster after Samuel left. Obviously she'd concentrated too much on the tremendous number of small items and neglected to pay attention to the furniture and large pieces. How could she have failed to notice that desk was a family heirloom? It didn't change her willingness to sell it, but she was glad it was going to someone she knew.

She had yet to find a complete inventory of everything in the great hoard of merchandise. After much searching, she had found a ledger listing inventory, but fewer than half the items on display were included in it. Did that mean they were also family heirlooms, like the desk, or had her sister been too busy or too careless to record them? Ruth had been a tireless buyer, but where were the receipts from her purchases?

It didn't make sense. After their mother's death, Ruth had undertaken many household responsibilities. Their father was a pharmaceutical rep and traveled extensively, but he carefully oversaw the funds he gave her to run the house. Miriam was sure her sister had handled money well, always balancing her checkbook and accounting for expenses. As far as Miriam knew, there'd never been any friction with her husband, Al, over financial matters either. Why had she run her business in such a haphazard way?

Miriam went to the back of the store, determined to make the furniture section more accessible. It would be awful if a customer stumbled over a rolled carpet or the violin case—which might or might not contain an instrument of value—and sued. Samuel would have a hard time removing the desk until she brought some order to the jam-packed area, so she set out to clear a path. But after another hour of work she was famished.

To save time, she'd packed a sack lunch to eat at the worktable in the office at the rear of the shop. Before she could finish her sandwich, someone knocked on the front door she'd locked while she ate. Hurrying to the front, Miriam's first thought was that Samuel might have returned to arrange for the moving of the desk.

Instead, she saw a woman waiting outside. When she pointed toward the Help Wanted sign in the window, Miriam opened the door and invited her to come in.

"I'm Mrs. Clark. I'm interested in the position you've advertised," the woman said in a cultured English accent.

"Come back to my office, and we'll talk," Miriam said, immediately impressed by the woman's neat navy pantsuit and sensible low-heeled shoes. Her hair was cut short with straight bangs, and what makeup she wore was applied sparingly.

Maybe her luck had turned. She'd sold her first piece to an old friend, and this woman looked eminently employable. Miriam loved her accent, a reminder of her family's English heritage.

"I'm sorry for the clutter," Miriam said, leading Mrs. Clark to the office. "I just inherited the business from my sister, and there hasn't been time to put everything in order."

"Your sister had quite an eye for antiques and collectibles. That little figure from New Guinea is rather special." Mrs. Clark stopped in front of the bizarre carved piece that had puzzled Miriam earlier.

"I wasn't sure of its origin," Miriam admitted. "You must really know primitive art."

"I worked in a small private museum in East Anglia before my husband and I came to this country. I've always had a knack for identifying objects."

Miriam invited Mrs. Clark to sit when they reached the office. She was awestruck by the Englishwoman's qualifications. What could she ask someone who seemed to know more than she did?

"I probably can't pay you what your qualifications deserve," Miriam said.

The woman waved a hand languidly. "Salary isn't my main consideration. I'd just like to get out in the community and do something worthwhile," Mrs. Clark said, sitting calmly with her hands folded in her lap.

Miriam couldn't believe the perfect person for the job might be sitting across from her. Would she be willing to do some of the cleaning and rearranging the shop needed? Her tactful question brought just the answer she'd hoped to get.

"You'll find I'm willing to do what the position requires," Mrs. Clark said in her pleasing accent.

"This is a full-time position," Miriam explained. "We won't open until ten, but you would need to be here by nine."

"Oh, I'm afraid I couldn't do that." Mrs. Clark sounded apologetic but firm. "My husband likes his breakfast promptly at eight thirty, then I have to make a different one for my elderly mother. She lives with us, and I rarely have her settled in for the day before eleven."

"What about Saturday? Do you have the same schedule on the weekend?" Miriam knew it was likely to be her biggest sales day, especially in the summer, and she might have to leave an employee in charge while she attended shows or auctions. She could be flexible on the hours if she had dependable help on Saturdays.

"My husband wouldn't hear of me working on his day off."

"When can you work?" Miriam was frustrated, but possibly she could use Mrs. Clark part-time to help identify and price the countless items on the second floor.

"Wednesday afternoon is good for me, and some weeks I can manage Monday and Friday after 2:00 PM."

"I'm sorry. You seem well qualified, but I need a person who's able to work more hours," Miriam said.

"Your sign didn't indicate it's a full-time position," Mrs. Clark said, sounding churlish. "Given the location of the shop and the size of the town, I don't expect you'll be doing much business."

Thank you for the vote of no confidence, Miriam thought as she ushered the Englishwoman to the front door. When Mrs. Clark drove away in a green Mercedes, Miriam went outside and tried to see the front of the shop as a stranger might. Ruth had painted the old brick facade white, but the paint was flaking away in spots. Her sister had always said collectors preferred to explore shops that didn't look too fancy. If an antiques store looked shabby, they expected to find better bargains inside.

Unsure of that theory, Miriam decided to hire a painter to spruce up the exterior.

"Are you the new owner?" A red-haired woman in a purple-and-white striped uniform rushed across the street just as Miriam was going inside. "Is your job still open?"

"It is," Miriam said, surprised to have another person interested so soon after the first.

"I'm Karen Decker. My sister and I own the Candy Corner Shoppe." She gestured at a store half a block down from where they stood. "I can't work with her another day. I want to apply for your job. That will show Jackie she can't boss me around."

At a loss on how to react, Miriam took a deep breath and invited Karen into the store. She was the exact opposite of cool, calm Mrs. Clark. Her cheeks were flaming pink with anger, and she hardly seemed to notice the antiques packed into the display room.

"Maybe you'd like to think this over a little while," Miriam said, using the rational voice she'd used when a student in one of her classes was upset. Karen Decker was at least twenty years beyond high school age, but her anger was unsettling.

"No, our partnership is over. She'll have to find a way to buy me out. That's all there is to it." Karen tried to untie her little purple apron but only succeeded in knotting it more tightly around her waist.

"Why don't you come back to the office?" Miriam asked. "I have a small fridge with some bottled tea and water. We can talk there."

The younger woman followed her to the rear without looking at any of the items in the shop.

"Do you have any experience with antiques or collectibles?" Miriam asked when Karen had cooled off and calmed down.

"If I can sell Jackie's horrible green tea fudge, I can sell anything," she said, finishing a bottle of mineral water in several big gulps.

"There's a bit more to it than that," Miriam said, trying to be tactful. "I'm trying to reorganize the whole store. Mostly I need someone who doesn't mind hard work and is willing to learn about what we have. I'm new at this, so we'd be learning together."

The bell over the door chimed, and a woman who could only be Karen's sister charged into the store.

"Karen Decker, you come back to work right now," the newcomer said, hurrying to the back. "I had to lock the store to come look for you."

There was no mistaking their relationship, though Jackie was taller, heavier, and louder.

"I'm not going to make those dreadful anise candies, no matter what you say," Karen said, folding her arms across her chest.

"Okay, I understand. You don't like them, but our customers do."

"One customer! Old Jake Jordan doesn't know candy from turnips. He only comes into the store because you flirt with him."

"Flirt! He's old enough to be our grandfather." Jackie seemed to notice Miriam for the first time. "I'm sorry to bring our little dispute to your store. I'm sorry about Ruth too. She was a swell person."

"Yes, she was," Miriam said. "Sisters have a relationship like no other. I miss her very much."

Miriam sighed with relief as the Decker sisters resolved their differences and left. If she'd known how complicated her life would become, would she have left Indiana? She wanted to know her sister better than she had in recent years, but was running her antiques shop the way to do it?

She missed her family, she regretted taking early retirement from teaching, and she wasn't sure she could make a success of her second career. The only bright spot in her day had been seeing Samuel Bentley again. He'd changed, of course, but he still had the same low, mellow voice and lovely smile she remembered. More importantly, he was as friendly and outgoing as the high school boy she'd adored. When they went their separate ways after graduation, she'd lost an important part of her life. She never cared deeply for another man until she met her beloved Ray. He'd been taken from her much too soon, though he lived on in her heart.

What would Ray think of her plan to run Ruthie's Antiques? He might be surprised by her decision to leave Lisa and her family, but he would applaud her determination to start a new life for herself.

She and Samuel had been much too young to plan a future together. Fortunately they'd both found others, and the past was past. She had to concentrate on her future.

Chapter Three

On Sunday morning Miriam found great satisfaction in going to the church she'd attended as a girl. Old Mariners was the oldest place of worship in Maple Landing and still had a thriving membership.

As she walked up to the entrance of the Gothic Revival church, bells in the tower summoned people to worship. They were a warm memory from her childhood and a reminder of the original mission of the church: to provide spiritual support for the men who took their living from the sea. She would never forget the mournful ringing when a fisherman was lost at sea, the bells marking each year of his life, but this morning they broke the morning silence with a welcoming peal.

Many years had passed since she last sat here with Ruth and her father, fascinated by her favorite stained-glass window of Jesus calling the fishermen to follow Him. This morning the bright June sun was directly behind it, brilliantly illuminating the scene. Behind her the magnificent pipe organ in the balcony played a familiar hymn, and Miriam closed her eyes and drew in a deep breath as she savored the peace and presence of God that she sensed there. She'd been lonely for her family since moving back to Maple Landing, but this morning she felt less alone as part of a worshipping congregation.

"Good morning, Miriam. How are things going at Ruth's shop?" the minister asked at the door as people filed out. The Reverend Paul Blackhurst greeted everyone at the service by first name. Combined with his shock of unruly salt-and-pepper hair and infectious smile, his friendliness made her feel even more at home.

"It's a challenge," she admitted.

"Yes, I've been there a few times myself. Ruth certainly had a gift for amassing antiques." He gave her hand a firm squeeze. "She's greatly missed by everyone who knew her."

Miriam carried the warmth of his comments down to the pavement in front of the church, but then her thoughts were interrupted by a voice calling out to her.

"Miriam, Miriam Maxwell!"

Turning to see who was calling, Miriam recognized one of her best high school chums, Bess Watkins. They had long been Christmas-card friends, but it still took a moment to connect the woman coming toward Miriam to the vivacious cheerleader and special confidante she'd once known so well.

"I heard you were back," Bess said, hurrying up and engulfing Miriam in a hug. "Charlie and I have been on vacation, our first in ages. We went to Florida, just the two of us, and had a ball. How are you? I'm so sorry about your sister. I wanted to go to the funeral, but I had to be in Baltimore to help settle my aunt in an assisted living facility."

It was so like Bess to spill out news without taking a breath that Miriam couldn't help grinning at her.

"It's so good to see you," Miriam said, feeling the years slip away as she remembered all the good times they'd shared.

"There's a lot more of me to see," Bess joked self-consciously. It was true her curves were well-padded now, but her round, smiling face was as pretty as ever. She wore her hair in a halo of curls, not unlike the hairstyle of her youth, only now blonde and gray were equally mixed.

"Can you come for lunch? Charlie and Randy, our son, went out on his boat—the rascals. They left Janice and me to take care of the inn—Janice is our daughter-in-law. The reason we could take a vacation from running our B and B is because Randy and his wife are gradually taking over the management, with the dubious help of our granddaughter, Phoebe. I love her to pieces, but she can be a trial. The day she decides what to do with her life is the day the rest of the family will sigh with relief."

Miriam had kept up with Bess and her family through her lengthy Christmas letters, but she was thoroughly entertained by her friend's update. It was almost as though they'd just said good-bye yesterday.

"I'd love to have lunch with you," Miriam said. "Why not come to my place? I made chicken, grape, and walnut salad as a Sunday treat for myself, but there's way too much for just me. I'm afraid I still haven't gotten the knack of cooking for one."

"It's just not fair!" Bess blurted, nearly startling Miriam. She sounded on the verge of tears. "First, your mother dies when you're an adolescent, your father dies when you're still in college, then you lose your husband in the prime of life. And now your sister passed away so suddenly."

Miriam patted Bess's hand. "I do miss Ray and Ruth terribly, but I feel so fortunate to have Lisa, my daughter. Her husband, Brent, is a wonderful man, and, of course, I adore their twins, Becky and Abby. It was a hard decision to move here," Miriam admitted. "But when I learned Ruth had left me her business, it was a challenge I couldn't resist. I want to make a success of it as a way to honor her memory."

"You were so close when you were growing up," Bess said.

"Yes, I was fortunate she always had time for my problems even though she was so much older than I am," Miriam agreed.

"Unlike my little brother! He dedicated his life to getting into trouble."

"Where is he now?" Miriam guided her friend onto the lawn because they were blocking the flow of people leaving the church.

"Alaska. He's working on a fishing boat to save up enough to retire in Costa Rica—but that could change."

"He always was adventurous," Miriam recalled. "Let's go to Ruth's—I mean, my house. I still have a hard time thinking of it as mine even though I grew up there. Did you walk to church?"

"No, I was running late, so I drove. You know me, 'a day late and a dollar short,' my father used to say. Can you believe I married a man who arranges the tools in his workshop in alphabetical order?"

Miriam laughed with her old friend, remembering how much fun they used to have together even though Bess had been a cheerleader and Miriam a flute player in the band. But their friendship had started in the third grade and never grew stale. Bess had married the football quarterback, and for many years they'd run the Apple Street Inn, the town's nicest bed-and-breakfast, according to Ruth.

"Anyway," Bess said, digging into a large tapestry bag, "yes, I'd love to come to your house for lunch. Let me call Janice on my cell."

It never took long to get anyplace in Maple Landing, so in a matter of minutes Miriam had her dear friend seated at the scrubbed oak table in the kitchen.

"Fortunately Ruth's slapdash ways didn't extend to the kitchen," Miriam said with a smile. "The house is almost as crowded as the shop, but she did keep this room tidy."

"I went to her store a few times," Bess said. "It was … cluttered."

"It's a disaster!" Miriam was glad to be able to vent with her longtime friend. "She accumulated more items than she could process and sell. I'm having a hard time understanding why. It's especially puzzling that I can't find a complete inventory. She must have kept one to pay her taxes, but it's nowhere obvious. It's almost as if she were hiding something. That doesn't make sense either."

"At least she had a lovely kitchen," Bess said. "I like the blue-and-white theme. I wouldn't have thought of painting the cupboards that shade of blue, almost cobalt, but the wallpaper was an inspired choice. It's so cute, with all those Dutch people in wooden shoes standing by windmills."

"Ruth had a gift for decorating. Her artistic eye helped her choose some lovely items for the shop. The trouble is, she bought much too much. I'm at my wit's end, trying to organize everything." Miriam brought a bowl of chicken salad to the table. "I hope you like croissants."

"What don't I like?" Bess joked. "I'm the exact opposite of a picky eater."

While Miriam warmed the pastries in the oven, she sat at the table with her old friend, delighted to have her company. "Tell me about your bed-and-breakfast."

"We bought the old Webster house and did most of the renovations ourselves. You should've seen me installing drywall and cementing floor tiles. It was not my finest hour! Fortunately Charlie is a born handyman. In fact, it was quite a few years before he could give up his full-time job in construction to help run the inn. Now we're both happy to turn the management over to Randy and Janice."

Miriam went to the oven and took out the pan of crusty croissants, sliding them into a basket lined with a blue-checkered linen napkin. "Do you like iced tea? I don't remember you as a tea drinker."

"I am since I learned there are no calories in tea," Bess said with a chuckle. "So, enough about me. How are things going at the shop?"

"I'm overwhelmed," Miriam admitted. "I've advertised for a shop assistant and put a sign in the window, but so far the best applicant only wanted to work about two hours a week. I really could use a full-time employee. They don't even need to know about antiques. Anyone who can operate a cash register and help with the volume of cleaning would be welcome."

"I'm trying hard not to micromanage my daughter-in-law," Bess said thoughtfully. "Charlie said I needed to find other things to do, but it's hard after running the inn for so many years. Maybe I could give you a hand until you find someone more qualified."

"Are you serious? If you are, I'll put you on the payroll immediately. I'd be grateful for any hours you can spare," Miriam said, forgetting about the tempting chicken salad in front of her.

"No, absolutely not. You can't pay me. I mean, what are friends for? I would love to get into all the drawers and cubbyholes in the shop and find the treasures," Bess insisted.

"There are more than little hidey-holes," Miriam said. "The second floor and the basement are full of things Ruth never had time to sort and put on display. And she got way behind on cleaning and dusting, not to mention mopping and scrubbing. It won't be a fun job, at least not until the hard work is done. I was thinking of having a grand reopening when I get everything cleaned up and sorted, but it's not going very fast."

"We owned the bed-and-breakfast for ten years before I had any help cleaning and cooking. In peak season that meant taking care of eight guest rooms and the carriage house in back. Some guests are lovely—you hardly know anyone used their rooms. Others are not." Bess took a generous helping of the salad and spread raspberry jam on a croissant. "That's how I kept my girlish figure—or what's left of it. If I don't find something active to do, I'm afraid I'll end up a blimp. But the real reason I'd like to help is to enjoy your company. We did have fun together when we were young, didn't we?"

"Yes, we certainly did," Miriam agreed. "And you're more than welcome to help out whenever you like. Just having you in the shop would be delightful, but I still need to hire someone to help with all the work. Maybe a younger person would be best. Ruth had an employee, but she retired after Ruth passed away. I don't imagine she could do any lifting or heavy cleaning."

"I know someone—if you're really desperate," Bess said hesitantly.

"Oh, I definitely am!" Miriam couldn't be more emphatic about that.

"My granddaughter, Phoebe, is a hard worker, but, well, she is a little flighty. More than a little sometimes."

"Isn't she working at your inn?" Miriam asked.

"Yes, but sometimes she drives her parents nuts. They want her to go to college—she's only nineteen—but she doesn't have a clue what she wants to do. Maybe it would be good for her and for them if she worked someplace else. But I'm not sure I should foist her off on you," Bess said doubtfully.

"You wouldn't be foisting her off! You'd be doing me a huge favor. I don't know how your granddaughter could be anything but a delight to have in the store. I'm desperate for help. Last week I was almost ready to lock the door for good. Of course, I can't give up that easily, not after I sold my house and moved here."

"If you're sure…" Bess sounded doubtful.

"I am!"

"Maybe you could hire her on a trial basis. That way if she doesn't work out, you can let her go without making a big deal of it. Yes, I think that might work."

"If you think so," Miriam said, "although I'm willing to take her on without that."

"Of course, I'll have to ask Phoebe if she's interested. She does have her own ideas about things. She's tried several other jobs and disliked them, one as a waitress and another as a nanny. I don't blame her, though. The restaurant manager wanted her to work all the slow times when there were no tips, and the children's mother expected her to do all the housekeeping and laundry besides watching three preschool children. Neither was a good introduction to the work world."

"I should say not!" Miriam said with a light laugh. "Maybe Ruthie's Antiques won't seem so bad."

"I'll have her come talk to you tomorrow if she's interested," Bess promised. "Needless to say, I adore her. I hope the two of you get along well. Who knows, maybe she'll like the antiques business."

"We'll be learning it together," Miriam said. "I can promise you that."

"I love garage sales and auctions," Bess said. "We furnished much of the inn that way and saved a lot of money. Maybe it runs in the family."

"If she has your charming personality, I'll be more than satisfied." Miriam told her.

After Bess left, Miriam felt more relaxed than she had since the movers unloaded her furniture and possessions. Part of her good mood came from reconnecting with an old friend, but if Phoebe Watkins worked out, that was one big problem solved.

Still, as Miriam reflected on her conversation with Bess, she couldn't help but hope Bess was exaggerating her granddaughter's flighty tendencies.

Chapter Four

Was there anyplace more pleasant than the Chesapeake Bay on a sunny June morning? Miriam took a detour on her walk to the shop Monday so she could enjoy the tranquility of the water. Halfway between the Susquehanna River and the Atlantic mouth of the bay, Maple Landing was a historic seaport that still provided the bounty of the sea to Washington, DC, Baltimore, and other large urban cities.

Now, of course, the town was a favorite destination for tourists, and even this early in the day she spotted the graceful white sails of several yachts on the shimmering blue water.

Turning toward the business district, she walked through a neighborhood with neatly manicured lawns and massive trees that had presided over hundreds of years of history. The houses represented the passing of time in the historic town, a mix of Colonial, federal, Victorian, and post-Victorian, much older than the mid-twentieth-century homes in her Terre Haute neighborhood. She felt as though she'd stepped back into the past, both her own and the nation's.

As much as she enjoyed her walk, it was a reminder of her own dilemma: Could she make a success of a second career? Had it been a mistake to sell her home and try to follow in her sister's footsteps?

At least she was looking forward to seeing more of Bess and possibly hiring her granddaughter. Maybe the shop wouldn't seem so overwhelming when she had someone to help—and keep her company.

After unlocking the door, she pulled up the shade. Although she wasn't officially open, she was ready to start selling if anyone dropped in. Samuel had boosted her confidence, although she didn't believe many customers would be so easy to please.

She went to the furniture section, where more items needed to be cleared before Samuel could move the desk. An adorable wicker doll's carriage caught her eye, just what she needed to display an adorable teddy bear and a well-loved rag doll in a calico dress. Before she could extricate it, the bell on the front door chimed.

"Good morning!" her first customer called out. "Hope we're not too early."

"Samuel, I was just trying to clear a path to the desk," Miriam said, hurrying to greet him.

Samuel gestured to the man standing next to him. "This is my cousin, Bill Bentley."

"I think we must have crossed paths back in the day," Samuel's husky, clean-shaven cousin said.

"Yes, I think I remember. You were a few years behind us in school," Miriam said, searching her memory. "It's nice of you to help move the desk. I'm afraid there are still some things in the way."

"No problem," Bill said.

"I've been researching online for ways to open a stuck drawer," Samuel said, making his way to the desk. "If worse comes to worst, I'll have to remove the back, but I'm going to try running a dehumidifier first. The wood may be swollen from the humidity. What's unusual is that only one of the three is stuck. If I can get a small opening, I can use a thin tool to see if something inside the drawer is causing the problem."

Miriam smiled, remembering how a younger Samuel had methodically approached problems. Certainly that talent had helped his rise to admiral in the navy. She moved the little doll buggy and stood out of the way while the two men hoisted the desk and made easy work of maneuvering it free of the surrounding furniture. They found a clear spot between two rows of merchandise and set it down for a minute.

"You can take it out the back if that's easier," she said. "There's a double door for large things."

"Just as easy to go out the front," Bill said. "My trailer's out there."

"I hope you enjoy it," Miriam said as they carried out the desk. As happy as she was to have Samuel own it, she felt nostalgic about the family heirloom. Ruth had always treasured the things handed down from their ancestors, so it was surprising she'd brought the desk to the store to sell.

Before she could give this puzzle more thought, the door opened again. Bess breezed in, dressed in faded pink capri pants and a big green plaid shirt that might once have been her husband's. She looked ready to tackle any kind of work, no matter how dusty, and Miriam was reminded of her friend's willingness to try anything at least once. They'd had many fun times together—and some that were better forgotten, like the time they'd taken care of a local farmer's pig while he went to his daughter's wedding in South Carolina. Instead of the cute little piglet they'd expected, they'd had to pig-sit a huge sow with a sour disposition.

"You look happy this morning," Bess said.

Miriam laughed. "I was thinking of the time we took care of the Abernathy pig."

"Don't remind me! What on earth made you think of that?" Bess asked.

"You look ready for some heavy cleaning," Miriam said. "I can't ask you to get down and dirty."

"You won't have to. That's work for the young, so I brought Phoebe with me." Bess looked behind her as though expecting her granddaughter to be there. "Well, I almost brought her. She stopped off for a lemonade at Salty Sam's. You know, it used to be Harold's Hot Dogs."

"I hope she's not reluctant to take the job," Miriam said. "I really need help. I didn't expect it to be so hard to find someone."

"There are lots of jobs in the summer," Bess said. "Once the tourists go home after Labor Day, it will be different. Here she is."

A willowy young woman in faded and patched jeans strolled into the store, bearing a large paper cup. Phoebe Watkins had her grandfather Charlie's reddish-blond hair and Bess's clear blue eyes, but she was at least six inches taller than her grandmother. She moved with casual grace in a crinkle-cloth lavender tunic, but the effect was somewhat spoiled when she tripped on the floor mat and her drink sloshed over the edge of the container.

"Phoebe! You didn't get a cover on your drink?" Bess rushed over to blot up the spill with some tissues from her bag.

"I'm sorry. I didn't want to use plastic. It never biodegrades, you know. There are places where waste from the sea has ruined beaches."

She sounded so earnest and concerned Miriam had to smile. Phoebe seemed to have a sweet disposition like her grandmother, but was she a good prospect for the job? Her doubt grew when Phoebe backed up and tripped on the mat a second time.

"I'd better replace that with something that will lie flatter," Miriam said, although she had walked across it many times without any problem.

"In case you haven't guessed, this is my Phoebe," Bess said with a mixture of pride and hesitation. "She said your job sounded interesting."

"I like the idea of recycling old stuff," Phoebe said earnestly. "Imagine what a great magazine rack that baby bed would make." She walked over to the Colonial-era cradle and rocked it experimentally.

"Careful, dear," her grandmother cautioned. "Some of the things here are quite valuable. You have to be gentle with them."

Torn between amusement and concern, Miriam watched as Phoebe picked up a Dresden figurine, one of the more expensive smalls—as Miriam had learned they were called—in the shop.

"This is cute," she said, picking up a Royal Doulton character mug. "It reminds me of Great-uncle Horace."

"It's actually Rip Van Winkle," Miriam said, a little concerned about the safety of her ceramics as Phoebe picked up one after another. At least she showed an interest in the items for sale.

"It's probably better not to handle the merchandise," Bess said in a firm but kind voice. "You wouldn't want to break anything."

To her credit, Phoebe didn't seem to resent her grandmother's admonition. She backed away from the shelf of breakables as though something there could bite her.

"Do you sell online, Mrs. Maxwell?" Phoebe asked.

"Not yet, but I wouldn't rule it out," Miriam said. "Why don't you come back to the office and we can talk?"

"All right," Phoebe said in an agreeable tone.

Apparently Bess's granddaughter didn't walk in straight lines. She wandered over to the cabinet with the grotesque little figurine Mrs. Clark had identified as valuable folk art coming from New Guinea.

"Poor little thing looks like he has a tummy ache," Phoebe said. "Can't you just see a medicine man carving away at him while a patient waited?"

"Mrs. Maxwell is waiting," Bess prompted.

"It's fine," Miriam assured her. "A big part of the job will be learning the stock. I have a lot of that to do myself."

"Wow!" Phoebe said, picking up the New Guinea figure for a better look. "I've never found shells like the ones in his eyes on our beach."

"Phoebe has a shell collection. She started it when she was little," Bess said.

"I like to look at them and imagine where they came from," Phoebe said dreamily.

"Let's go talk in the office," Miriam repeated. She nodded at Bess to show her the situation was under control, telling herself it would be good to have an employee who was interested in the items in the shop.

"Oh, you have books," Phoebe said as Miriam led the way to the rear. "I always thought it would be so special to have a bookstore. I must have a hundred Nancy Drew mysteries. Mom keeps suggesting I donate some to the library, but they're so cool."

"You enjoy reading?" Miriam asked, glad to find common ground with her old friend's granddaughter.

"I've never seen such an avid reader," Bess said, obviously trying to show Phoebe in a good light.

The young woman nodded and crossed to the other side of the store, stumbling over a Victorian piano stool with a faded green velvet seat. "Oh, sorry."

"Did you forget to put your contacts in this morning?" Bess asked.

"Yes, but I have my glasses." Phoebe started digging in a tapestry shoulder bag with half of one side unfinished. She pulled out a pair of red frames without a case and propped them on her nose.

"They're left from Phoebe's crimson phase," Bess murmured to Miriam. "She wanted to prove a red-haired woman could wear red."

Smiling to herself, Miriam decided to give Phoebe a chance as her assistant. She wasn't going to be put off by the unfinished tapestry or the garish glasses. From her teaching experiences, she'd learned to work with all manner of young people. It was good that Phoebe was curious about the items around her.

"I'll just look around while you two talk," Bess said when her granddaughter had finally reached the office. "Charlie says it's time to sell, not buy, but I'm not going to give up my collection of antique buttons. Some date back to Colonial times. I think I saw a card with silver buttons sewn on. I'll just have a look."

"Now, Phoebe," Miriam said when they were seated beside the oak schoolteacher's desk Ruth had used for book work, "would you be able to work full-time for me, especially Saturdays? I'd give you another day off when you were needed on the weekend."

"I'll work anytime as long as I don't have to make another bed," Phoebe promised emphatically. "I don't know what possessed my grandparents to become innkeepers."

Miriam didn't try to explain what a great opportunity it had been for an energetic young couple to start a business. Bess and Charlie probably seemed ancient to their granddaughter. She remembered one of her darling twin granddaughters, Becky, telling a friend that her grandma was really, really old.

Instead she went over the wages, the hours, and the responsibilities. It felt a bit strange putting into practice things she'd only taught in her high school classes, but she gave Phoebe credit for being a good listener.

"Would you like the job?" Since Phoebe was the only candidate Miriam had for the position, there was no reason to delay the decision, not that she would turn down her old friend's granddaughter.

They went back to the display area after Phoebe accepted the job. Bess was pacing, certainly more nervous about the interview than her granddaughter had been.

"I think this is going to work out just fine," Miriam said with a smile.

Bess sighed with relief. "Where do we begin, boss?"

"In the furniture area, I think," Miriam said. If—when—she sold more furniture, she wanted the buyer to be able to look it over without navigating an obstacle course. "We need to dust everything here, sweep the floor, and arrange things more attractively."

Phoebe picked up the wooden ox yokes that blocked the way to some Windsor chairs. Surprised by how heavy it was, she staggered under the weight and nearly dropped it on a painted chest from eighteenth-century Pennsylvania.

"Sorry, Mrs. Maxwell." Phoebe managed to lay the yoke down without crushing her toes.

"No harm done, but don't try to lift heavy things by yourself. And you can call me Miriam now that we'll be working together."

"Do be careful, dear," Bess said.

"Yes, I will," Phoebe promised, nearly backing into the wicker doll carriage.

Maybe it was a mistake to hire Phoebe when her own grandmother didn't have confidence in her, but Miriam was desperate for help. She couldn't ask her friend to do heavy work, and Phoebe seemed more than willing to tackle whatever was needed. She had to think of her as a student and hope she'd work out. It was true when she'd said they'd be learning together. She had much to learn herself if this fresh start in life was going to work out for her. Meanwhile, she was thankful to have companionship with Bess and help from Phoebe.

"Let's move all the smaller items to the side and get started on rearranging the furniture," Miriam said, sounding as cheerful as possible in spite of Bess's worried expression and Phoebe's faraway gaze.

As the morning wore on, Miriam's only complaint about Phoebe was that she continued to attempt moving heavy pieces by herself. Perhaps she was a little too eager to prove herself in the job. She also knocked over a shaving mirror, but it landed on the seat of a sofa and wasn't broken.

"I have to meet Charlie at the bank," Bess said. "Would you like me to bring something back for your lunch?"

Miriam declined, but Phoebe asked her grandmother to get a sprout sandwich at Salty Sam's.

"She's a vegan this week," Bess whispered to Miriam as they walked to the door together. "I love her to pieces, but good luck on teaching her the business. And bless you for giving her a chance!"

Smiling as she watched her longtime friend walk away, Miriam knew Phoebe wasn't the only one taking a chance on a very different lifestyle. Things were starting to look up, though, now that she'd reconnected with Bess and Samuel.

Chapter Five

Samuel stood on his deck looking out at the bay, daydreaming about the boat he hoped to buy in the near future. There was no hurry, though. He was still getting used to the leisurely pace of his retirement, and his first priority was to furnish his cottage.

He'd refinished the hardwood floors himself and painted all the walls eggshell white. Cerise would've laughed at the spartan interior of the place, preferring bright colors to display the array of souvenirs she'd acquired during his career. Before moving to Maple Landing, he'd put the contents of their most recent home in storage for his sons when they were ready for them. Difficult as it was, he had to put aside mourning for his wife and start a fresh life. The cottage was the first step.

The living quarters were on the second story with a roomy garage and workshop on the ground level. He went there now to check on the desk, hoping two days of running the dehumidifier had loosened the stuck drawer. He wasn't sure why the other two moved smoothly while the third stubbornly resisted.

"Well, let's give it a try," he said, wondering if talking to himself would become a habit. He wasn't used to being alone all day, but he was excited about beginning the book he'd been planning for many years.

The dehumidifier ran with a noisy hum, and he emptied more than a gallon of water from the tank.

"If that doesn't do it, I'll have to take the desk apart."

Removing the top or the back were possibilities, but he hated to use tools that might mar the beautiful patina of the wood. He'd been fortunate to find the Queen Anne desk so quickly, and what a nice coincidence that Miriam had returned to their hometown just as he had. He appreciated the desk even more knowing it was her family heirloom. Hopefully she wouldn't regret selling it.

Taking a deep breath, he gently tugged on the brass handle of the third drawer, trying to jiggle it very gently from side to side. Much to his relief, he felt a little give.

"Time for plan B," he said, finding the thin metal ruler on the workbench. He'd bought it especially to probe the inside of the drawer once he'd loosened it. Maybe there was some obstruction.

He wiggled the drawer a little more. It seemed to give, and he carefully inserted the ruler in the minute opening.

The tip of the ruler didn't find any obstacle. He ran it along the top of the interior, pushing a little harder when it was a tight fit. Withdrawing the ruler, he tried to open it again, encouraged when the drawer moved several inches.

He wiggled it again and was gratified when the drawer finally slid out its full length.

Something was different. The wood on the bottom of this drawer was higher than that of the other two. Using the ruler again, he was able to pry the bottom board up, revealing a hidden compartment and its contents. He carefully sorted through them, astonished by what he was seeing.

This was something he had to share with Miriam. Feeling as excited as a boy finding some lost bit of treasure on the beach, he went to the garage, backed out his classic convertible, and headed toward town.

As he parked near the store, he realized it was the lunch hour. Hopefully Miriam was there. What he had to show her was too good to wait.

"Samuel!" she said when he hurried into the shop. "It's good to see you again."

"You too," he said, realizing how much he wanted to share his find with her. "You won't believe what I found in the desk."

"You got the stuck drawer open?" She watched as he laid a plastic bag on the countertop.

"Yes, the dehumidifier did the trick, I guess, but I never expected to find something like this. There was a false bottom in that drawer, and you won't believe what was in it."

"It's money," she said as he removed a wad of bills from the plastic bag.

"Confederate money, only valuable as souvenirs or collectibles," he said, "but there's quite a bit. Someone went to a lot of trouble to hide it. The false bottom was neatly made with wood thin enough to fool a casual observer. But there's more."

He carefully unfolded a yellowed sheet of paper, revealing a map. Actually, it was half of a map, with one ragged side that showed it had been torn. It was crudely drawn in faded brown ink.

"What does it show?" Miriam asked.

"I haven't a clue. We'd probably have to match it to a more modern map of the same area to decipher it. But the best is yet to come." He handed her a letter, a folded piece of paper with an address on the outside, a method used long before envelopes were invented for postal use.

She gingerly unfolded it and looked up at him. "I recognize the signature."

"An ancestor of yours?" He wondered why she looked so pale and stricken.

"My great-grandfather, unless I'm mistaken. Thomas Davis, a captain in the Confederate army."

"That's wonderful!" Samuel said. "I'm glad I bought the desk so I could return it to you."

She only shook her head, not at all the reaction he'd expected.

The door opened before she could explain her distress. Samuel vaguely recognized the older woman but not the tall young woman with her.

"Samuel, you remember Bess Watkins, Maple Landing's most enthusiastic cheerleader ever. And Phoebe, her granddaughter."

"Nice to see you," Samuel said, offering his hand to both of them in turn.

"They didn't have the brand of furniture polish you wanted," Bess said, holding out a plastic bottle, "but I can return this if you don't want it."

"Phoebe is my new shop assistant," Miriam explained. "Bess is just being a very good friend and helping out."

Miriam wasn't herself. Samuel could tell even after all the time that had separated them. Whatever was bothering her, he was beginning to wish he hadn't shown her the letter.

"Samuel bought a desk that used to be in our house," Miriam said. "One drawer was stuck, and he found a letter along with some Confederate money and part of a map."

"How exciting!" Bess said. "Have you read it?"

"I'm not sure I want to."

"What's upsetting you?" Samuel asked.

"I guess there's no reason not to tell you," Miriam said. "My great-grandfather disappeared during the War Between the States. Family tradition says he was a deserter, a traitor to the Southern cause. His family lived in disgrace when word circulated in the town."

"Oh dear," Bess said. "That must have been hard on your family. But it was a very long time ago."

"I think I understand," Samuel said. "A stain on the family honor is hard to live down. I can see why you don't want to dredge up the whole story again, but a lot of bad things happen in war. It may have only been a rumor that he deserted."

"Have you read the letter?" Phoebe asked.

"Not yet," Miriam said.

"Maybe it will explain why he disappeared," Samuel suggested.

"Maybe he was a spy and couldn't reveal what he was doing for the cause," Bess said.

"He may have been protecting his family when he dropped out of sight," Samuel said. "Would you like to read the letter in private? It's yours now. I wouldn't dream of keeping a cache that belonged to your family."

"Thank you. I guess I'll read it now. It may not be as damaging as I expect." Miriam picked up the letter. After reading for a few moments, she managed a weak smile. "He didn't get high grades in penmanship. I can't make out all the words."

"Maybe a magnifying glass would help. Nancy Drew always carried one on the covers of older books," Phoebe said.

"It's pretty vague," Miriam said after reading it through. "What would you say this word is?"

She spread the letter out on the counter where all of them could see it.

"Unless I'm mistaken, it's *riches*," Samuel said, frowning at the difficult writing.

"That's the way I read it too," Bess said. "He apparently didn't bother to dot the letter *i*."

"Or he was in a really big hurry," Phoebe helpfully added.

"It's really hard to make out some of the words, but there's an urgency about it that intrigues me," Miriam said. "He sounds concerned about protecting something. The person who was supposed to read it must have known why he was writing."

"Even the name of the addressee is hard to make out," Samuel said. "This letter seems to have been written in a rush. Look, here are a couple of blobs where his feather quill leaked—if that was what he was using."

"I wonder why he bothered to hide the letter," Miriam said. "I can understand secreting away money, but he picked a really secure place to put this letter. If you hadn't been the one to buy the desk, no one in our family would ever have seen it."

"I'm intrigued too," Samuel said. "There's the military angle, of course, but he went to a great deal of trouble to make a hidden compartment—if he was the one who made it."

"I suppose it could've been an earlier ancestor, but he would have had to know about it. Maybe the person who was supposed to find the letter met a tragic end."

"There were a lot of tragedies in that war," Bess said. "Brothers fighting brothers, whole divisions wiped out, all those young men dying. I never like reading about bad times like wars."

Samuel didn't comment, instead picking up the map and studying it. "Look at the odd symbols on this. I can't decipher them. Maybe I could after more study, but this isn't a kind of map I've seen before."

"I'd like to be able to tell my family their ancestor was a hero, not a deserter," Miriam said. "But I wouldn't begin to know where to start looking. Maybe it's better to let the past stay in the past."

"I'm not sure it can," Bess said. "Now that you've seen the letter, can you forget it ever existed?"

"I suppose not," Miriam agreed, "but I might like the true story even less than what I believe now. What if the riches he mentions were stolen? I could learn my ancestor was a thief as well as a deserter."

"Looting in war certainly isn't unknown," Samuel said, feeling protective of Miriam. "But there's not enough in the letter to suspect your ancestor was guilty of anything. He wanted to protect something. That much we can make out. Maybe I can help unearth some facts about him."

"How?" Bess asked. She seemed more curious about Thomas Davis than Miriam was. Or maybe it was easier for her to treat it as a puzzle to be solved because her family wasn't involved.

"The answer may lie in regimental records," Samuel said.

"Where can I find something like that?" Miriam asked, sounding a little less upset.

"I'm sure they must have quite a few at the county library. It's always a challenge to pin down a particular ancestor because there weren't nearly as many names in the Civil War era. The same name can appear again and again for different soldiers. Fortunately there are a lot of resources available. I'll be happy to take you to the library and help you look. There are online sources too."

"I don't want to take up a lot of your time," Miriam said. "I know you want to work on your book."

"It would be my pleasure. There's nothing that interests me more than military history," Samuel assured her.

"I may take you up on your offer someday," Miriam said. "For now, I really have to get the shop ready for the grand reopening."

"I'll leave the contents of the drawer with you," Samuel said. "But I'd certainly like to know more about Captain Thomas Davis."

"I can't thank you enough," Miriam said, walking him to the door after he told Bess and her granddaughter it'd been nice to see them.

"There's nothing like a little mystery to get the brain working," Samuel teased her. "And I'm glad you have help now."

"Me too. I shouldn't get upset about something an ancestor did a hundred and fifty years ago, but I'd like to tell my family he wasn't a deserter."

She touched his arm, a surprisingly warm gesture, and he smiled down at her. "Let me know when you'd like to go. My schedule is pretty flexible these days."

"I'm really glad to see you back in Maple Landing," she said.

He couldn't agree more. In his opinion, a home wasn't a home until you had friends there.

Chapter Six

Still stunned by Samuel's find, Miriam put the Confederate money and map in the safe but slid the letter into a clean envelope and stowed it in her purse. She wanted to take it home and try reading it again, but right now she had to tell Phoebe what to do. And since Bess was still eager to help, she needed to find a job for her too.

"Can you believe that?" Bess was cleaning the glass front of the counter. "I'd heard on the grapevine Samuel was back in town, but what a coincidence he bought a desk with your ancestor's things hidden in it."

"Yes, a happy one," Miriam said, although she wasn't at all easy in her mind about the find. "I'm not sure why Ruth brought it to the shop to sell, but it might have sat at home for many more generations. I never would've found the cache myself."

Phoebe popped up from behind the counter with a polishing cloth in hand. "What would you like me to do next, Mrs. Max?"

The young woman wasn't comfortable using her first name, so Miriam had decided to let her do as she liked, although not even her high school students had come up with a nickname like that.

One thing she'd learned already about her new assistant: it was safer not to let her work with breakables. As contrite as Phoebe had been when she broke the handle off a relatively inexpensive Depression glass creamer, it seemed better to keep her away from more pricey glassware and ceramics.

"Come take a look at these," Miriam said. "We have three George III dining chairs. I'm pretty sure they're 1920s reproductions, but they're still nice." Miriam had been doing her homework, spending the evenings with Ruth's extensive library.

"I like the tapestry seats," Phoebe said.

"The trouble is, most people want sets of six, or at least four chairs. If there are more on the second floor, it will be much easier to sell them. Go to the second floor and see if there are any more just like these. Don't worry if the upholstery isn't the same. It's the style of the wood that's important."

"More chairs like those," Phoebe repeated to herself.

"And do be careful," Miriam warned. "Everything up there is all jumbled together. I don't want you falling."

Or breaking anything else, she thought.

"You're lovely to be so patient with Phoebe," Bess said when her granddaughter was upstairs. "I think she's enjoying her time in the store."

"She can be very helpful," Miriam said.

"When she's focused," Bess qualified. "I hope she'll turn out to be a real help to you."

"She tries hard," Miriam said. "We're both learning the business, but I'm hopeful. She does seem to appreciate beautiful things. She just has to handle them more carefully."

"What else can I do for you?" Bess asked.

"I don't want to overwork you. It's your company I appreciate the most."

"But I'm having fun getting into everything," her friend assured her. "In fact, I've had my eye on that mason jar full of buttons. Ruth marked it five dollars, but the old canning jar alone must be worth more than that. I collect buttons, so maybe I could sort through them to see if there are any valuable ones."

"Good idea," Miriam said. "I feel overwhelmed by everything I have to learn. It's comforting to know my sister wasn't up on everything. I don't see how one person could be. And by the way, if you find buttons you'd like for your collection, please take them as a thank-you gift for all you're doing."

"I wouldn't dream of it, but maybe we can make a trade. The attic of our inn is full of things we have no use for. Charlie thinks it's all junk, but I bet there are some nice old things."

Miriam couldn't help but laugh. "If there's one thing I don't need right now, it's more stock for the store. I still don't know why Ruth was out buying more merchandise when she passed away. There's so much here that hasn't even been sorted. So for now, take any buttons you like. Why not spread them out on one of the desks so you can sit while you do it?"

"I have to admit my legs don't have that cheerleader spring any-more," Bess said with a giggle.

She reached up to get the jar of buttons from a shelf above her head just as the bell on the front door sounded. Miriam looked at the newcomer, trying to decide why she looked familiar.

"You remember me, don't you?" asked a rail-thin woman with dark hair pulled back in a severe bun.

"Natalie Spencer." Bess sounded guarded. "You remember, Miriam. She was in our chem class."

"It's Natalie Downs now."

"Yes, I remember you," Miriam said, although she couldn't say Natalie had been one of her friends. She'd made a big fuss when Miriam got first chair in the flute section of the band instead of her. Funny how long-forgotten incidents came back to her since she'd moved to Maple Landing.

"Are you still indulging in your little hobby, Bess? I can't imagine it's much fun cleaning up after tourists, but I guess someone has to run a hotel."

"It's not a hotel. It's a bed-and-breakfast, and it's hardly a hobby," Bess said in a tone of voice that told Miriam exactly how she felt about Natalie.

"You've probably noticed our store right next to yours: Downs and Sons?" Natalie said, directing her question to Miriam. "It's been in my husband's family for generations, although it's only since WWII, the big one, that they added appliances to the fur-niture inventory. They originally started making coffins, if you can believe that."

"I have no trouble believing it," Bess said, looking unusually sour. "And around here, we think the War Between the States was the big one."

Miriam was surprised by her friend's rancor. It was totally unlike Bess to be argumentative with anyone, but she did remember that Natalie had been something of a loner. She hadn't moved to Maple Landing until they were in the tenth grade, and perhaps other students, Miriam included, hadn't been as welcoming as they might have been. Miriam couldn't remember where Natalie's family came from, but it was definitely north of the Mason-Dixon line. She remembered how comical Natalie had sounded when she tried to speak with a Southern accent.

Natalie shrugged off Bess's comment and came to the point of her visit. "It must be hard on you, Miriam, losing your sister and taking over her unsuccessful business. You have my condolences."

Miriam had to force herself to say, "Thank you." After all the time she'd spent settling her sister's estate, she knew Ruth's business had been very successful in spite of her rather unorthodox methods.

"You're planning to sell out, aren't you?" Natalie spoke in a matter-of-fact tone.

"Why would she do that?" Bess was quick to ask. "Ruthie's Antiques is the pride of Maple Landing. She's already hired help to get ready for the grand reopening."

"Oh, I'm surprised to hear that," Natalie said, her face looking more pinched as it registered disapproval. With her sallow skin she should have never worn black, but she was covered in it from her frilly blouse to her shiny pumps.

"I have no plans to sell," Miriam said as pleasantly as she could manage, hoping this would put an end to the conversation.

"Well, when you do decide to unload it, please give my husband and me first refusal. We've been wanting to expand our floor space for some time, but Jamison Banks—he has the men's haberdashery on the other side of our store—absolutely refuses to sell. You can see our dilemma. I've told my husband, George, that we should build a new place outside of town, but he doesn't want to give up the long tradition of the Downs family dominating business in the heart of Maple Landing."

"I'll keep you in mind if the store is ever for sale," Miriam said, giving Bess a warning look. She didn't want to get off to a bad start with the owners of the adjacent business, although she could see why Bess didn't like Natalie.

"Please do," Natalie said. "I'm sure we could offer you a fair price, especially if you don't list with a Realtor. There's no reason to pay a commission when you have a ready buyer right next door."

"Nice seeing you again," Miriam said, a little ashamed of herself for the white lie.

"Pretty cheeky," Bess said when Natalie had left. "Offering you terms on a property that isn't for sale."

"You seem to have a bad history with her," Miriam said mildly.

"She fancies herself an interior decorator. When we were renovating the inn, she practically insisted it would be a failure unless we let her decorate it the 'proper' way. Of course, we were doing most of the work ourselves with limited financing. Paying her to do the job would have ruined us. Her ideas were outrageous anyway. She must have watched *Gone with the Wind* too many times. She wanted to add columns and a circular staircase—and rip out walls all over the place to change the floor plan. She's held a grudge ever since."

"I hate to see you upset," Miriam sympathized. Bess was one of the most forgiving people Miriam had ever known. Miriam was shocked at her friend's enmity, although Natalie wasn't a person she'd want as a friend.

"I know I'm being uncharitable," Bess said gloomily. "Something about her rubs me the wrong way. I'd hate to see her take over Ruthie's Antiques. I love having you back in Maple Landing, and I can't wait to see what you learn about your ancestor's letter. I can't believe anyone in your family would be a deserter."

"I guess war makes people do things they'd ordinarily never consider," Miriam said. "But it's in the past. I'm so happy to reconnect with you. We did have fun together when we were young, and I'm sure we will again."

"I found some! Come see!" Phoebe's eager voice called from the rear of the store where the stairs were hidden from the public.

"Great!" Miriam moved toward the back of the store.

"I didn't try to carry any downstairs. I wanted you to check them out first," Phoebe said, tripping on the bottom step when she started to lead them to the second floor.

"Careful, dear," Bess cautioned, making Miriam smile. Bess had been the most agile cheerleader on the squad, but apparently her granddaughter hadn't inherited her grace. But Miriam was getting attached to Phoebe already.

The light in the second story left a lot to be desired, but Ruth had kept a fairly powerful flashlight on a table near the top of the steps. Miriam followed Phoebe, keeping the beam of light on the floor to avoid hazards.

"Here!" Phoebe proudly announced. "I only pulled out two because they're a little hard to reach. I didn't want to scratch them, but there are a total of five."

Miriam bent down for a closer look and confirmed her assistant's find. There were indeed five chairs to match the ones on the main floor.

"It took a keen eye to spot them, Phoebe. And you were right not to try getting them out. We'll have to move some things first, but there's no doubt they match. Now we have a set of eight, the perfect number for anyone wanting them to go with a formal dining table."

Phoebe beamed with happiness, and Bess looked even more pleased. It had been a day of surprises and upsets, but Miriam was more than happy with her first employee. Later, when she had time, she'd give more thought to Samuel's find. Had the Confederate money been devalued to almost nothing when Thomas Davis hid it? What was the significance of the map and its odd symbols? And would she better understand the meaning in his letter when she deciphered the words that were difficult to make out?

Maybe she should take Samuel up on his offer to help search regimental records for her ancestor's role in the war. Was there anything to justify his blackened reputation? Or was his reputation completely unfounded?

"They aren't too heavy," Miriam said, lifting a chair to gauge its weight. "I think if we move them carefully, one step at a time, we can get them downstairs without any scratches. I'll take the first, and you can follow my lead, Phoebe."

Soon all three of them were busy polishing the chairs, taking time out to visit with several people who dropped in to see if the shop was open. Phoebe made her first sale, an old tin cookie cutter in the shape of a camel. She was thrilled, and it gave Miriam a chance to show her how to work the antiquated but not antique cash register.

Later, when she was home, Miriam studied her ancestor's letter and tried to decide whether she should try to learn the truth about him after so many years. She wanted to be proud of her relative. Was the cache Samuel found under the drawer's false bottom the key to doing that? Maybe God had directed her to Maple Landing to clear a good soldier's name, but she braced herself for a disappointment.

After thinking it over for several hours, she decided to take Samuel up on his offer to help research Thomas Davis's role in the Confederate army. It was a small thing to do for an ancestor who'd never been honored by his own family. She might not find anything honorable in his record, but she'd rest easier knowing she'd tried.

Chapter Seven

Miriam had one more thing she wanted to do Wednesday evening after her eventful day at the store. Lisa hadn't called in several days, and Miriam tried to talk to her daughter at least once a week. She punched in the Indiana number and was pleased when Lisa answered on the first ring.

"You must have been sitting by the phone," Miriam said.

"Well, sort of," her daughter admitted. "All my chicks are out of the nest, so I'm keeping the phone nearby."

"Oh, that's right! The girls are at a church summer camp for the first time ever." Miriam felt a bit guilty forgetting such a major event in their young lives. "How are they doing?"

"Becky is loving it. Let her into a pool of water, and she couldn't be happier. I'm a little worried about Abby, though. When I talked to her yesterday, she was homesick."

"Oh dear," Miriam said. "You were hoping she'd be all right if she went with Becky."

"Yes, usually the twins enjoy the same things, but I guess a week away from home is a little too long for Abby. I offered to come get her, but she decided to tough it out. She was excited about the crafts program, though, so maybe she'll enjoy the experience."

"You said all your chicks are out of the nest. Do you mean Brent too?"

"Actually, he's the one I'm expecting to hear from. He's in California checking out the housing situation, the commute to his new job, and schools for the girls. There's so much to think about when you move—but, of course, you know that," Lisa said.

"It's not as complicated when one person does the moving, although I don't really feel settled into the house yet," Miriam admitted, thinking of all the things she wanted to do to the home where she'd grown up.

"How about Aunt Ruth's shop? Are you enjoying yourself? Did you find someone to work for you? I wish I could be there to help."

"Fortunately, I have a full-time employee and a dear friend from high school who's volunteering her time. In fact, it's her granddaughter who took the job. She's a little on the flighty side and tends to drop breakables, not to mention stumbling over her own feet, but she's trying hard. I think she'll work out," Miriam said.

"You never give up on anyone," her daughter teased. "Who was that boy who could barely write his name, and you discovered he had a gift for numbers? I remember how proud you were when he earned an A in your accounting class."

"Mason Engle," Miriam said. "I really can't take credit. He was diagnosed with autism while he was in my class."

"Because you insisted on getting tests for him," Lisa said proudly. "Compared to the red tape you had to go through for him, it should be a snap to train an employee."

"Not exactly." Miriam laughed. "There is something I wanted to tell you. I sold a Queen Anne desk that had been in our family—Ruth had it in the store. By coincidence, a friend from high school bought it. When he unstuck—"

"He?" Lisa interrupted. "Was he a good friend?"

"Yes, but that was ages ago," Miriam said, wanting to continue her story about the cache. "He found a false bottom in one drawer."

When she finished relating the details of the find, her usually talkative daughter was quiet for several moments.

"Wow!" she said. "Brent will be thrilled to hear about this. He's the history buff in our family. Imagine, a Confederate captain is one of the twins' ancestors."

"If I can find out more about him, it may not be good," Miriam warned. "There's a possibility he was a deserter. In fact, that's the story my great-aunt told about him. Do you want your daughters to learn the truth if he was dishonorable? I don't have to take this any farther."

"If you don't, you'll always wonder whether he was unjustly accused," Lisa said in a practical tone. "If he wasn't, there may have been a good reason for what he did."

"You always see the glass as half-full," Miriam said. "Since you don't have any objections, I'm going to find out as much as I can. The old friend who found the cache has offered to help."

"Go for it, Mom."

It was the reaction she'd expected from her daughter. Miriam ended the call in a happy frame of mind.

* * *

Thursday dawned with the promise of another perfect early June day. Miriam was tempted to work in the neglected flower beds surrounding the house. The square, boxy lines of her childhood home cried out for a flowery setting even more than a paint job, but she had to get to the shop. Now that she had an assistant, she had to be there to let her in. Maybe it was time to have a key made for Phoebe—although Miriam herself still needed to go into work.

By the time she walked to work for her daily exercise and unlocked the front door of Ruthie's Antiques, both Phoebe and Bess were there.

"Bess, how can I ask you to come here every day if you won't let me pay you?" she asked her friend.

"Believe me, it's better if I let Randy and Janice take full charge of the inn. If they're going to make a success of the bed-and-breakfast, they have to make their own mistakes. Anyway, Charlie will be in and out all day. That's more than enough supervision."

"Well, I won't pretend I'm not delighted," Miriam said. "One of the best things about getting the shop in shape is having you and Phoebe here."

"Aren't you sweet," Bess said, hugging her. "But I have to confess, I still want to go through those buttons. I never did get to them yesterday. I took a look in the attic last night—it's like an oven in the summer, so I wanted to go there on a cool evening. I think you'll like my trade goods."

She pulled an old candy box out of her carryall and handed it to Miriam.

"Old valentines," Miriam said with pleasure, starting to look through them.

"Not terribly old. Maybe the 1930s with a few from the 1940s. Here's one that says 'To My Pal in the Service.' That has to be World War II."

"They're charming, but I don't want to take your family mementos," Miriam said.

"They were in the attic when we bought the house. We really don't have any interest in them, so they're perfect to trade."

"Why don't you take the whole jar of buttons for the box of valentines?" Miriam suggested.

"Not until I see what's in it. There could be a button from George Washington's inauguration or a really old enamel. One button could be worth more than all the valentines," Bess insisted.

"Have at it," Miriam said with a laugh. Her friend's enthusiasm was contagious. "Now, Phoebe, you and I need to go through that stack of picture frames behind the office door. Maybe my sister bought them as an auction lot and never had time to sort and price them. I'm not expecting much, but some have paintings in them."

It proved pretty much impossible to sort in the confines of the small office, so Miriam spread a raggedy quilt on a dining room table and helped Phoebe put them on it.

"This looks familiar," Phoebe said, standing over a fanciful painting with a dragon-like creature. "I used to read science fiction. This looks like a book cover."

"Original art for a book?" Miriam mused. "Or it could be an advertising poster. I have so much to learn!"

She had laid it aside to study later and perhaps have appraised when the bell on the door chimed. Her first thought was Samuel was coming to discuss going to the library, but instead a young man came into the shop. She didn't have a chance to ask if she could help him. Phoebe darted to the front and greeted him with more animation than Miriam had ever observed in her.

"Would you mind if I take a short break, Mrs. Max?" she asked, her ponytail bobbing.

"That's fine," Miriam agreed. Who was she to impede the course of young love, if that's what it was?

As soon as the door closed behind the young people, Bess stepped away from the buttons and watched them through the glass in the door.

"I didn't know Phoebe had a boyfriend," Miriam remarked. "He's nice-looking—taller than she is, and I always did like dark curls."

"He's not her boyfriend!" Bess said emphatically. "He's the last person in Maple Landing I want to see hanging around Phoebe."

All Miriam could say was, "Oh?"

"Don't be fooled by that innocent look," Bess went on. "Guess who he is."

"I don't have a clue," Miriam said, wondering why her friend thought she could identify a boy she'd never seen before.

"Think! Who do we know with black hair—though she must dye it now—and that cunning look?" Bess's face was flushed, not a flattering look with her bright-red T-shirt imprinted with Apple Street Inn, a Family Bed-and-Breakfast.

"He looked like a generic young adult to me," Miriam said. "Maybe a little thin and sloop-shouldered, but certainly attractive to girls."

"He's Natalie's grandson, Jason Downs!" Bess said. "It would be terrible if Phoebe married him. Imagine having to share grandchildren with the one person I disliked in high school. She'd be at family picnics, holiday celebrations, all the big events in Phoebe's life."

"They only went out for a few minutes," Miriam reminded her. "I'm sure a pretty girl like Phoebe has plenty of opportunities to be with young men. And as you told me, she really hasn't decided what to do with her life yet."

"That's why this is a dangerous time," Bess insisted. "She doesn't know what she wants. What if she decides to marry that Jason Downs? I'm never sure what she has in mind."

"Oh dear, Bess," Miriam said. "I know what a stressful time it can be when young men come courting—I guess they don't call it that anymore."

"It's not just that. Phoebe hardly dated at all in high school. I urged her to get involved in school activities, but her only interest was the French club. She was president of it her senior year, but almost all the members were girls. She doesn't have the experience to see what Jason is."

Miriam hadn't seen Bess so riled up since she'd had to sit out a football game for getting a D in geometry.

"Jason seems courteous enough," Miriam said in a mild tone.

"Someday he may take over that wretched store next to yours. Can you imagine Phoebe stuck working there for the rest of her life?"

"Whoa, girlfriend," Miriam said, trying to think of what she could say to calm her. "They went out to talk for a few minutes, and you have them walking down the aisle."

Bess laughed at herself, one of her really good traits. "I did get carried away. I knew I wanted to marry Charlie the first time he sat beside me in the school lunchroom. That's no reason to believe Phoebe has any such idea."

"Of course not," Miriam agreed. She remembered how much Samuel had meant to her when she was still in her teens. She'd never thought of seeing him again in Maple Landing. Were they destined to be friends again, or would their connection end after he helped her investigate her ancestor's past?

"Oh, I got distracted," Bess said in her usual cheerful voice. "Look what I found!"

She held out a small button that appeared to be brass and quite old.

"You found one you'd like for your collection?" Miriam asked.

"Look closely. It's a Confederate uniform button. See the initials: CSA." Bess held it practically under her nose.

"That's nice." Miriam said, not sharing her friend's excitement about an old button.

"Don't you see?" Bess insisted. "This button could've come from your great-grandfather's uniform. The young officers wore them at the beginning of the war in two rows of seven buttons. What if this one came from the jacket of Captain Thomas Davis? Isn't it exciting!"

"I guess we can never prove that, but it is a nice one to find, isn't it?" Miriam took the button to examine it. "Please add it to your collection."

"I wouldn't dream of it," Bess said. "You should keep it with the other keepsakes from your great-grandfather. It's not certain it was his, but surely he wore similar ones."

After staring at the button for a long moment, Miriam put it in the pocket of her jeans. Was this one more piece of the puzzle involving her ancestor? She doubted it, but the button made her even more eager to find out the truth.

Chapter Eight

Friday began with heavy clouds hanging over Maple Landing. The promise of rain was welcome, and Miriam opted to take her small compact car so she wouldn't get soaked walking to the shop. Sometime soon she had to practice driving Ruth's big van, but she was still a bit intimidated by it. She had to admire her sister for driving all over the Eastern Seaboard in search of antiques, although it did seem she'd been overstocked already. Maybe the thrill of the hunt was the thing she liked best.

Saddened because she hadn't known her sister as well as she would have liked in recent years, Miriam parked in the alley behind the store and hurriedly unlocked the back door.

Phoebe certainly deserved kudos for promptness. She was waiting by the front door when Miriam turned on the lights.

"We need to get you your own key," Miriam said when she let Phoebe into the store. "Where's the best place to get one made?"

"The hardware store has one of those machines that duplicate keys," the young woman said. "Would you like me to get one during my lunch break?"

"No, you can go later this morning. First I have to make a few phone calls. I need someone to appraise the artwork we found yesterday," Miriam said.

"It would probably be quicker to do it online. That way you can get several estimates," Phoebe said matter-of-factly.

Though Miriam was computer literate, a necessity to a business teacher, she had zero experience finding prices on the Internet. She wasn't even sure what category to check.

"You make it sound easy," she said.

"If you like, I can do it for you. I looked through some of my old science fiction paperbacks last night, so I actually have a pretty good idea who the artist is." Phoebe made it sound as easy as looking up a number in the phone book.

"That would be really helpful," Miriam said, happy with her shop assistant's offer. Apparently Phoebe had hidden talents, and she was delighted to tap into them.

"Oh, and my grandma is coming as soon as she checks out the last guests," Phoebe added. "Mom had to go to the dentist, and Dad is helping Granddad spread new redwood chips around the shrubs. They were trying to get done before the rain starts. You don't know how much I appreciate working here. Dad thinks I was born to be his gofer."

"I'm certainly lucky to have you," Miriam said. "Sometimes I look around this place and think I'll never get it in shape for a big reopening.

There's a month's work on the second floor, and I don't even like to think about going through all the boxes and shelves in the basement."

"Maybe you can have someone haul it all to an auction house," Phoebe suggested.

"That's a really good idea, but my sister bought good things mixed with pure junk. I really have to go through it all before I can make any decisions."

"If you need someone to lift heavy things, I think Jason Downs would be glad to help. He doesn't like working in his parents' store," Phoebe said.

"I'll keep him in mind," Miriam said, although she didn't want to upset Bess.

Her friend usually loved everyone she knew, or at least she had in high school. There was no reason to believe she'd changed. In fact, she suspected the success of the inn could be credited as much to Bess's warm personality as her husband's skill as a handyman.

As if on cue, Bess came through the front door wearing a yellow slicker over khaki walking shorts.

"It's starting to rain," she announced, taking off her wet-weather gear and giving it a shake. "I put the calico buttons you gave me in my collection. I love to think of them sewed on the dresses ordinary women wore. If I had unlimited space—and funds—I'd look for calico dresses to match. But one reason I love buttons is they're small and easy to store. Charlie isn't keen on collecting—except for his shed full of tools. That man must have fifty hammers. They all look alike to me, but he knows the approximate time each one was made."

"Good morning, Bess," Miriam said with a smile in her voice. Her friend brought sunshine into the shop even when the sky was dark and ominous.

"Hi, Gran. I'm going to do some price checking online," Phoebe said, hurrying back to the office without an answer from Bess.

"That's one thing she's really good at," Bess said with pride. "If you want to know how many high schools in the United States have football cheerleaders, she'll find it for you."

"I'll pass on that," Miriam said, smiling, "but anything she can do to save me time is really welcome. Would you mind watching the store while I work upstairs?"

They hadn't been overwhelmed by customers, but a few people drifted in every day, some buying and others only looking. Miriam was planning to do some advertising for her big reopening, but she was nowhere ready yet. She wanted people to see a rather elegant and very well organized antiques shop, not a flea market jumble. If she wanted shoppers to purchase the good things Ruth had stocked, she had to make the store look like a place where quality antiques could be had.

"Glad to," Bess said. "Charlie had that look in his eyes—the one he gets when he wants me to help him with a dirty job. Puttering around the inn is his idea of fun, not mine. When I left, he had Randy installing a new showerhead in a guest bathroom. Both my men are good at plumbing, but they think cleaning up afterward is women's work!"

"Thanks. It's only until Phoebe is through on the computer," Miriam said.

"If I know my girl, she'll not only find the price, but she'll locate a buyer. Computers aren't my thing, but she's a whiz—if her grandmother does say so."

"I believe you," Miriam said, edging her way toward the stairs in the rear.

Alone in the stuffy second story, she looked around for a window to open. Ruth had added air-conditioning to the main floor, but apparently only intended to use the upper level as a storage area. Miriam stifled a sneeze as she tried to open a window at the far end, but it seemed to be painted shut. She really could use a strong young man like Jason, at least on a temporary basis, but she wouldn't dream of upsetting Bess.

After less than a half hour of searching and sorting, she heard Bess shouting up the stairs.

"Miriam? Can you come down?" her friend asked without giving a reason.

Miriam's first thought was that a customer wanted to bargain on the price of an object. Accustomed as she was to going into stores where every item had a firm price, she had to get used to collectors trying to get better deals. Ruth had put a letter code on many price tags as a reminder of what she'd paid, but Miriam still wasn't comfortable with her system.

Hanging on to the rail, she hurried down the aged wooden steps, being careful not to stumble on the indentations where many generations of feet had worn wavy surfaces onto the wood.

"Sorry if I'm interrupting something," a familiar voice said even before she reached the bottom.

"Samuel, any excuse I have to leave that mess," she said, gesturing upward, "is a welcome break."

His hair was damp from the rain, and the shoulders of his navy-blue jacket were wet. She'd heard the rain battering the roof, so it was surprising he'd come out in it. Or maybe a navy man was immune to the vagaries of the weather.

"I thought this might be a good afternoon to visit the county library. You probably won't have many customers while it's raining so hard," he said.

"You're the first person to come through that door since I've been here," Bess said as a way of urging Miriam to accept his offer. "Anyway, you have Phoebe, and I'd be happy to stay as long as you like."

"Tell you what," Samuel said. "I have a few errands to do. Why don't I pick up some sandwiches when I'm done and bring them here? We can have lunch, and maybe by then the rain will slow down."

"Oh, you don't have to get anything for Phoebe and me," Bess was quick to say. "You and Miriam could go out for lunch."

Bess was trying to play matchmaker! Miriam didn't know whether to laugh or scold her.

"Your plan is perfect, Samuel. It will give me time to finish a few things," she said.

"Isn't it nice you've becoming reacquainted with Samuel after all this time?" Bess asked when he was gone. "You two were the sweethearts of the homecoming dance. Everyone thought you were the perfect couple."

"That was high school," Miriam said, hoping Bess didn't notice the flush on her face. "Anyway, it was all over when he went away to

Annapolis. It was always his dream to go to the naval academy. And I was set on being a teacher. That's a decision I've never regretted."

"Yes, I was sad when you got a scholarship to that teacher's college in Indiana. It felt as if you were going to the ends of the earth. Not that I didn't want you to do what you wanted, but it was lonely here after you were gone."

"But you had Charlie," Miriam reminded her.

"Yes, and I still adore him even when he's being a pip about not letting Randy make more decisions about the inn. I guess it's harder for men to retire than women."

"Samuel seems to be enthused about being a civilian again," Miriam pointed out. "He's writing a book about naval history. That's why he's already familiar with the county library."

True to his word, Samuel returned shortly after noon with a sack full of hero sandwiches. Miriam had forgotten to mention Phoebe was a vegan, but it didn't turn out to be a problem. All the sandwiches were loaded with lettuce, tomato, sprouts, olives and enough other ingredients to allow her to remove some thin-sliced ham and cheese and still have a nice lunch. Bess was quick to add the discarded meat and cheese to her own long, crusty bun.

Samuel's classic car was parked at the curb, a reminder of how much he'd liked to work on automobiles when he was young. He opened the passenger door for Miriam, doing it with a gallant flourish that made her feel special.

"I don't know what we'll find at the library," Samuel said, pulling out on a rain-slicked street almost devoid of traffic. "But they have the best military collection on the Bay as far as I've been able to determine. It's amazing how many records have survived, considering the chaos after the war."

When they got there, the library's reading room had a smattering of patrons, perhaps some of them only seeking shelter from the inclement weather. Samuel led her beyond the large circular desk, their footsteps echoing on the marble floor. It always amazed her how high the ceilings were, given that the building was built at a time when fireplaces were the main source of heat. She followed him to a small elevator, added when the library was renovated before she was born.

"The good stuff is on the second floor," he said. "One of the first things I did when I moved here was get a library card. They're wonderful about getting information for me on interlibrary loan, although the Internet has much of the research I need."

Although Miriam had visited the venerable building many years ago, she still had a feeling of awe when she passed the murals on the walls depicting famous battles and soldiers in the War Between the States. Even after years of living in a Northern state where most people had forgotten all about what they called the Civil War, she felt a kinship to those who had suffered so greatly.

Samuel pushed the button to summon the elevator, a small box that Miriam was glad to leave after a labored ascent to the second floor. Here a long corridor bisected the building with dark stained wooden doors on either side.

"I wouldn't know where to begin," she said, walking beside Samuel.

"Most of the important military documents are available online. It makes a writer's job so much easier. I may actually finish my history within a year or so, although that's being optimistic. Here's the room we need."

He opened a door in the middle of the corridor and let her enter ahead of him. She was surprised he didn't knock or request special permission, but he seemed to be very familiar with the available resources.

A pleasant-faced woman in her late fifties or early sixties stood up from behind a desk when they entered.

"Admiral Bentley, it's nice to see you. As you can see, the rain has kept our patrons away today."

"This is my friend Miriam Davis Maxwell." he said. He turned to Miriam. "Mrs. Beauregard has been immensely helpful in my search for information on the Confederate navy."

"It's my pleasure as well as my job," she said, taking off a pair of glasses attached to a chain. Her neat salt-and-pepper curls and rather long face with high cheekbones were vaguely familiar, but Miriam had given up trying to identify everyone she might have crossed paths with in the distant past. "Davis—now that name is familiar."

"Captain Thomas Davis is my ancestor," Miriam said, wondering how much background to tell her.

"Mrs. Maxwell would like to see the records from his regiment," Samuel said.

"Do you know what it was?" the librarian asked.

"No, but I'm pretty sure he would have enlisted in Maple Landing."

"As a general rule, we don't allow patrons to examine the original records, but fortunately almost our whole collection is available online. Would you like to search on one of our computers?" she asked. "I'd be glad to get you started."

Miriam's palms felt damp, and she was almost afraid of what she'd find. Without Samuel's help she might not have had the nerve to trace her ancestor.

After Mrs. Beauregard helped them get started, Samuel assured her he could manage.

It proved fairly easy to access enlistment records, but after that even Samuel had trouble tracing what had happened to individual soldiers.

"Are you sure he survived the war?" Samuel asked. "So many didn't."

"As sure as I can be of anything," Miriam said. "My only real source was my great-aunt, and I'm not one hundred percent certain her mind was still sharp when I knew her."

She sat beside Samuel, mesmerized at his speed and competence on the computer. It would've taken her much, much longer to find half the information he did.

"Your great-grandfather seems to have disappeared from his unit, as far as I can determine," he said, sounding disappointed.

"Does that suggest he never made it home?" she asked, wondering if it was good news or bad. Perhaps he hadn't lived to deny the rumors about his desertion.

"The whole South was devastated," Samuel said. "Maryland wasn't the Deep South, but the first thing most people think about after a disaster is survival. Writing the history of the time is often put off till years later. It wouldn't be hard for your ancestor to slip between the cracks, so to speak."

"If he was a deserter while the war was still going on, wouldn't he be listed as a criminal or something?" she asked, not entirely sure she wanted the answer.

"Let me check some more," Samuel said.

Feeling too agitated to watch the screen as he searched, she wandered along the shelves in the room. Storage boxes and volumes with shabby spines were crowded onto full but orderly cases. She couldn't imagine how many tragic stories were told there, or what an effort it had been to assemble all of them for future generations. Did she really want to know the truth about Great-grandfather? In spite of what she might learn, she was convinced he deserved a chance to have his reputation cleared.

"Miriam, come see this," Samuel said.

She hurried to peer over his shoulder, not knowing what to expect on the computer screen.

"It's hard to prove a negative," he began thoughtfully, confusing her a little. "But I haven't been able to find any charge of desertion leveled against Captain Thomas Davis. He disappeared from the regimental record, but there doesn't seem to be any stain on his reputation, at least not that I can find."

"Does that mean he wasn't a deserter?" Miriam asked hopefully.

"I wish I could say yes, but it only means there's no record of any dishonorable conduct. When men are dying by the thousands, mistakes are made. I'm afraid that's the best I can do for you here."

"I really appreciate it," Miriam said. "I wouldn't have known where to begin without you."

When they walked out, the sun was making a valiant effort to emerge from behind the clouds. The rain had stopped, and Miriam decided not to let Samuel's inconclusive search disappoint her. After all, they'd had a pleasant afternoon together, a reminder of how much she used to enjoy his company.

"If I get any bright ideas, I'll let you know," he said. "I don't believe a man with the rank of captain would just disappear. Certainly relatives would have searched after the war ended."

"You've already been a huge help. The more I learn—or don't learn—the more I want to find out what happened to him. I didn't tell you, but Bess found a Confederate army button in the store yesterday. I wanted to give it to her, but she insisted I keep it. There's no reason to believe it belonged to my great-grandfather, but it does encourage me to keep looking."

"I'd be disappointed if you didn't," Samuel said. "I'm intrigued myself. If there's anything else I can do, be sure to let me know."

"Thank you so much," Miriam said.

"It was my pleasure." He escorted her to the car, and it felt surprisingly good to lean on the strong arm of an old friend.

Chapter Nine

As soon as Samuel got home from taking Miriam to the county library, he went to his own computer. It was set up on the kitchen table because he still wanted to give the Queen Anne desk a final polishing with some beeswax. He'd decided not to refinish the spot on the side with the scratch. After all, even that bit of damage had Miriam's family history behind it.

His search for a desk had led him to an old friend, but he almost wished he hadn't decided to buy one of her heirlooms. It seemed more fitting to keep it in her family, although he was pleased to have found the secret cache. The question was whether this search for the truth about her great-grandfather would make her more or less happy. He fervently hoped it was the former.

Before he could start work, his landline phone rang. A quick glance at caller ID showed his younger son was calling.

"Scott, how's it going?"

"Pretty well, Dad. How do you like your new home?"

"No near neighbors and a great view of the bay. What more could an old salt want?" Samuel asked. "I didn't expect to hear from you. Aren't you going overseas soon?"

"My unit is being deployed, but I may not go with it. I've been offered a chance to train on a new weapon—can't tell you what it is."

Samuel suspected his clearance was high enough to hear anything his son might say, but he respected his discretion. "I wouldn't want you to."

"The bottom line is that I'd become an instructor. But I'm not sure I want to leave my unit."

"What does Ginny think?" Samuel asked, pretty certain what Scott's on-again, off-again girlfriend would want.

"I haven't mentioned it yet, but we both know she'd want me to stay in the States," Scott said.

The last thing Samuel wanted to do was give advice about his son's personal life, but he'd learned by trial and error Scott only wanted a sounding board. He'd been making his own decisions since high school, when he'd decided to quit football and run cross-country.

"Whatever you decide, I'm sure you'll do great," Samuel said, giving his marine son a closing vote of confidence.

Scott didn't call that often, and he wasn't glued to electronic communicators. It was always a treat when Samuel heard from him. Fortunately Colin's family was just the opposite. His wife, Laurie, and their children, Katie and Kevin, loved to Skype, especially when Colin was at sea. Samuel loved seeing his grandchildren on the computer screen, and Laurie kept him informed about their life in Spain as she waited for Colin's ship to return. It took a strong woman to be a navy wife. Samuel was grateful for all the support Cerise had given him, and his daughter-in-law was following the same path.

Returning to the kitchen, he decided to plan his dinner before he did anything on the computer. Cooking was a new interest, and he'd invested in a pile of books and was learning every day. He smiled when he thought of how matter-of-fact he'd always been about his meals. Cerise had been an excellent cook, and at sea, good meals were the norm. He had a lot to learn, but he was having fun, just as he'd had fun with Miriam years ago.

In high school he'd had a huge crush on her, but that wasn't what stuck in his mind. They'd been good friends, always able to talk and laugh together. He was finding her easy conversation and innate kindness both refreshing and stimulating now. And truth to tell, he would've been disappointed if she'd rejected his help searching for her ancestor.

What about Captain Davis? A lot of men deserted in the War Between the States, some with severe health problems or pressing family business. Others just weren't able to rise above the horrors of war. He liked to think he would've stood fast to the bitter end, but it was impossible to put himself in the place of a desperate, defeated man. Without knowing his story, Samuel was inclined to sympathize with the missing man. There was very little record of his life and none of his death. Where should he look next to dredge up some concrete information?

In Thomas Davis's day, births were often recorded in churches and deaths in cemetery records. Although an amazing amount of information was available online, there was always a chance that something pertinent lay hidden in unexpected places.

Smiling at his fanciful notions, Samuel started assembling ingredients for a pasta dish heavy in fresh vegetables and light on meat. It might not be as tasty as the sandwich he'd had at noon, but he credited Miriam for making the takeout lunch seem especially good.

* * *

Saturday morning Miriam was alone in the shop. She'd given Phoebe the day off after she was exceedingly helpful the day before. Not only had she found a price for what turned out to be the original illustration for a book cover, but she'd found a buyer willing to pay the full retail amount. Miriam was hopeful about using online sales in her overall plan for the business, but she had some work to do catching up with her young employee's computer skills.

Apparently word of mouth was spreading about new management in Ruthie's Antiques. All morning Miriam kept busy helping customers and, of course, giving attention to "lookers," who always seemed to outnumber buyers. At least she was getting a good idea of the antiques people hoped to find in the shop.

Around noon the shop emptied out, but another woman came in just before Miriam decided to lock the door. She only planned to close for a short time so she could eat the contents of her sack lunch in peace.

"You're Miriam, Ruth's sister, aren't you?" the new arrival asked.

"Yes, that's right."

"I'm Sally Weber. I was terribly sorry to miss Ruth's funeral. We were in Florida and didn't hear until it was too late. She talked about you so much I almost feel I know you."

Miriam searched her memory but was pretty sure Ruth had never mentioned the woman. Of course her sister had had many friends after living her whole life in Maple Landing. Miriam knew she could've forgotten this one.

"That's nice," Miriam said a bit weakly.

"I have a shop in St. Michaels. We often went on buying trips together before my husband and I became snowbirds."

"Ruth seemed to travel a lot," Miriam said. "She certainly had a lot of stock in the store."

"Oh, I can believe that. I don't know how many times we went to auctions and came home with her van loaded to the brim. I special-ize in glassware, so I pretty much limit my buying. I used to ask her what she was going to do with all the miscellaneous stuff."

"She stored it on the second floor and the cellar here. I haven't begun to go through it," Miriam said. "I have to admit, I've been wondering why she bought so much."

"We became good friends, but she never explained. I assumed she was a compulsive buyer. She didn't seem to have any collections of her own. My big problem is I always want to keep the best glass for myself."

"I don't think she collected anything. I've even found family heir-looms in the stock here," Miriam said.

"I just wanted to stop in and tell you how much I miss Ruth," Sally Weber said. "She was such a kind, caring person, but she had a great sense of humor too. I really miss her."

"Thank you. I do too," Miriam said, although it was a little disconcerting to realize this friend had spent so much more time with her sister than she had in recent years.

"If you ever come to St. Michaels, do stop in and see me. We're only open from Memorial Day to Labor Day. The shop is on our family farm, so we're not paying rent while we're gone."

"I'd like to do that," Miriam said, wondering if she could feel closer to Ruth by getting to know her friend.

"Oh, and if you find a hoard of old glass, I'd be glad to make an offer on it. Here's my buy list." She handed over a computer printout. "Sandwich glass literally flies off my shelves—without the breaking, of course. It was made in Sandwich, Massachusetts, on Cape Cod in the nineteenth century. My customers are crazy for the pressed glass in colors, although I also sell a lot of free-blown and blown three-mold."

"I'm afraid you've lost me," Miriam had to admit.

"That's right, you're new to the business," Sally said. "Don't worry. You'll learn fast. Ruth was always proud of how smart you are. Oh, and I can use almost any Depression glass. My customers try to complete sets to use. My own favorite is Lalique, the French glass. If you've ever seen any, you'll understand why."

"You can look around the shop if you like," Miriam offered. "I haven't begun to study glass."

"I don't see anything I can use offhand," Sally said. "Just keep me in mind if you find anything special. I sell online, so you can look up my interests that way."

Shaking her head after her sister's friend left, Miriam wasn't sure whether she'd come to offer condolences or buy glass. Maybe both.

What little Ruth had told her about the business, most dealers and collectors were pretty intense about their interests.

Before she could get to her lunch, Bess was at the door with a covered casserole dish.

"I didn't expect you today," Miriam said. "You've been working here as much as Phoebe."

"My daughter-in-law made a wonderful breakfast casserole for the inn's guests this morning," her friend said. "I heated this up for your lunch. If it isn't hot enough, I thought you could pop it in that little microwave in the office."

"That's sweet of you," Miriam said. "Can you stay while I eat?" Bess's offer was much better than a cold sandwich.

"Love to," Bess said. "I want to hear all about your trip to the county library—and Samuel."

"I don't know what you want me to say. We didn't find any proof that my great-grandfather was a deserter. Or that he wasn't. Samuel was very helpful." She led the way to the back.

"You two still make a cute couple," Bess said as she took a seat next to Miriam's office chair.

"Bess!" Miriam said. "Cute couples are for people Phoebe's age."

"Don't mention it! She's going to the movies with that Jason, and her parents don't even seem to mind."

"I had a visitor," Miriam said to change the subject. "Sally Weber from St. Michaels. She used to go on buying trips with Ruth."

"Did she know why Ruthie bought such huge quantities of stuff?" Bess asked.

"Not a clue, really, unless my sister was just a compulsive buyer. I really regret not seeing more of her in recent years."

"Yes, I remember she was a wonderful sister after you lost your mother."

"She was, but as much as I loved her, I don't think it dishonors her memory to admit she was terribly disorganized. I thought I could take over her store using my skills as a retired high school business teacher. I just didn't know what it would take to run my sister's business."

"You're doing fine," Bess said.

"You're kind to say so, but between you and me, I'm feeling over-whelmed. Without you and Phoebe, I might put a For Sale sign in the window today."

"You won't do that," Bess cheerfully assured her. "Look at all the good that's happened so far. We've gotten reacquainted, you have clues about your ancestor, and Samuel has reconnected with you."

"Reconnected!" Miriam said with a laugh. "Oh, Bess, you have a unique way of putting things."

"I call them as I see them," Bess said with a peal of laughter.

"You're right about one thing," Miriam said. "I can't give up on the store. It's made me feel closer to Ruth, and I still have to figure out how and why she ran the store the way she did."

"For now, eat your casserole," Bess said. "How did you get to be our age without putting on an ounce of weight?"

"Leave it to you to ask that." Miriam took a big bite of the egg casserole with mushrooms and bacon bits. "This is so good I'm tempted to move to your bed-and-breakfast."

The years seemed to fall away as she talked and laughed with her old friend, but some nagging questions still stayed at the back of her mind. Why had her great-grandfather disappeared? And what had possessed her otherwise rational sister to stray close to being a hoarder? The answers had to be somewhere, but for now puzzles were all she had.

Chapter Ten

Monday morning found Miriam working at the counter to inventory a collection of silver spoons. Phoebe had discovered them on the second floor, and Miriam wasn't sure whether to clean them with silver polish or sell them in somewhat tarnished condition. Meanwhile, she examined each one for maker's marks, not that she expected to find one made by Paul Revere. Ruth did seem to put her best buys on display, but there was the distinct possibility she hadn't taken time to examine all her finds.

Her young employee was showing a real gift for discovering saleable items lost in Ruth's huge hoard. She was still upstairs poking through the stack of mildewed boxes where she'd found the spoons when the bell on the door sounded.

Too intent on what she was doing to look up immediately, Miriam was surprised to see Samuel standing on the other side of the counter. Something was different about him, but it took a moment to realize he must have come from the barber. His white hair was closely trimmed, and his beard was even shorter and neater. More importantly, he had a pleasing twinkle in his eyes, reminding her that blue was her favorite color.

"Samuel, nice to see you," she said, self-consciously tucking an errant lock of silver hair behind one ear. She liked to keep her hair in a short bob, but it was way past time for a haircut of her own. The more she struggled to get the shop in shape, the more disheveled she felt. At least today she was wearing beige linen slacks and a presentable print tunic in shades of beige and green.

"I've come to take you away from all this," Samuel said, gesturing around the store interior. "At least for a cup of coffee."

"Actually, I could use a break," she admitted, coming out from around the counter. "Let me put these old spoons in the safe and call Phoebe down to watch the shop."

Normally, Miriam would have been hesitant about his offer to leave the shop when she was in the middle of something—even though she really enjoyed spending time with Samuel—but she needed a breath of fresh air. Although she'd dreamed of running her own business someday, she'd never imagined the amount of work it actually took to operate a retail business. Or, in the case of the shop she inherited, to organize a disorganized jumble of stock.

"Phoebe, I'm going out for a bit," she called up the stairs. "Would you mind coming down to watch the store?"

"Okay, Mrs. Max," came the muffled reply. "I'll be right there."

Phoebe bounded down from the second floor while Miriam watched a bit nervously. Her shop assistant was wearing a long black crinkle-cloth skirt and seemed in danger of tripping over it on every step. So far she hadn't done herself or the store any major damage, but it had proved futile to warn her about being careful. For now, Miriam just kept her away from the high-priced glass and ceramics and hoped for the best.

As soon as Phoebe took over behind the counter, Samuel held the door open for Miriam so they could walk out into the late morning sunshine. So far the June weather had been mild and mostly sunny, and a virtual flotilla of sailboats was skimming the waters of the bay. Business was good for all those who depended on summer visitors, and Ruthie's Antiques was benefiting from the tourist trade, at least in a small way. Miriam had sold more than enough to meet expenses in the first week of June, including Phoebe's salary. It was a good start, but every sale meant an empty spot to be filled from Ruth's huge hidden inventory.

"Where would you like to go?" he asked, offering her his arm.

"Do you mind if we just stroll up the street for a few minutes?" she asked as he linked his arm in hers. "I've been too busy in my own shop to enjoy all Maple Landing has to offer."

"Good idea," Samuel agreed. "Things have changed since we were kids, but it's nice to see a few older businesses have survived."

Tourists roamed picturesque Main Street, wandering in and out of the shops and cafes on either side. A breathless young couple coming out of Foster and Sons Fine Jewelry nearly bumped into Miriam and Samuel. They murmured hasty apologies before scurrying on their way.

"I can guess what they were in doing," Miriam laughed.

"Probably not buying a jeweled dog collar," Samuel joked as they passed Happy Tails, a local pet-grooming center. "Have you thought about changing the name of your shop?"

"No, it'll always be Ruthie's Antiques to me. I can't imagine renaming it. Sometimes new customers ask me if I'm Ruthie. It's a nice connection to my sister."

"I imagine it is," he said, smiling at her.

The years may have added lines to his face, snow to his hair, and a tad more width to his waist—but when Samuel smiled she was instantly transported back to their youth by his boyish grin.

Careful, Miriam, she silently chided herself, *or you'll start giggling like a schoolgirl.*

"A penny for your thoughts?" he asked, steering her around a gaggle of small children. The towheads were clamoring for their beleaguered parents to take them into the Candy Corner Shoppe.

"I'm sure the going rate is at least a quarter during tourist season," she laughed.

"Are you ready for some coffee yet?" he asked as they neared Cooler Beans, Maple Landing's version of a trendy coffee shop.

"I think so...oh, look!" she said, pointing to a placard outside one of her favorite childhood places. "The Orbit Theater is reopening. My sister mentioned it closing years and years ago."

"I loved going there as a kid," Samuel said. "Remember the double features with movies that went back to our parents' time?"

"Sometimes they ran specials, and we could watch different oldies all afternoon on Saturdays," Miriam said.

"Of course, my dad always insisted all my chores had to be done first. I sometimes wished I had a whole gang of brothers to share the work."

"I had a sister, but sometimes I felt like an only child. She was more mother than companion. And, of course, my dad traveled in his work, so I was home alone with Ruth a lot. It was a special bond, but I was the kid and she was the adult after Dad died."

Miriam felt a lump in her throat at the sight of the restored marquee. "They're showing *The Wizard of Oz* as their first feature," she said. "Ruth and I used to have heated debates about what was scarier, the Wicked Witch of the West or the flying monkeys."

"Hands down, the most terrifying thing is a tornado lifting up your house and dropping it down on the other side of the rainbow," Samuel said.

"You know, we never considered that," Miriam said, laughing.

"Samuel? Samuel Bentley?" a booming voice called out.

Miriam turned to see someone she definitely recognized in spite of the years since she'd last seen him. It was Mikey Royers roaring down the sidewalk the way he used to race down the football field when they were all in high school.

"And Miriam, I heard you were back in town!" Mikey said as he caught up with them.

Miriam couldn't help smiling. Mikey made it sound as though she'd been gone a few months instead of many years.

Mikey seemed even shorter and rounder than he had in his youth when he and Samuel had been best friends.

"I just got back from a trip to New York City," he said. "Mikey Jr.'s been getting everything ready for the grand reopening of the theater. Say, you want a sneak peek at the inside?"

What Mikey Sr. lacked for in stature he made up for in volume. *He was the perfect foil to the much taller and quieter Samuel,* Miriam had always thought.

"Miriam, do you have time?" Samuel asked.

"I'd love to. Thanks, Mikey."

Miriam knew the Royers family had owned the movie theater since it opened in the early 1930s, although they went on to other investments when television and changing times had made the movie business unprofitable.

"You know, Mikey," Samuel said, "Miriam and I had our first date here."

"How could I forget? Leroy Mayer and I sat behind you in the back row." The shorter man roared with laughter as he held the door open for Miriam and Samuel. "Here, just let me flick on some lights."

"I wondered if you'd remember," she whispered to Samuel. She was glad they were standing in the dim light of lobby so he couldn't see her blushing. The movie had been dreadful, the popcorn stale, but he'd held her hand in the darkened theater.

"How could I forget?" he echoed Mikey as the lights glared on.

"Oh my!" Miriam gasped as she gazed at the heavy brass wall sconces lining the walls. "I just love the old art deco style," she said, awed by all the lobby renovations. The old threadbare rugs had been replaced with rich-looking crimson carpet imprinted with golden-colored diamond shapes.

Mikey beamed at her words. "Wait'll you see the inside. The missus and me were inspired by the Empire State Building. We love the art deco style. We went to the top of the grand old building while we were in the Big Apple."

"How much restoration did you have to do?" Samuel asked.

"We did extensive electrical work, replaced the roof, rebuilt some interior walls, added a digital projector and sound system…you name it, we probably did it," Mikey said proudly.

"I love the reproductions of old movie posters you have hanging on the walls," Miriam said.

"The ticket booth and concession stand look like they must have in the thirties," Samuel said. "Not that I'm old enough to know!"

"Yep, they match the period," Mikey beamed. "We also have new plumbing and refurbished bathrooms. Now follow me to see the interior of the theater."

"Isn't the marquee new too?" Miriam asked, as she and Samuel followed Mikey.

"It sure is," he said. "We use more eco-friendly bulbs now. Saves a lot on electricity too."

Miriam remembered that back when they were in high school, the only thing that ever made Mikey gloomy was holding the ladder for his dad to change burnt-out bulbs.

With a grand gesture, he opened the doors leading into the theater proper and ushered them in. Miriam stood by Samuel as they waited for the lights to come on, and she couldn't help oohing and aahing as the refurbished interior was revealed.

"Mikey, this is just amazing," she said. The light fixtures on the walls were classic art deco and the seats had been recovered in a plush red fabric that looked like velvet. A crimson curtain with braided gold pulls covered the screen. The woodwork was newly polished mahogany, and faux marble statues stood watch in niches on either side.

"She seats 350," Mikey said proudly.

"You'd think you were an old navy man yourself," Samuel joked at his friend's reference to the building as a *she*.

"Some days 'she' nearly did me in," Mikey admitted.

"Oh my, look at the organ," Miriam said.

She didn't think their old friend's smile could get any wider, but it did.

"It's a historic 1926 manual theater organ. Cost me a pretty penny and worth every cent of it. I plan to play live music before the shows. We're going to feature a mix of old classics and family movies. Plus, I plan to rent out the theater for weddings and anniversary parties. We redesigned the floor plan to include a room big enough for a couple of hundred guests. Are you planning to come to see our first feature, *The Wizard of Oz*?"

"We may have to do that," Samuel said to his old friend. "What do you think, Miriam?"

Before she could answer, Mikey burst forth with more information.

"It's the perfect first movie, see? The sets for Emerald City were based on the art deco style. From a distance all you see are domes and tall, thin towers. The walls are polished green marble set with emeralds. Pure deco! Just like the Orbit! Gotta love it!"

"That never occurred to me," Samuel said.

"Me neither," Miriam said. "And I loved the movie when I was young. In fact, I've watched it quite a few times on TV with my daughter and her children. It would be fun to see it on the big screen again."

"We'll be sure to see it," Samuel said with a wink at Miriam.

Miriam nodded, pleased by the prospect. "I probably should get back to the shop to see if Phoebe is overrun with customers."

She and Samuel thanked Mikey for the sneak peek at the new theater, promising they'd see him again soon.

"Rain check on the cup of coffee?" he asked as they got close to Ruthie's Antiques. "Maybe we should see *Wizard* again."

"Yes, definitely. Thanks for stopping by. That turned out to be a wonderful break," she said.

"Mikey hasn't changed at all, has he?" Samuel laughed.

"Not a bit," she agreed.

"I'm glad we got a glimpse of the old place," he said.

Miriam was sure Samuel was going to say more—after all, she hadn't given him her answer about going to see *Wizard*—but Phoebe frantically waved at them through the shop window.

"Oh dear, I better see what Phoebe needs," Miriam said, glancing over to see her shop assistant standing by an irate-looking woman holding a large vase.

"Thanks again," she said to Samuel.

"My pleasure."

Miriam went into the shop, wondering wistfully if her first date with Samuel at the Orbit Theater all those years ago would be their only date there. Would they stay casual friends, or was this a second chance at something more?

"I saw this very same vase online for only 220 dollars," the customer was saying.

"I'll have to stand by our pricing," Miriam said. "My sister was very knowledgeable about Roseville."

She smiled at Phoebe as the woman stormed out. Running an antiques shop was proving to be more complicated—and more contentious—than she'd ever suspected. Was her personal life going to be that way too?

Chapter Eleven

Phoebe has been invited for a sail on the bay," Bess said when Miriam opened the front door Tuesday morning. "I was sure you wouldn't object if I came to help out in her place."

"Not at all," Miriam said. "She's been immensely helpful lately. She seems to have a gift for finding things—on the computer and in Ruth's unsorted stock."

"She did feel bad about breaking the salt shaker," Bess said. "I know she's trying to be more careful, but it doesn't come naturally."

"I'm just glad she didn't hurt herself when she slipped. So much is packed into the second story, I should give her hazard pay for working up there. Anyway, a salt shaker without the pepper shaker isn't saleable, so it's no loss to the store."

"Ordinarily I would have insisted she call you," Bess said, "but the boy who asked her is only here summers. She met him last year."

"And you're eager for her to go out with someone besides Jason Downs." Miriam felt torn between sympathy for Phoebe and sympathy for her old friend.

"You got me," Bess said, managing a broad smile. "How was your date? We didn't get a chance to talk when you got back."

"It wasn't a date!" Miriam insisted. "We were lucky to see Mikey Royers. He's reopening the Orbit Theater. The first feature will be *The Wizard of Oz*. I've watched it dozens of times on TV with Lisa and her children, but it's interesting to think of it on a big screen again."

"Oh, are you and Samuel going to see it?" Bess asked, abandoning any attempt at sounding casual.

"Bess! Are you trying to be a matchmaker? Samuel is a friend, but that's all."

"*Mm-hmm*," Bess said.

"Would you mind watching for customers while I do a few things in the office?" Miriam asked.

"Of course not. I'll do a little dusting while I wait."

Miriam felt more at home in the crowded little office than anywhere else in the shop, although Ruth's books were as disorganized as her storage areas. But Miriam was an accountant at heart, and she was trying to work through her sister's systems.

Today, though, she was too distracted to concentrate. Was her friendship with Samuel going to develop into something more? Did she want it to? She believed in second chances, but maybe not for herself.

Ray was seldom far from her thoughts, and she couldn't help but wonder how her beloved late husband would feel about her renewing old friendships in Maple Landing. She suspected he would like Samuel as a friend since both were men of faith concerned about their families and others. Would Ray agree with her decision to pursue a very different life in Ruth's shadow?

He'd often told her to do as she thought best, but they'd always planned to retire together. Neither of them had envisioned the single life she was leading now. Sometimes she missed Ray to distraction, but she owed it to her family and herself to cherish memories of her husband but move on with her life.

The phone broke into her thoughts, and she was happy to tell the caller that they were indeed open for business. Maybe it was time to start placing ads in the local paper, although people were coming without them. She'd planned a grand opening, but judging by the satisfying numbers of sales, customers were shopping for antiques without any promotion on her part.

Still, it would be foolish to be complacent. If there was one thing necessary to a successful retail business, it was advertising. She had to rethink the timing.

"Miriam, can you come out here now?" Bess asked, poking her head into the office. "Someone needs to see you."

Her friend looked a little harried, and Miriam hoped she wasn't needed to handle a difficult customer. Although she recognized bargaining as part of the game in antiques, she'd still been upset by a few people who grew angry or sullen when she wouldn't lower a price to half of the marked amount. So far, every price she checked was modest compared to guidebook recommendations. Ruth had seemed to pay more attention to what she'd paid for an item than to guides. Her sister always had a generous nature, and she gave her buyers a break when she could.

Bess led the way to a man standing at the counter.

"This is Jack Yester," Bess said when they reached him. "He's an auctioneer. This is Ruth's sister, Miriam Maxwell."

"I'm so pleased to meet you," the auctioneer said, reaching out to shake her hand, then handing her a business card with gold letters on black. "Everyone in the trade was extremely sorry about your sister's sudden departure."

Miriam tried not to judge people at first sight, but the description of this man that came to mind was *slick*. Yester had coal-black hair arranged in thin strands over his scalp and a thick mustache that curled down like an Old West gambler's. He was slender except for a basketball belly not concealed by his western-style shirt and bolo neckpiece. At least he wasn't wearing a cowboy hat, although Miriam knew that auctioneers nationwide sometimes wore one as part of a costume for work.

"Thank you," Miriam said, aware of Bess hovering at her elbow. Was her friend trying to be protective? "What can I do for you, Mr. Yester?"

"It's what I can do for you, Miriam. Do you mind if I call you Miriam?"

She did, although she couldn't put her finger on the reasons for her guarded reaction to the man. He obviously wasn't there just to offer condolences, but he also wasn't the first in the antiques trade to scope out the store for possible bargains. Or perhaps to take advantage of her while she was still learning.

When she nodded assent, he replied in a hearty voice. "Call me Jack, please. I think we can be very good for each other."

"How would that be?" Bess asked, still in protective mode.

"It's common knowledge in the trade—" he began.

There was that word again: *trade*.

"What is?" she interrupted.

"That your sister was a volume buyer. I can see the shop is overstocked, and rumor has it she stored a lot too. I'd like to help you dispose of excess inventory. Our auctions bring some of the best prices on the Eastern Seaboard, excepting big cities like Baltimore and Boston. We haul things back to our auction house and sort them to bring the highest possible bids. I can't tell you how important it is to group them in ways that appeal to collectors."

"You're getting ahead of yourself," Bess said.

"She's right," Miriam agreed. "I don't plan to liquidate any stock at this time."

Perhaps she sounded unnecessarily curt, but she wasn't comfortable with the auctioneer's aggressive sales pitch.

"Of course, I wouldn't expect you to get rid of the whole inventory at once. In fact, liquidating the shop alone would take a minimum of three sales. I'd prefer not to hold them on site. There's not enough floor space to accommodate all the bidders who typically attend a Yester auction."

"Perhaps you misunderstood," Miriam said, trying to sound pleasant. "I don't intend to sell any of my sister's stock at this time. I'm just getting into everything she has stored, and it could be years before I know exactly what's here."

"That's the beauty of selling at auction. We do the organizing for you to get the best possible prices. We'll even sort out the storage items and haul the junk to the recycling center or the dump. We pride ourselves on being a full-service auction house."

Miriam knew what a chaotic collection she had to process, and she was still mystified by her sister's overwhelming hoard. But she had no intention of letting any of it go until she knew what was hidden from sight. If the store succeeded under her management, she might need many of the things Ruth had put aside.

Glancing at the business card in her hand, she wondered what it would take to convince the aggressive auctioneer she wasn't ready to let him sell her inheritance.

"I realize this isn't good timing on my part," Yester admitted. "You're probably overwhelmed at this point. May I ask you to keep my card and consider our services when you're ready to sell?"

"All right," Miriam said, giving the weakest possible answer as she slipped his card into the pocket of her denim skirt. If it went through the laundry, it wouldn't be a great loss.

"Oh, I forgot to mention. Some auction houses are charging twenty percent commission with buyer's fees on top. If you consign a significant number of items at the same time, I can give you a much better rate."

"Thank you. I'll keep it in mind." By now, Miriam only wanted him to leave.

"The selling climate is really good now," he said. "With all the TV shows about finding and appraising antiques, everyone wants to get into the game. You know the vagaries of any market. It's better to strike while the iron is hot."

"Unless you burn your fingers," Bess said under her breath.

"We all have to make a living," Yester said, speaking more to Bess than Miriam.

It was beginning to seem as though he wouldn't leave until he wore down her objections, but at last he delivered a closing volley.

"My grandfather started Yester Auction House, and it's been in the family since the mid-twentieth century. We can do very well for you, Miriam. I'll check back when you've had more time to consider selling down at least part of the excess inventory."

The door shutting behind him was a pleasant sound.

"The cheek of that man! His family started by selling livestock at auction. You'd think he was some antiques mogul the way he talks." Bess quickly dropped the subject. "I bought myself a new *Antique Trader* price guide at the bookstore. It's great fun looking at the pictures and the prices. I know how busy you've been, but I think you need to look at some of the current values. You may want to up the prices on some of the items Ruth marked. I'm wondering if she spent so much time on buying trips, she didn't keep up on the value of things already in the store."

"You're probably right," Miriam agreed, although she was beginning to think she'd never get everything done. At least the front section of the display area was starting to look like a high-end antiques shop instead of an overcrowded thrift store. She'd always thought of Ruth as the more artistic Davis sister, which made the way she ran the business even more of a puzzle.

"I bet I could get Charlie to go to the *Wizard of Oz*," Bess said, jumping to another subject. "He owes me a night out, and we don't have to get up at 6:00 AM every day now that Janice and Randy are running the inn. He won't have that excuse anymore, although he'd probably fall asleep during the film."

"How could anyone do that!" Miriam teased.

"We could make it a double date," Bess said. "Then the boys could chat or eat popcorn in the lobby while we enjoy Dorothy walking down the yellow brick road."

"I feel as if I'm on the yellow brick road myself," Miriam said with a light laugh to avoid talking about her friend's suggestion. "Every day brings new adventures."

"And you're seeing old friends with new eyes," Bess said, leaving no doubt she was referring to Samuel.

Was she? Miriam wondered. She couldn't deny it was pleasant to be with Samuel after all the time that separated them. But would she stay in Maple Landing for his sake if her family weren't moving to California? Now she was rushing things as much as Bess had. She didn't know how she felt about Samuel, much less what he thought of her.

Letting her mind go back to the problems at the shop, she was beginning to think of her sister as a big—albeit friendly—spider who'd spread her web over a much bigger territory than her replacement could handle. Would it be a good idea to auction off some of the excess inventory? Miriam's heart was telling her no, even though her mind was toying with the idea.

Chapter Twelve

After convincing Bess to leave before closing time, Miriam worked on a small display of sewing items, moving them to a more prominent place on a shelf. A friend in Terre Haute collected antique thimbles, pincushions, scissors, and other objects a seamstress might have used a hundred or more years ago. Miriam suspected hers would sell well if people could see them better.

Just as she was ready to lock the front door for the day, a tall older woman with tight white curls and a pleasant pink-cheeked face came into the store.

"How may I help you?" Miriam asked.

Usually she liked to greet people, then give them time and space to look over her stock. Today, though, she'd had a long day and wanted to go home. Hopefully the customer wouldn't want to spend a lot of time looking.

"I'm Dora Henderson. Do you buy antiques?" she asked, looking a bit hesitant.

"Yes, I suppose I do." Miriam felt unsure because it was the first time someone had walked into the store to sell something. "This is new to me. I'm Ruth's sister, Miriam Maxwell."

"I understand," Dora said. "I used to serve lunch to your sister. I have a little snack place down by the bay. She liked my Reuben sandwiches."

"Yes, Ruth always did enjoy corned beef," Miriam said. People liked to reminisce about her sister when they came into the store. It was nice to know she was so well liked, but Miriam had been on her feet too long today to encourage a lengthy conversation. "What do you have to sell?"

"I have these little photographs," the woman said, taking a plastic bag out of her quilted carryall. "A friend told me they have a French name, *cartes de visite*. They're like the calling cards people used back in the day, only with photographs. They date back to the War Between the States, so I thought they might have some value. I'd like to help with my granddaughter's orthodontic work. I know they're not valuable enough to pay the whole amount but maybe a part of it."

"Let me see," Miriam said, carefully removing the small photos mounted on cardboard. They were only around two and a half by four inches, just the right size for mailing in a small envelope.

"They all show orphan children," Dora said. "Maybe an orphanage had photographs taken to show around in case a parent was looking for one of them. But that's only my guess. They are sweet-faced little ones, aren't they?"

"Yes, they certainly are," Miriam agreed. "Look at this little girl with her unkempt hair and unhappy expression! She looks like she's going to cry."

"That's a little boy," the woman told Miriam with a smile. "They dressed boys like that until they were out of diapers."

Miriam studied the picture and realized the woman must be right.

"Are they something you might buy?" she asked Miriam with a hopeful expression.

"I don't see anyone famous. There are no soldiers either. They'd be easy to sell if there were. My heart really goes out to the children, but I'm not sure about buying them." Miriam hesitated, realizing it was easier to sell than buy. If she paid too much, she'd lose money on them—or they wouldn't sell at all. If she paid too little, she'd feel guilty about cheating the woman who wanted to sell them.

"You're not interested then?" Dora sounded dejected.

"I like them, but I have no idea what they're worth," Miriam admitted. She'd decided it was better to admit what she didn't know than to bluff. "Do you have any idea what you want for them?"

"No." The woman shook her head. "I thought you would know. Ruth's sister would never cheat me, I know."

"Not on purpose," Miriam agreed, "but I don't know what to offer. Are you in a hurry to sell?"

"Oh no, my granddaughter will be in braces for a good long while, I imagine."

Picking up one of the most poignant images, Miriam's heart went out to the abandoned child. Countless children must have been orphaned by the horrors of the Civil War.

"If you don't mind, I'll look up some information about cartes de visite and get back to you," Miriam said. "I'm just not prepared to make an offer now."

"That would be fine. I'd rather sell them to Ruth's sister even if it means waiting awhile." Dora gathered up the cards spread out on the counter and returned them to the protective covering.

"Great! I'll take your phone number and e-mail address so I can get in touch with you."

"I don't have a computer, but I'll write down my phone number. I'd appreciate it if you call me at home after six. I close the shop at five, but I have to clean up, and I only have one helper, my server."

"I'll get back to you if I decide to buy them," Miriam promised, which seemed to satisfy Dora.

Instead of hurrying home for a simple salad dinner, Miriam started to go back to her computer to research cartes de visite. She was almost sorry she hadn't made an offer right away, but it wouldn't have been good business. She wanted a reputation for fair dealing, both in buying and selling.

Before she could settle down by the computer, she heard the front door open.

"It works!" Phoebe announced, holding up the duplicate key she'd had made.

"It does," Miriam agreed, "but I wasn't expecting to see you today. How was your sailing date?"

"Fine. My grandmother isn't here, is she?" Phoebe was red-faced from the wind and sun on the bay, and she wasn't exactly bubbling with enthusiasm.

"No, she went home," Miriam confirmed.

"Good." Phoebe sank down on a balloon-back nine-teenth-century chair Miriam had moved to the front of the store to better display it. Ordinarily she discouraged sitting on the antiques, but Phoebe looked totally done in.

"Did you have a good time?" Miriam was almost afraid to hear her answer.

"I had an incredible time," Phoebe said in a tone that seemed to belie her words. "Greg and his friends were really nice—they didn't seem at all bothered that I'm a townie. He brought a picnic lunch in an ice chest: pâté, lobster rolls, cheese I'd never even heard of, little horn-shaped pastries so light they nearly floated away. It was fantastic."

"Well, I'm glad you had so much fun," Miriam said.

Phoebe's face fell. "I had a terrible time," she admitted. "All I could think about was Jason. I'd rather be with him in a rowboat than on a yacht with Greg, not that he isn't a nice guy. My parents were practically doing handstands when he came to pick me up in his Corvette. And Gran! I hated seeing her so happy for no reason."

"I'm sure she wants you to be happy, no matter what young man you choose to go out with."

"I know." Phoebe slumped forward and rested her cheek on her palm. "Just so long as it isn't Jason Downs. Gran can't get over the feud she had with his grandmother in high school."

"Your grandmother is one of the best-hearted people I've ever known. When she gets used to your friendship with Jason, she'll be happy for you."

"No, she won't. You don't know the way she is now. When she gets an idea in her head, there's no way to change her mind."

Upsetting as it was to hear Phoebe's opinion of Bess, Miriam wondered whether she knew her old friend as well as she thought she did. Maple Landing had changed, and so had the people she remembered there. No matter how fond she was of Bess, she had to admit a lot had happened in their years apart.

Was that true with Samuel too? Was she kidding herself in thinking their friendship could pick up where it had left off? Maybe it was too late to retrace her steps with former friends. Coming to Maple Landing might be a detour, not a second chance.

"Things will work out." Was she reassuring herself or Phoebe? Maybe a little of both.

"Yeah." Miriam had taught high school long enough to know Phoebe meant, "No way."

"Are you in a hurry to get home?" Miriam asked, deciding to try distracting Phoebe. In truth, she really could use some help researching on the computer.

"Not at all," Phoebe said. "They'll want a blow-by-blow account of my day, but Gran won't believe I didn't have a fabulous time."

"If you have time, I need some information on cartes de visite," Miriam said. "A woman came into the shop wanting to sell some."

"One of those little pictures of Abraham Lincoln sold for nearly forty thousand dollars a few years back," Phoebe said. "Of course, he'd signed it himself."

Miriam never ceased to be amazed by the odds and ends of information Phoebe picked up. Maybe a career in antiques would be ideal for her. Miriam had a vague idea Phoebe should go to college and major in fine arts. Of course, as a teacher, she'd always tried to steer her students into careers where they could succeed.

Standing up, Phoebe nearly tripped over a child's table from the 1930s. She jiggled the stack of vintage board games displayed on it and narrowly missed colliding with a pedal car Miriam especially liked.

"Sorry," the young woman said, apologizing to the toys. "I'm a little loopy from all that sun on the bay."

Oh, my dear, Miriam wanted to say. *You're the proverbial bull in a china shop, and that's on a good day.* Instead she led the way to the office.

Rather than watch as Phoebe's fingers flew over the keys, Miriam went back to the front door and locked it, pulling down the shade. In a surprisingly short time, her shop assistant appeared in the office doorway, calling her to come see what she'd found.

"People were crazy for cartes de visite," Phoebe reported, resuming her place behind the computer. "It all started in Paris in 1854. People at the time used a lot of calling cards, but after then little cards with photos were the things to have. People collected them in albums, and not just pictures of their relatives either. Photographers sold ones of famous people. Look, here's one with John Wilkes Booth before he killed Lincoln. I guess he was as popular as a rock star."

Miriam wanted to know the value of Dora Henderson's cartes de visite, but she knew Phoebe would get to it in her own way.

"Did she have any soldiers?" Phoebe asked, still checking different sites.

"No, only orphan children," Miriam said.

"Too bad—well, too bad they were orphans," Phoebe said, "but soldiers had them taken to send home to relatives in case they didn't get home themselves. Collectors will pay quite a bit for those. And for famous people."

"And children?" Miriam prodded, with visions of going home and settling down in her slippers and housecoat with a good book.

"See for yourself," Phoebe said.

A few examples on the screen were worth the price of dinner out for two, so perhaps she should buy them. There was still the question of whether they would sell. Did Ruthie ever hesitate before investing her money in stock for the shop? From what Miriam had seen so far, it appeared she bought first and thought later—if at all. Or at least that was the impression she got from the huge amount stored above and below the shop.

"I'm glad you stopped by on your way home," Miriam said. "Someday you'll have to show me how you find answers so fast on the Internet. Although I have to admit, I'm perfectly happy having you as my computer expert."

"I'm having fun with it," Phoebe admitted, standing to leave. "And thanks for listening to me. You think Jason is nice, don't you?"

"He seems very nice," Miriam said, answering truthfully although she felt faintly disloyal to Bess. The last thing she wanted was to be in the middle of a disagreement between her valued employee and her longtime friend. The two of them gave her hope she might be able to make a go of Ruth's shop. The real issue was whether Maple Landing was the place where she belonged. Was she being unrealistic to think she could fit in again after so many years? Did she have any talent for running a retail business?

She walked home thinking of the abandoned children on the carte de visite photographs. Her problems were small compared to those of little ones orphaned by war. Would she be honoring them if she bought their little portraits? She could see them framed in a prominent place in the store, but now she was thinking like a museum curator, not an antiques dealer.

Ruth had been a sensitive, loving person. She must have suffered from dilemmas like this in the course of running her business. Was that what triggered her buying binges? Perhaps her antiques talked to her, linking her to the sorrows and disappointments of the people who'd owned them.

After many years as a teacher, Miriam felt like a beginning student again. What else would she find out about her dear sister in the course of running her business? Was this her most important motivation for coming back to her hometown? Whether she stayed or not, she was sure to learn some life lessons about herself.

Chapter Thirteen

Sitting in front of her dressing table Wednesday morning, Miriam thought back to the Christmas when her father gave it to her. He'd found it in a resale shop in Baltimore and had it shipped home to surprise her. As a teenager she'd loved primping in front of the big mirror in its tiger maple frame, but more importantly, it was art deco–style like the one her mother used to own. Father couldn't bring himself to move Mother's out of the room he was using alone, but his gift was a lovely substitute with honey-hued curved wood and a matching seat.

Now that she was running her sister's antiques shop, she looked at the piece with newfound appreciation. Why hadn't she taken it with her all those long years ago when she'd first married? Perhaps it was because she wanted to start fresh with Ray, selecting furniture together when they could afford it.

Ruth and her late husband had used the master bedroom throughout their marriage, so it was no surprise Ruth had stayed there until her death. Miriam thought of using it as her own now, particularly since it had a charming window seat with a distant view of the bay, but returning to her childhood room seemed more appropriate.

Someday she'd have to do some major renovating and redecorating if she intended to live in the house permanently. For now, she was enjoying the wallpaper with a delicate pattern of pink roses and the white woodwork that lightened the whole room. The broad oak floorboards were in keeping with the original décor, and she enjoyed the portraits of distant relatives in walnut oval frames, not that she could identify most of them.

When she was ready to go, she noticed the metal button Bess had found in the old canning jar. She'd tossed it in a porcelain pin tray with other odds and ends and forgotten about it. Could it have belonged to her great-grandfather? It was definitely a Confederate officer's uniform button, but there was no way of knowing where Ruth had found it.

Picking it up, she stared at it for a few moments, but it was only a bit of metal to her. Maybe she should've showed it to Samuel, but he was out of town for a couple of days. Incredible as it seemed, she was missing a man she hadn't seen since her high school days.

Slowly descending the staircase, Miriam tried to decide what to tackle at the store. There was no shortage of potential projects, but her mind kept going back to Captain Thomas Davis, her disgraced great-grandfather.

The trip to the county library hadn't turned up any positive information, although she was glad he hadn't been listed as a deserter by his regiment. Of course, that didn't mean he hadn't slipped through the cracks in the chaotic final days of the war.

After finishing her cereal and juice at the kitchen table, she closed her eyes and tried to imagine her soldier-ancestor. Had his hair been fair and curly like her grandfather's in his youth or tinged with red like her father's? The men in the Davis family were only a little over medium height, but they carried themselves well with broad shoulders and lean frames. If there was one trait her father and his father shared, it was an abundance of energy. Was Captain Davis a leader of men or a craven deserter? Or perhaps he was a combination of both, a man who'd given his all and succumbed to the horrors of the battlefield.

Although she'd always felt far removed from her great-grandfather, her curiosity was growing since she'd returned to Maple Landing.

Only a couple of customers visited the shop that morning, although Miriam was pleased to sell a nineteenth-century English flow blue platter that had gathered a thick coat of dust before she found it hidden on top of a hutch. The buyer had been so pleased to find it that she paid the full price without a bit of bargaining. Flow blue had never been Miriam's favorite because the design was blurry. It was made by firing stencils on white earthenware or sometimes porcelain. The pattern burned away and looked a bit smeary. Of course, the flow blue style had a huge following, and Miriam knew her opinion wasn't widely shared.

In spite of the successful sale, she couldn't get her ancestor out of her mind. Although the half map Samuel had found in the desk was promising, she hadn't made any progress on deciphering the clues. An *X* marked a town that didn't seem to correspond to any modern-day Maryland town. She couldn't help wondering if the *X* meant that's where the riches her great-grandfather wrote of were located. Her head was fairly spinning from all the unanswered questions.

"You okay, Mrs. Max?" Phoebe asked, real concern in her voice as she broke into Miriam's daydreaming.

"I'm fine, Phoebe. Thank you. I was just thinking about the map Admiral Bentley found in the desk he bought."

Phoebe nodded sympathetically, which made Miriam all the more thankful for Bess's granddaughter. What Phoebe lacked in grace, she more than made up for in helpfulness. She was sharp as a tack and a whiz at finding things in the shop. Now Miriam could add alertness to her other skills.

"Do you want me to do an Internet search for the town?" Phoebe asked.

Miriam, along with Bess, had scoured a current atlas looking for the town shown on the faded map. So far they didn't even know where it was, let alone the significance of hiding it in a false-bottomed drawer. Maybe it was time to put a twenty-first-century sleuth on the job.

"That's a good idea, Phoebe," Miriam said. "Why don't you go back to the office and see what you can come up with on the computer?"

The faint *X* on the map marked a town named Suetville, and so far neither she nor Samuel had turned up a town with that name.

"Here's the map," Miriam said to Phoebe, handing over the fad- ed parchment. "Be careful with it." So far her shop assistant had a better record with paper items than glass, but a word of caution was still in order.

"Don't worry, Mrs. Max. I won't let any harm come to it. I won't even drink soda while I'm working on it."

Gratefully, Miriam watched Phoebe head toward the office computer. Maybe the younger woman could figure it out where she and Samuel had failed.

Tourists swarmed the shop all afternoon, and Miriam was exhausted when the doorbell signaled the exit of a group of customers, several sun-bronzed women who'd come to Maple Landing to enjoy sailing. They discussed her merchandise in critical terms and bought nothing, but she was learning not to take people's comments to heart.

Free for the moment, she was curious to see if Phoebe had found anything useful. Going back to the office, Miriam found the dejected girl staring glumly at the computer.

"No luck, I take it?" Miriam asked, already knowing the answer from the expression on Phoebe's face.

"I tell you, Mrs. Max, I'm stumped," the younger woman said.

Miriam knew Phoebe prided herself on her Internet skills. If her Web-savvy employee felt defeated, it didn't bode well for finding answers.

"Why don't you tell me what you've done so far?" Miriam asked.

"Well, at first I thought the faded name on the map might say 'Stewartstown' because there is a modern-day town with that name. But looking more closely, I saw it couldn't possibly be that. The name on the old map is definitely Suetville," Phoebe said.

Phoebe was warming to her subject, and Miriam couldn't help finding the girl's enthusiasm contagious. *Surely*, she thought, *they'd suss this out.*

"Then," Phoebe said, "I looked for meat-packing towns because of the name *Suetville*. Who would give a town a name like that unless they were into pigs? But still no luck. The Civil War town of Suetville seems to have vanished into thin air."

Even though Miriam felt frustrated by the lack of results, she didn't want to discourage Phoebe's enthusiasm for the project. "Keep going…"

The bell on the door signaled the arrival of more customers and interrupted Miriam before she could finish her sentence. "I'll be back as soon as I can," she said.

"I'll figure this out, I promise," Phoebe vowed, not looking up from the computer.

Miriam hurried out to greet her customers, pleased by Phoebe's determination. She knew her own patience with computer searches wasn't up to her employee's.

The couple who came in wanted to add pieces to their Fiesta collection of ceramic dishes. They were knowledgeable and wanted only the early colors, especially the original ones from the 1930s: royal or cobalt blue, turquoise, yellow, and a distinct reddish-orange. Miriam knew them well because her family had still been using the long-lasting dishes when she was growing up. She couldn't forget eating spaghetti from a cobalt blue plate, never an appetizing combination.

"Are you sure this tumbler is the right shade of red?" the wife asked.

"If you're not sure, don't get it," her pragmatic husband said.

"Yes, but I haven't seen this one before," she argued.

Although she wanted to see if Phoebe had learned anything, Miriam stayed patient and was rewarded by a sale of over three hundred dollars. She was relieved when the shop was empty again so she could check on Phoebe's progress. Before she could get back to the office, the bell chimed again, but this time it was Bess.

"How's it going?" her friend cheerfully asked.

"Sales or sleuthing?" Miriam replied with a welcoming grin.

"Either," Bess said.

"I was just about to check on the sleuthing," Miriam said. "Phoebe is working on the old map, trying to find where Suetville is—or was. Care to join me?"

"You don't have to ask me twice," Bess said.

"Eureka!" they heard Phoebe cry out.

"What is it?" Miriam asked as she hurried to the office with Bess right behind her. "Is everything okay?"

Phoebe was grinning from ear to ear, a triumphant look on her face. "More than okay, Mrs. Max. Hey, Gran, how are you?"

Bess was theatrically clutching her heart. Miriam knew Phoebe had that effect on her grandmother.

"I'm okay, just don't scare me like that, dear," Bess chided.

"Sorry," Phoebe apologized. "It's just I found what we're looking for!"

Miriam could tell the younger woman was beside herself with excitement.

"Tell us," she urged. Phoebe's excitement was contagious, and Miriam was eager to decipher the map. It might be too much to hope that she could clear the stain on her great-grandfather's character, but she wasn't going to give up as long as there was any hope.

"Well," Phoebe said, pausing for dramatic effect, "I finally hit pay dirt."

Miriam had to smile at the younger woman's use of the old cliché. She worried Phoebe was spending too much time around old things—and old people.

"I found a map from the 1890s at the online archive at Dixon State College, a small school south of Baltimore," Phoebe said, gesturing at the computer screen. "Suetville was an old town that never grew very big. After the War Between the States, a new town was founded nearby to build railroad cars."

"I've heard that railroads would do that—start new towns where their tracks went. It makes sense they'd do that to build the cars too," Bess said.

"That new town was Stewartstown. It still exists today," Phoebe said triumphantly.

"What about Suetville?" Miriam asked.

"It's simple," Phoebe continued as the two older women hovered over her shoulders. "During the recovery that followed the war, the two towns—Suetville and Stewartstown—grew together. You know, like big cities swallow up the little villages around them. In 1901, the two towns merged and became known as just Stewartstown."

"I can see why they wouldn't choose Suetville as the name for both towns," Bess said.

"When did this happen?" Miriam asked, still wondering what the significance of the map was. "Why was Suetville so hard to trace?"

"It was really hard to figure out because the two towns were only on the same maps for less than forty years from the end of the war until 1901," Phoebe explained. "Modern maps are useless in locating Suetville."

"I understand," Miriam said. "When my great-grandfather made the map, Stewartstown didn't exist. Unfortunately he didn't include any indications of where it was located, like nearby towns or rivers."

"As soon as I found the history of the two towns, I realized Suetville was the western edge of Stewartstown. It just wasn't called that anymore," Phoebe said.

"You've done a great job, Phoebe. Thank you so much," Miriam said, knowing they now had a starting point to trace her great-grandfather's history. Was Suetville his last destination? Why was it so important that he made a map? And even more puzzling, what were the obscure symbols that still meant nothing to any of them?

"In other words," Phoebe said, "Stewartstown swallowed Suetville. They became one town and wisely got rid of the Suetville name. Imagine going to a high school football game today and yelling, 'Go, Suetville, go.'"

"The cheerleaders would love being called Suet girls," Bess said with a giggle.

Miriam laughed at her old friend's comment. "I really appreciate both of you helping me."

Her next thought was to pick up the phone. She couldn't wait to share this new information with Samuel, but maybe it would be more fun to wait until she could tell him in person.

Chapter Fourteen

For the first time since she'd reopened the shop, Miriam felt free to leave it in someone else's care for an extended period. It was wonderful to be able to trust Phoebe to take care of the business, and Bess had taken the hint to let her granddaughter solo.

After doing a few necessary chores at home, Miriam briskly walked to the main shopping area of town where she had a much-needed hair appointment. Shaggy manes were fine for young women, but Miriam was beginning to feel like the rag doll in her shop, hair going in all directions.

"How would you like your hair styled today?" the young beautician asked when Miriam settled into a chair at the Hair Emporium.

Gigi, as her name tag indicated, had a huge mop of hair that was black at her scalp and faded down to bright orange at the tips. Taking a deep breath and hoping for the best, Miriam requested a simple bob and rejected a suggestion for platinum coloring.

In spite of a few misgivings about her stylist, Miriam felt relaxed and happy in the hair salon. Fortunately it was soon obvious Gigi's skill with scissors was better than her taste in personal hair styling as small snippets of silver hair fell on the purple cape.

"You have such beautiful patrician features," Gigi said. "I'd give anything to have a nose like yours. I've thought of getting a nose job, but my boyfriend is afraid it might make me look like a baboon."

"That's unkind of him," Miriam sympathized. "But you certainly don't need surgery. You have a perfectly nice nose. I like a face with character."

Smiling inwardly, she felt like a teacher again. Although she'd never officially been a counselor, her students had come to her with personal problems when they thought the world was against them. Being able to help was what made teaching so satisfying. She missed it but was firmly resolved to keep the future in the forefront.

Watching the beautician style her hair with a rounded brush and a dryer was a revelation. After seeing how well her hair turned out, she purchased a similar brush and some styling gel from a shelf of beauty products in the waiting area. She stepped out onto the street feeling too good for a mundane Thursday morning.

Idly window shopping, she wasn't in any hurry to get to the shop. It would be good for Phoebe to have full responsibility for a bit longer, so she ducked into a coffee shop to treat herself to a white chocolate mocha, her favorite self-indulgence.

There was no table service, so she waited at the counter until her drink was ready. Just as the server handed over the cup, she heard a familiar voice behind her.

"Good morning, Miriam. You're looking fine this morning."

Flushing with pleasure, she turned to look at Samuel, smiling broadly. "Why, thank you, Samuel."

"May I join you for coffee?" he asked with a pleasant expression. "I never did like indulging alone."

"My pleasure. I'll find a table," she said.

Not surprisingly, he carried a big white mug of freshly brewed black coffee when he joined her a few minutes later. She couldn't visualize the retired admiral with a frothy sweet drink.

"I'm glad I ran into you," he said, sipping the scalding coffee without hesitation. "I just got back to Maple Landing last night."

"Did you have a nice trip?" she asked.

"As nice as it could be bucking traffic all the way to New York City and back. I do have some good news, though."

"About your book?" She had a vague idea it was the reason for his absence.

"Yes, I have an agent who might want to represent me. Publishers are especially interested in the War Between the States because of the 150th anniversary of the surrender is coming up. The agent I talked to is big on history. He suggested I narrow the focus to the Confederate navy."

"That won't make a very long book, will it?" Miriam asked, sipping her mocha with pleasure. "I didn't think the South had much of a navy."

"Not compared to the United States Navy," he said with a smile. "But our sailors deserve more credit than they usually get. Not only did they help break Union blockades, they made the war more expensive for the North by attacking their merchant ships anywhere they could find them. And of course, they protected our coasts from invasion by sea."

"I can see where there's an important story to be told there," Miriam said, genuinely intrigued by Samuel's take on history. "Maybe if Thomas Davis had been in the navy, we could find more about him."

"I haven't given up on him," Samuel said. "I still want to help you find any information that may be available."

"I don't want to interfere with your book. It sounds like a daunting project," she said.

"Not as daunting as you might think," he said, taking a big swallow of the hot coffee. "I've been studying naval history for a long time. Now I just need to bring it all together. Even if I don't work more with the agent, he gave me valuable advice to narrow my focus. I can do other historical periods in other books."

"I'm excited for you," Miriam said with a smile.

The handsome white-haired man across from her still had the boyish enthusiasm she'd loved in high school. But were either of them the same people they'd been?

"Here I am, rattling on about my book," he said sheepishly. "How are things going at Ruthie's Antiques?"

"Pretty well so far," Miriam said. "I've left Phoebe alone in the store this morning. She's been giving her all to the job—and we've gone two or three days without any breakage. But more importantly, she made a breakthrough on finding Suetville. It's part of Stewartstown now. Phoebe was able to find it on the computer."

"Good for her!" Samuel said. He had a knack for showing he cared about everyone he met. "I tried calling you earlier. You probably have a message from me at the shop."

"Oh, do you have any new ideas about tracing my great-grandfather?"

"Not yet, but I have been thinking about Mikey's old theater. The opening night is tomorrow, and I just happen to have two tickets, compliments of my old buddy. Would you be interested in going?"

Was he asking her on a date? Did people their age actually "date"?

"I always liked *The Wizard of Oz*," she said without committing herself. Maybe he was only offering her one of the tickets.

"Mikey will be disappointed if I don't show up," he said. "But I'll enjoy it a lot more if you go with me."

"I would like to see it again on a big screen," she admitted, not wanting to seem as eager as she felt. She was happy to renew her friendship with Samuel, but she wasn't quite ready to commit to any new relationship, especially not one with roots in the past.

"I'll take that as a yes," he said, smiling as though he'd read her thoughts. "There are showings at seven and nine. My tickets are for the later show. Does that work well for you?"

"Fine," she said. "I'll look forward to it."

"As long as we're going to the movies, how about having dinner first? I haven't begun to try all the restaurants that weren't here when we were kids. Never did care much for eating out alone," he confessed.

Miriam had to agree with him. She always felt conspicuous eating alone in a restaurant, just as she'd never gone to a movie in a theater by herself.

"That would be nice," she agreed. Did having dinner first make it an official date? "I can trust Phoebe to lock up now, so I won't be pressed for time."

"Put on your party clothes, and we'll make an evening of it," Samuel said.

When she got back to the store, she checked with Phoebe. "Will you be able to close the store tomorrow evening?"

"No problem. I have a Friday-night date with Jason, but he's picking me up here. Saves him having to make small talk with my family."

* * *

On impulse, Miriam stopped to have her nails done on her way to work Friday morning. Apparently early-morning appointments weren't popular with the summer crowd, so she was able to get in right away. She walked out of the shop admiring her blue fingernails. This was the first time she'd ever tried any color not some shade of red or pink, and it made her feel younger and more daring. She planned to wear her best white jersey dress with turquoise earrings and necklace. Hopefully her nails wouldn't clash with her jewelry, but she could always wear something else if they did.

"You look happy this morning, Mrs. Max," Phoebe said when Miriam got to the shop. "I hope you'll be even happier when I tell you what I just sold."

"Don't keep me in suspense," Miriam said, glancing around to see whether she could spot what was missing.

"That weird little statue with the shell eyes," Phoebe blurted out, too excited to wait for Miriam to guess. "I'll be glad not to have it staring at me all day."

"Well done," Miriam said, almost as glad as Phoebe was to have it off the shelf. She didn't see herself specializing in primitives anytime soon.

"I had to give a ten percent discount," Phoebe admitted. "A dealer in primitive art bought it to take back to his shop in Boston."

"That's fine. Every time we sell something, that's a little more shelf space to bring something down from upstairs. And we've hardly looked in the basement yet."

By late afternoon, Miriam realized her whole day had gone well. Was it because she was anticipating her evening with Samuel? Or maybe it was the relief of having her old friend's granddaughter work out so well.

Bess came into the store just as Miriam was planning to leave.

"Hello, stranger," Miriam teased, although there was no reason for Bess to come in every day. She was, after all, a volunteer.

"I've had the most fantastic day," Bess raved. "Our bed-and-breakfast was reviewed by an incognito food expert a few weeks ago, and we're going to be featured in a regional magazine."

"Congratulations!" Miriam said. "You deserve it."

"Actually I have to give most of the credit to my daughter-in-law. Janice's breakfasts really measure up to the standards we've set. Randy is bursting with pride. In fact, we thought the family would go out for a celebration dinner this evening. We'd like you to join us. You too, Phoebe," Bess said.

"Oh, I'm really sorry," Miriam said. "I already have plans."

"For tonight?" Bess sounded surprised.

"Me too, Gran," Phoebe said while her grandmother was still re-acting to Miriam's refusal. She went back to the office, perhaps to get out of range when Bess wanted to know what she was up to.

"Samuel and I are going to the reopening of the Orbit Theater," she explained. "Mikey Royers gave him a pair of tickets."

Did she mention the free passes because she needed an excuse for going? Her life was getting too complicated when she had to put spin on her activities for Bess.

"You have a date with Samuel! I'd say join us, but you two prob-ably have lots of catching up to do."

"I'm going to leave early," Miriam interrupted, a little too unsure of her decision to talk it over with her friend. "I'm sure Phoebe can manage until closing time. You have a wonderful granddaughter, Bess. You did me a big favor when you introduced us."

No grandmother could argue with a compliment like that. Miriam took advantage of her friend's proud glow to make her exit.

* * *

Samuel came for her exactly when he'd said, not that she was sur-prised. She'd been dressed and ready to go for half an hour, know-ing he was never late. Now that she was with him, she worried what he might think about her nails. After all, bright-colored polish was for younger women and even children, not someone her age.

At least she wasn't sorry for wearing one of her best dresses when he complimented her. Samuel had dressed up too. She loved the way he looked in a navy blazer with a white turtleneck under it. His beard looked newly trimmed, and he'd used a particularly aromatic sandalwood aftershave. Maybe this was a real date, odd though the idea was.

By the end of their dinner at a small Italian restaurant near the bay, she was enjoying herself too much to analyze their evening together.

"Great pasta," Samuel said over small cups of apricot gelato, an Italian frozen dessert almost too good to be believed.

"It's a good thing they serve small portions of this," Miriam said. "I don't think there's a nicer flavor anywhere."

Over dinner they'd talked about their children, his book plans, her store, and old friends. She couldn't quite get over the strangeness of being with him after so many years, but the delightful movie helped her relax.

"We should do this more often," Samuel said as they were walking out of the beautifully refurbished theater.

"It's been a lot of fun," she agreed. "I wonder what other movies Mikey plans to show."

"Did I hear my name?" Their rotund friend suddenly appeared before they could reach the door. "What did you think of it?"

"The theater is a wonder," Miriam said.

"It was like going back in time," Samuel agreed. "We were wondering what's up next. Are you going to show more old classics?"

"Depends on what you call old," Mikey said, drawing them to the side. "I'm looking at a run of the movies we saw here when we were teenagers."

"I would call those old," Miriam said.

"Or not," Samuel said, giving her a wink.

A wink! What did that mean?

"We may stroll down to the bay. See if it's cooled off outside," Samuel said. "Maybe we can get together sometime soon. I'd like to meet your wife, Mikey. Thanks again for the tickets."

"Great to have my old bud here—and lovely Miriam," Mikey said in his usual exaggerated way.

As she walked out on Samuel's arm, Miriam couldn't help but wonder if the *we* meant they were a couple again in Samuel's eyes. It seemed improbable, but how did she feel about it?

* * *

Samuel breathed in the fresh, salty air on the walkway overlooking the bay. It felt nicer than he liked to admit to himself to have Miriam on his arm, obviously enjoying herself as he was.

"This is gorgeous weather for the first half of June," she said, stepping carefully on the boardwalk in her high heels.

The weather was always a safe subject, he thought with a secret smile. He'd worried Miriam might not be ready for dinners and movies out together, but they'd talked nonstop over dinner without running out of conversation. It was great to catch up, and even better to enjoy her company.

"I'd like to buy a sailboat," he said. "There's nothing like sailing on the Chesapeake Bay. Can't let the summer people have all the fun."

"What did you have in mind?" she asked.

"I really haven't had time to do any shopping, except online. I guess now I'll have to get serious about my book—I like to think of it as my first book."

"It sounds like you're doing the same thing I am," Miriam lightly teased. "Starting a new career."

"Yes, I'm excited about it, but there's one drawback. I'm used to having a lot of people around," he admitted. "Working alone is the hardest part."

"Yes, being alone is hard. Our old family house is pretty big just for me. I've been thinking of ways to utilize some of the space, but I'm not quite ready to take in boarders." Her light laugh was a lovely sound.

"A lot of old homes have been converted into apartments," he said to keep the conversation going. "I'm not sure I'd like having renters though. It's a big job just keeping a historical home in good condition. Painting your foursquare with those dormer windows will be a monumental task."

"Well, you won't see me up on a ladder trying to paint up high by the roof, that's for sure," she said.

"I would hope not!" he said, distressed at the thought of Miriam risking her neck. "Shall we head back to my car?"

"I do have to open the shop tomorrow," she said, although she sounded hesitant to end their pleasant evening.

As much as he would like to prolong their parting, he knew it wasn't sensible. They'd had a wonderful evening, but there would be other times together—hopefully soon.

He wanted to help her track down her ancestor, especially if Thomas Davis turned out to be an honorable soldier. He didn't want her to go through the disappointment of knowing her great-grandfather had been a deserter, or worse, a turncoat. The lack of information worried Samuel. Was it possible the captain wasn't what he seemed to be? He wouldn't be the first young man who'd sold out to the other side, if that was why he'd disappeared.

Chapter Fifteen

When they reached Samuel's car parked on the street near the theater, he opened the door for her. The top was down, and she hadn't thought to bring a scarf. Fortunately her newly styled hair held up in the almost windless evening. She could remember a time when she loved riding with him in his convertible, her hair streaming in all directions as the ocean breeze whipped against them.

"You always did like convertibles," she said, snapping the seat belt.

"I like them even better now," he said. "They're much safer with seat belts and a roll bar, but we did take chances when we were young."

"We called it having fun," she mused.

She'd never felt in any danger with Samuel. Even in high school he'd been a skillful driver, never one to take risks. Mikey had been just the opposite. When they double-dated with him, Samuel usually insisted on driving. His friend's favorite game was roaring down Bayside Road in his old pickup with four of them squeezed in the cab, his date and Miriam screaming at him to slow down.

"This was a fun evening," Samuel said. "All that was missing was a jumbo-size popcorn during the movie."

"Sorry, I wasn't up to it after our dinner," Miriam said.

"Neither was I," he agreed as he started the car.

"Before you take me home, would you mind stopping by the shop?" Miriam asked, rummaging in her white leather handbag for her keys. "I forgot to give Phoebe the combination to the safe, and we made a few big sales today. I'm sure she locked the proceeds in the register, but I'll sleep better if I pick up the cash before I go home."

"No problem," he said as he headed to the shop only a few blocks away.

When he stopped at the curb beside her store, she quickly got out. "I'll only be a minute or two."

"Wait, I'll come with you." He got out from behind the wheel before she could protest.

Although she never felt afraid at night in Maple Landing, she appreciated having him beside her as she went to the door. This part of town seemed deserted, and the closest streetlight was way down on the corner, too far away to illuminate her storefront. Only the faint glow of a security light inside helped her find the lock on the door.

"Oh my," she said when she tried to insert her key in the lock. "That's odd."

"What's wrong?" Samuel asked.

"The door isn't locked." It swung inward with no help from her.

"Here, let me see." Samuel sounded tense.

He stepped ahead of her and pushed the door all the way open. She could tell by the swishing sound that the shade was still pulled down. Phoebe would ordinarily have lowered it right before locking the door from the outside.

"There's a light switch on the wall to the right," she said.

"Wait here," he said.

She held her breath while he felt his way along the wall until he found the switch.

"Got it," he said as welcome light flooded the interior.

"Oh!" Miriam gasped, shocked by what she saw.

Evidence of intruders was everywhere. A Windsor chair had been overturned at the front, and the display of sewing antiques had been scattered in all directions. A leather-bound set of Charles Dickens volumes were pulled from the bottom shelf of an oak bookcase and tossed around for no evident reason. In fact, the front part of the display room looked as though it had been hit by a small tornado.

"Wait!" Samuel said, reacting to the chaos in front of him. "Don't go any farther. They could still be here."

"I don't hear anyone," she said, hoping the silence meant the intruders had left. Samuel didn't need to warn her to be cautious. She had to clench her jaw to keep her teeth from chattering from the shock of seeing such devastation.

Samuel stood silently beside her for a minute or two as they listened for the telltale shuffling of strange feet or muffled breathing. Miriam was afraid the intruders were hiding upstairs but didn't really want Samuel to investigate. She wasn't prone to imagining things, but this was real and scary. Unknown assailants could be lurking in the shadows or on the second floor.

After a few silent moments, she managed to breathe normally. It helped that Samuel had instinctively reached for her hand and was holding it in a gesture of comfort. He slowly exhaled and relaxed a bit since no intruder had leaped out at them. A formidable player on the football field in his youth, he might try to confront the intruders if they were still there. Fortunately her fear was unfounded. He stayed beside her at the front of the store.

"Can you tell if anything has been taken?" he asked, looking over the mess someone had made at the front of the store.

"Not at first glance," Miriam said. "Let me check the drawer where we keep the receipts."

With a heavy heart, she headed toward the glass-fronted counter. Had Phoebe forgotten to lock the front door? And if so, did she remember to secure the day's proceeds in the vinyl pouch kept in a locked drawer of the register?

With a sigh of relief, Miriam found the drawer was still locked. When she inserted her small key to unlock it, she found the pouch and its contents intact.

"Everything okay there?" Samuel asked.

"Yes, this drawer hasn't been touched."

"Do you think Phoebe forgot to lock the front door when she left for the evening?" he asked, voicing her fear out loud.

"I can't believe she would. She's a tad awkward, but she's not absentminded. She takes her responsibilities very seriously."

Samuel nodded in agreement. "We'd better call the police."

Miriam took out her cell phone and thought of punching digits for an emergency call, but this wasn't an emergency. The person or people who'd broken in could be long gone. She rummaged around for the phone book, located the number of the local police, then patiently explained to the dispatcher about the break-in. While she did this, she watched Samuel pace around the store, being careful to skirt around the overturned objects.

She felt helpless until the police came, and she could tell Samuel did too. It would be folly to start picking up before the police dusted for fingerprints—or maybe they only did that on television and in the movies.

"I feel like I should be doing something," Samuel said, frustration in his voice.

"I know," Miriam said. "But I'm afraid to start cleaning up. I don't want to disturb any clues."

He laughed, and Miriam decided if she had to be the victim of a crime, she couldn't have a better companion. Samuel's presence was reassuring, and his sense of humor mood lightening.

The bell over the door rang, signaling an arrival. Miriam turned and was surprised to see the chief of police taking the call instead of one of his officers. She recognized the man in spite of the fifty extra pounds he carried. Chief Lewis Camden had been a few years ahead of her and Samuel in school. He'd been officious as a teenager, and she was afraid he might still focus on irrelevant details and miss the big picture. She almost wished an officer fresh out of the academy had shown up.

"Well, well," he said, rubbing his hands together as though warming them on a cold January night instead of a mild June evening.

His posture and actions seemed so theatrical, she wondered whether he spent way too much time watching old detective shows to hone his procedural style.

"Samuel, good to see you," Camden said heartily, recognizing him and extending his hand. "I heard you were back. Had enough of the navy, did you? I thought of enlisting once myself, but someone had to keep order on the home front."

"As you can see, Mrs. Maxwell has had a break-in," Samuel said.

"Miriam, Miriam Davis, if I'm not mistaken," he said, seemingly more eager to talk than investigate. "I heard you took over your sister's place. That's my job, knowing what goes on in Maple Landing."

Miriam was pretty sure he was being paid to fight crime, not keep track of who moved to town. "About the break-in…"

"What's the problem?" Camden finally asked.

"I've been burglarized," she said trying not to lose her patience with the man. As a hall monitor in middle school, he'd once given her a detention demerit for not having a proper restroom pass. Was it her fault a teacher's assistant didn't know the procedure?

The chief surveyed the room. "Yep," he drawled. "Looks like some kids had some fun with you tonight."

"Kids?" Samuel asked.

Miriam knew he was trying to keep quiet and let her handle things, but he looked as impatient with the chief as she felt.

"There's been a rash of break-ins around here, petty stuff, little bit of vandalism," Chief Camden said. "It doesn't look like they did any real damage here."

"Lewis…I mean, Chief Camden," Miriam amended when he raised one eyebrow at her familiarity, "why would kids break into an antiques store?"

"Just for something to do," he said. "Does anything appear to be missing? Although I'm not sure how you could tell," he added. "Your sister sure kept her shop filled to the brim."

Miriam bristled but kept her cool. "I'm not sure."

"Tell you what, let me take a look around here—there's an upstairs, isn't there?"

"Yes, and a basement. Someone could be hiding either place."

"I'll check them out while you see if anything's gone missing. Any cash missing?"

"No." Miriam glanced at Samuel. No doubt he could handle things immensely better than Lewis Camden. The police chief still acted like a hall monitor with more authority than sense.

"Now don't touch anything until I get back," Chief Camden said as he walked away.

"Well, how am I supposed to tell if anything's missing if I don't touch anything?" she grumbled her under her breath.

Samuel heard her and laughed. "He hasn't changed a bit since junior high school, has he?"

"Not one bit," she agreed. "You'd think I was the guilty party." She sighed, looking around at the debris.

"Do you think anything was stolen?" She could hear the genuine concern in his voice.

"I honestly don't know," she admitted.

"Do you want me to help you straighten everything up tonight?" he offered.

"You know," she said, "I think I'll just wait and tackle the mess in the morning with Phoebe's help. She's working tomorrow morning because she had a day off to go sailing this week."

He looked so crestfallen that she added, "If you want to stop by, I'd appreciate it. But only if it doesn't take away from your writing time."

"I have time to help you."

Miriam expressed her gratitude, and they quietly talked about the fun they'd had before they found the break-in. Chief Camden must be opening boxes and looking behind old furniture judging by how long it took him to survey the shop. When he finally finished, he didn't have anything to report.

"Find anything missing?" he asked as he scribbled in a notebook.

"Not that I can tell. I'll check more in the morning," she said.

"It sure looks like the work of some young hoods," he said, snapping his little book shut. "Not much I can do unless they stole something and try to sell it. Better be sure your door is locked from now on."

"Hoods?" Samuel gave her a quizzical look after the police chief left. "Does anyone actually use that word anymore?" He shook his head.

"I don't believe kids did this," she said. "It doesn't look random enough. The books are piled around, not thrown. Nothing is broken. I don't even see any scratches or dents."

Samuel thoughtfully pulled on the tip of his beard, looking as perplexed as she felt.

"I might even say it looks staged," he said. "As though someone wanted to send you a message."

"That's what I think," she said. "But we might as well go home now."

A dejected Miriam made sure the door was locked as she followed Samuel out. It had been such a lovely evening until she stopped at the shop.

* * *

As promised, Samuel stopped by Ruthie's Antiques early the next morning. He balanced a cardboard carrier of coffee as he approached the door. The door chime signaled his arrival, but he doubted Miriam could hear the musical jingle over the cacophony of raised voices.

"Gran, I did lock the door up when I left. I know I did," Phoebe was protesting. The distress in her voice was apparent.

"Maybe you just thought you did," her grandmother said.

Samuel himself was distressed to see Miriam looking as though she had hardly gotten any sleep. She had faint violet shadows under her eyes, and the corners of her mouth seemed to point downward.

"Well, nothing appears to have been stolen, so there's really no harm done," Miriam said. "Oh, good morning, Samuel. I told Bess and Phoebe about Chief Camden's theory: juvenile delinquents on the prowl for some fun."

Did her eyes momentarily light up when she saw him? "Brought you ladies some caffeine," he said heartily, placing the carrier on the counter.

A glum Phoebe said thanks but no thanks, but Miriam and Bess accepted his offerings gratefully.

Before they could even lift the lids, the bell sounded again. A woman rushed in as though the place were on fire. Samuel recognized her as Natalie Downs because she'd introduced herself when he'd gone to her store looking at furniture. Otherwise he wouldn't have remembered her from high school. He hadn't bought anything from her.

"Did I hear you were robbed?" Natalie excitedly asked.

"No robbery, just a little B and E," Bess said sourly.

Samuel suppressed a small smile at her tone. He suspected Bess Watkins felt the same way about the furniture store owner as he and Miriam felt about the chief of police. Old school ties didn't mean much when people had never been friends.

"What if the robbers had targeted my store instead?" she asked. "I have brand-new merchandise, not just old castoffs."

Obviously Natalie hadn't come to offer sympathy. He'd always told his children to turn the other cheek, but with some people it was much easier said than done. He debated whether to intervene for Miriam but suspected she could take care of herself.

"There was no robbery, only vandalism," Miriam said.

"Well," sniffed Natalie, "I'd heard there were some incidents lately. Maybe this neighborhood isn't as safe as it used to be. Perhaps you should think about liquidating and putting the building up for sale."

"I'm hardly going to close up shop because of this," Miriam said with conviction.

Samuel congratulated her in his mind.

"Well, when you decide to quit, you know my expansion ideas," Natalie said before she huffed out of the place.

"Grr," Bess said to no one in particular. "That woman really has nerve."

"So you're sure nothing was taken?" Samuel asked. Changing the subject was the best way to calm his friends down.

"Not to the best of my knowledge," Miriam said, sipping her coffee. "We straightened everything up and double-checked inventory. The only item damaged is a vase that has a hairline crack."

"Mrs. Max," Phoebe interjected, "I know I locked the door when I left. I just know I did."

"I believe you," Miriam said.

Samuel didn't miss Bess shaking her head at no one in particular.

"Let me take a closer look at the door now that it's daylight," Samuel offered.

The women crowded around him as he examined the metal plate around the lock. He knew Miriam had the utmost faith in Phoebe and didn't want to believe the young woman had made such a bad mistake.

"Look," he said triumphantly. "The area around the lock shows unmistakable scratches. This door was jimmied by someone who knew how. I would say that eliminates young kids out for a thrill."

"I told you I locked it!" Phoebe said. This was directed at Bess.

Bess looked stricken for having doubted her granddaughter. Samuel felt sorry for both of them, but he was glad to absolve Phoebe of blame. He knew Miriam hadn't wanted to believe Phoebe had been lax about locking up.

"I believe you," Miriam said, "but I'm glad the person who did it left proof."

"I'm sorry for thinking you were careless, dear," Bess said, putting her arms around her lanky granddaughter.

"Now, ladies and gentleman," Miriam said thoughtfully, "we have to figure out who breaks into an antiques store, tosses things around and yet doesn't break anything but one lone vase."

"My thoughts exactly," Samuel said.

"I've broken more things by accident than those so-called teenage vandals," Phoebe added sorrowfully.

"Which means it wasn't teenagers," Samuel said.

Why would anyone want to distress Miriam? What did one or more vandals have to gain by making a mess in her store without taking anything? A robber could've carried away her cash register on the chance there was something inside. And he didn't have to be an antiques expert to know there were some valuable pieces in Ruthie's Antiques.

For now, he had to talk to Miriam about a security system. His biggest worry was she might come to the shop by herself some night and find she wasn't alone. He was surprised—though pleasantly so—to find himself feeling so protective toward his friend.

Chapter Sixteen

So far, the book was lining up well—at least Samuel was pretty sure it was. His strength had always been in dealing with personnel, but he was also confident of his ability to grasp complicated situations. That certainly applied to the Confederates' effort to maintain and deploy a navy.

After getting up at dawn Tuesday for a run along the bay, he'd worked diligently until noon. Now it was time to save what he'd written and do some household chores.

His cousin had helped him move the Queen Anne desk to his office area several days ago, but he hadn't taken time to put his supplies in the drawers. It was an organizing task he'd looked forward to.

The stuck drawer was working smoothly, thanks to an application of liquid beeswax on the runners. He started unpacking the contents of a bin he planned to transfer to the desk, but his mind wasn't at ease. He kept thinking about the break-in at Ruthie's Antiques.

Miriam had been calm and level-headed, insisting the store open as usual. She'd also found a company to install a security system, something her sister had neglected to do. Samuel wasn't so much worried about her immediate safety as he was the reason why someone would scatter things around in the store. There was a message in the mess, he felt certain, but what was it?

When hunger pangs sent him to the kitchen for lunch, he plugged in the panini grill, a sandwich press given to him by a friend as a parting gift when he retired. As soon as the green light showed it was hot, he put one of his favorite sandwiches in it to brown: rye bread with thin-sliced prosciutto, sliced tomato, Swiss cheese, and mayo thinned with lime juice.

Sandwiches were his favorite meal to prepare himself, and he prided himself on creating some tasty ones. But delicious as his hot sandwich was, he couldn't get Miriam out of his mind. As he sat at the kitchen table with his lunch, he glanced through a shopping paper left in his mailbox. The news content was nil, but one advertisement did catch his attention.

Less than an hour later, he biked down to her store, using the opportunity to get more exercise. He had a plan to take Miriam's mind off the break-in, but he also wanted to spend more time with her.

* * *

The nice thing about the Internet, Miriam thought, was how easy it was to keep in touch with family and friends. The downside came when it substituted for personal contact. Although Samuel sent her entertaining little notes on a regular basis now, she would've preferred to see him. She wanted him to look at the plans for a security system before she signed the contract, but mostly she just wanted to be with him again. In spite of the traumatic ending, the evening they'd spent together had made her happier than she'd been in quite some time.

A short time ago she'd sent Phoebe to the five-and-dime, one of the few left on the Eastern Seaboard and a charming reminder of shopping in days past. Phoebe was supposed to buy a list of things, including vinyl gloves to use with caustic cleaning products and a new plastic bucket to replace the battered tin one Ruth had been using. When the bell on the door sounded, she turned expecting to see her assistant.

"Samuel!" Her day got sunnier when he walked into the shop.

"Hello, Miriam. It looks like you have the place in good shape after the break-in."

"It wasn't too difficult with Phoebe's help. And Bess came on Monday to lend a hand. The odd thing is we couldn't find a thing missing except a corkscrew with a dachshund top. I only noticed because it was in a box with a matching bottle opener that was still there," Miriam said.

"Maybe the intruder collects them. Was it valuable?" Samuel asked.

"Ruth must have thought both pieces were reproductions. She only had a price tag of ten dollars for the set. Odd the burglar took the corkscrew when there are so many genuinely valuable antiques in the shop," Miriam said with a frown.

"Everything about the break-in is odd," Samuel said. "Have you heard anything from the police?"

"Not a word. I doubt I will when the chief of police didn't take it seriously. But my instinct tells me the culprits weren't teenagers doing it for thrills. Wouldn't they target someone who'd angered them? I don't remember any young people coming into the store—except a friend of Phoebe's. And I wouldn't dream of suspecting him. He's a very nice boy." *Despite what Bess thinks.*

"I can't help you figure out who did it or why," Samuel admitted. "But I do have an idea. How would you like to go to a country auction with me?"

"Sounds like fun. When is it?" she asked.

"Tomorrow. Can you get away from the store? It starts at ten in the morning and will probably go until late afternoon. Of course, we don't have to stay for the whole auction."

"I'm sure I can." She smiled broadly. "It's a weight off my mind to know Phoebe can take over when I want a day off."

"The auction is being held on a farm about forty-five minutes from here. They listed stuff from the barn to be sold first, so there's no hurry to get there."

"I wouldn't mind going early," Miriam said. "Ruth spent so much time and money at auctions that I'd really like to see what the appeal is. Sometimes I feel as though I didn't really know my sister— at least in later years."

"How will it be if I pick you up around nine at your house?" Samuel asked, looking pleased by her acceptance.

"Wonderful! I'll look forward to it," she said.

* * *

Wednesday morning Miriam woke up with a smile on her face. Not only would she get out in the countryside to enjoy a lovely, sunny day, she'd be doing it with Samuel.

Bess had volunteered to help Phoebe during the afternoon, so she didn't have to worry about the shop. Who knew? Maybe she'd even find an interesting item to add to the store's inventory, not that she was likely to run out of stock anytime soon.

For the outing she decided to wear a full cotton skirt with a ruffle around the bottom. The blue print reminded her of a square-dancing costume, although she'd never tried any kind of folk dance. To help ward off the sun, she decided to take the shawl that matched the skirt to drape over a short-sleeved white knit top. Her old beat-up running shoes would probably be the best choice for walking around a farmyard, but instead she slipped her slender feet into a pair of three-strap sandals. She hadn't thought much about her wardrobe in recent years, but maybe sometime soon she could go to Baltimore on a shopping trip.

Samuel was ten minutes early, but she was ready. Old habits die hard, and he'd always been one to show up before the appointed hour.

"You look lovely today," he said, escorting her to the car. "I have the auction notice here if you'd like to see what they're selling."

While he buckled up and started off, she scanned the page of newsprint.

"It says here Jack Yester is the auctioneer. I thought he had an auction house just outside of town," she said.

"He probably goes to the site when there's too much to haul to his place," Samuel said.

"I guess."

"Do you know him?" Samuel asked.

"Not really. He came to the store and offered to auction off my excess stock or the whole contents of the store. I guess Ruth had a reputation for buying huge amounts, but I don't know why he showed up so soon after I took over the shop."

"Just trying to line up business, I assume," Samuel said, turning to pick up the county road west. "You sound troubled."

"No, not really," she said. "I just didn't expect to see him at this auction. No doubt he'll just ignore me since I haven't gotten back to him."

Putting aside her misgivings about Jack Yester, Miriam was determined to enjoy everything about the day. Soon they were driving through the lush Maryland countryside where field after field was planted in neat rows. With her scanty knowledge of agriculture, she couldn't identify many of the early crops.

Cows she did know, and they were out in abundance grazing in the fields. It was also fun to see a pen of sheep and a young woman riding a white horse along the highway.

"I always liked barns," Samuel said as they passed a weathered red one. "My uncle had a farm, and I spent hundreds of hours playing with my plastic animals."

"I didn't know that," Miriam said.

"That was when girls were still the enemies," he teased.

"Like the time you grabbed the knit hat my grandmother made and ran around the playground pretending to be an airplane pilot," she said.

"Did I do that?"

He grinned but kept his eyes on the road, giving her a chance to admire his outfit, light tan pants and a green-and-white striped polo shirt. She was glad she hadn't worn jeans and a man-style shirt, her first thought when she contemplated going to a farm.

The drive passed quickly, even though Samuel made one wrong turn and had to backtrack to find the location of the auction. The man could navigate the globe, Miriam thought with amusement, but the Maryland countryside managed to confuse him.

They had to park a long way down a dirt road lined with other vehicles. Apparently the auction had drawn a big crowd, although only half the folding chairs set up before a podium were occupied. Most people were still wandering around the yard and checking out the inside of the house, although all the selling would be done outside.

Miriam wondered why a farmer was selling out in the early summer instead of after the fall harvest, but she picked up snatches of information from conversations. Apparently the elderly owner of the farm had been forced by failing health to go to a care facility, and his wife was moving in with one of their sons, none of whom wanted to farm the place.

"I didn't expect to find so many books," Samuel said, going over to one of the many long tables holding sale items.

He stooped to examine the contents of several boxes pushed under a table, immediately finding some of interest.

"My favorites—mysteries," he said.

"I've noticed at garage sales they always put the books on the ground where they're hard to see," Miriam teased. "Do you see any books on home decoration? Some day I'm going to spruce up the house, although not until the shop is under control."

"None here," Samuel said, straightening up and noticing the crowd moving toward the barn where the selling would begin. "We'd better get our numbers."

At the check-in point, they opted to get separate numbered bidding paddles to simplify things if Miriam wanted to buy anything for the shop.

She'd been to a few country auctions in Indiana, and she wasn't immune to the excitement of the auction-goers. The day could be a total bust when it came to finding anything, but she knew spending time with Samuel was the real prize of the day.

Jack Yester was standing by the broad entrance to the barn, rattling off the customary instructions, most of them concerned with paying. He was wearing a different "costume" today, perhaps trying to look like his idea of a farmer with jeans belted halfway up his chest and a silver buckle that looked vaguely Native American. His red plaid shirt made his complexion look even more florid under a wide-brimmed straw hat.

The selling started with his helper trying to coax bids on a row of well-worn implements including rakes, shovels, and an old hand plow that actually brought a good price. Bales of wire, tangles of leather harnesses, a steel drum, and other miscellaneous lots seemed to take forever to sell. Samuel and Miriam were among the many who wandered off to wait for more interesting merchandise.

They bought cans of soda at a food truck parked on the property to sell lunches and refreshments to the crowd, then looked for places to sit.

"Taken," one woman in a cotton housedress said when they tried to choose a chair in her aisle.

It turned out almost all the folding chairs set out in front of the podium had someone guarding them, or the seats were covered with a personal item to mark territory.

Laughing at the inconvenience, Samuel found two old kitchen chairs and started a row of their own at the back. So far Miriam had no idea what had attracted her sister to so many auctions.

"Ruth's sister!" A vaguely familiar voice rang out across the yard, and Miriam looked up to see Sally Weber, the glass dealer who had gone to many sales with Ruth.

"You don't want to sit back here," she said after Miriam introduced her to Samuel. "Come sit in my row. I'm not sure all my people are going to show up anyway."

"Her row" turned out to be the front one. Miriam sat at one end, feeling a little self-conscious since Sally threw several cloth bags on the ground to clear seats for them. She chatted nonstop with Samuel until the auctioneers finally made their way to the podium. Then she seemed to turn into an entirely different person, totally focused on the sales crew and the lots put up for auction.

Samuel put his arm across the back of Miriam's chair and whispered into her ear. "Having fun yet?"

Oddly enough, she was. The sights, sounds, and smells on this small family farm made her delighted to be outside, and she couldn't have asked for better company than Samuel.

Miriam took a few minutes to decipher the auctioneer's spiel, but when she did, bidding seemed easy. Or it would've if there'd been anything she wanted to buy.

"That is one sweet price," Sally whispered into her ear after she won the bid on a box of glass haphazardly thrown into a corrugated cardboard box.

When one of the auction workers brought it to Sally, Miriam looked into the box with interest. It appeared to be full of amber-colored Depression glass, but as far as she could see, almost every piece was chipped or cracked.

"Looks like a bunch of stuff to recycle," Sally said, reaching deep into the box. "But look at this. It's an end-of-day glass basket. It won't make my fortune, but it will cover my gas and time today."

"End-of-day glass?" Miriam took the little purple-tinted glass piece and admired the clear twisted glass handle.

"When glassblowers finished for the day, they were allowed to make whimsical items with the leftover molten glass. I think they were even allowed to take them home."

"It is cute," Miriam agreed, wondering if she would ever know as much about the antiques trade as her sister had.

After Samuel bought his box of mystery novels, pleased because he found a few Little Golden Books on the bottom, they decided to leave.

"My daughter-in-law collects them," he said. "These look to be mid-twentieth century but still good to read to my grandchildren."

Miriam turned in her bidding paddle without having used it. She was still a bit overwhelmed by the rapid-fire selling, but Jack Yester's style made her even more determined not to let him auction anything for her. He seemed to pick bids out of the air, and he definitely favored some bidders over others. One poor woman had waved her paddle any number of times before he acknowledged her.

"Sorry you didn't find anything to buy," Samuel said when they were headed back to Maple Landing.

"I'm still on a learning curve," Miriam admitted. "Fortunately there's no immediate need to restock my shelves at the store."

"When I saw how old the farmhouse was—late-nineteenth-century, probably—I was hoping to see some artifacts from the War Between the States. The longer a family has been in the same home, the better the chance of finding something left by an ancestor."

"Maybe the family removed all the historic artifacts to keep for their children and grandchildren," she suggested.

"Most likely," Samuel admitted. "I just have a hunch Captain Davis left a journal or a diary of some kind somewhere in all of your things. During wartime, soldiers did a lot more waiting around than fighting. It was pretty common to keep a record of what they saw and experienced."

"Maybe the contents of the desk were all he left," she said.

"Could be," Samuel said. "Anyway, we'll keep looking. You deserve to clear the name of your great-grandfather."

Smiling to herself, Miriam was at a loss to tell him how much she appreciated his support.

Chapter Seventeen

W hen the bell rang for the first time Thursday morning, Miriam looked up to see an elderly man in worn overalls approaching the counter.

"Good morning," she said. "Can I help you with something?"

"Clarence Windham here," he said, pulling on his scanty beard. "I got some signs you might want to buy."

"What kind of signs?" This was a new area for her, but she'd learned to keep an open mind when people wanted to sell.

"From old gas stations. Wanna come out to my truck and take a look?" he asked. "They're too heavy to carry inside unless you want them for sure."

"I'll take a look," Miriam said, following him out to his truck parked in front of the shop.

The elderly man didn't look as though he could lift an old gas station sign. He wasn't much taller than Miriam, and his shoulders were rounded with age. She didn't know if she could sell old petroleum signs in her shop, but she was willing to check whatever he'd brought to show her.

The paint on his truck had worn away, leaving only dull gray on the metal parts. He pulled down a crude wooden loading ramp on the back of the pickup as an invitation for her to climb up for a better look. Miriam preferred to see his signs standing firmly on the ground.

"Where did you get them?" she asked, knowing provenance was essential if she did decide to buy.

"Mostly Stewartstown," he said a bit defensively. "My farm is just down the road past the old cemetery. Mind, when I bought the signs, folks didn't think they were good for anything but scrap metal. They thought I was crazy for taking them. In fact, some I got just for hauling them away. That must have been in the sixties. I'd just taken over the farm from my father."

His mention of Stewartstown immediately piqued her interest. Thanks to Phoebe's mastery of the computer, the town was almost certainly the one on her ancestor's map. There could hardly be two towns in Maryland that had annexed a place called Suetville.

The signs were familiar ones from the past: a big red Pegasus, a red star for Texas, and several other familiar ones. There was even one advertising tires and another for motor oil. Unfortunately she didn't need to climb up on the truck bed to see the damage. One looked as if it had been used for target practice. Another was so rusty it was ready to fall apart. The only one in decent condition seemed to be the tire sign, but she couldn't visualize giving it space in her shop.

"What's under the canvas?" she asked, wanting to talk more with a man who knew about a cemetery in Stewartstown.

"Clocks," he said without enthusiasm. "You can have all three for a hundred and a half."

When he uncovered them for a better look, Miriam made a quick decision. All three had auto-related advertising, and they looked in much better condition than the signs.

"I'll take them if you'll carry them inside for me," she said.

Maybe she should've bargained before agreeing to his price, but she was confident at least one of them would sell for enough to make buying them worthwhile.

"Do you have ancestors buried in the Stewartstown cemetery?" she asked as he unloaded the clocks.

"Yup, a whole passel of 'em going back to the 1820s. 'Course, it's the soldiers' graves everyone wants to see. No idea why. Just a bunch of old stones. Some you can't even read anymore."

"Is there a special section for the men who fought in the War Between the States?" Miriam asked as she followed him through the entrance to the store.

"Reckon so, but I was never one to go disturbing the dead. Where do you want these?" he asked.

"Just put the clocks on the floor over there," Miriam said, going to her purse to get her checkbook. Since the break-in, she didn't feel secure leaving it in plain sight in the office—even though nothing of value had been taken.

"Sure you don't want any signs?" the old man asked.

"No, I'm sure someone would want them, but as you can see, I don't have space to display them."

Mr. Windham grunted his understanding and waited in silence while she wrote a check.

"I can take this to the bank?" he asked in what may have been an attempt at joking.

"All day, any day," Miriam said in a light tone, although her mind was on the information he'd given her. "Do the people in charge of the cemetery have an office?"

"Can't say. A bunch of Confederate ladies tend the graves, put out wreaths and such. Guess they do it to show respect for the men who gave their lives for the South." He suddenly sounded less like a shambling old man and more like a patriot.

"Would it be all right if I visited it?" Miriam knew he wasn't the one who could give permission, but he did live nearby.

"Never heard of ghosts chasing folks away," he said with a lop-sided grin. "Don't know that I'd walk through the place at night, though."

Watching him drive away with a puff of exhaust smoke, Miriam couldn't help feeling excited. Most small towns had a cemetery, but the elderly man had confirmed Confederate soldiers were buried there. There was at least a slim chance her great-grandfather was among them.

At the counter Phoebe had just sold a Seth Thomas kitchen clock in the shape of an apple and was wrapping it. Miriam waited until the customer left, then told her the news.

"I shouldn't be surprised there's a cemetery," Miriam said, "but it was interesting to hear about the Confederate military graves. Do you think you can pull up a plot map on the computer?"

"I can try," Phoebe said with enthusiasm, loving any chance to work online.

Miriam followed her to the office to look over her shoulder. She should try to update her computer skills, but Phoebe was fast and competent.

"Yes, there's a cemetery association," Phoebe said after a few minutes. "But there's no plot map or record of burials."

"Maybe I can get one from the Ladies of the Confederacy. Mr. Windham mentioned they care for the soldiers' grave sites."

"Why not go look for yourself?" Phoebe suggested.

Laughing at herself for overlooking the obvious, Miriam thanked Phoebe for her expertise.

"I have an idea about all those odd symbols on the old map," Phoebe said, never in a hurry to leave the computer.

The bell sounded as someone entered the shop, but both women ignored it for a moment. Most customers liked a little time to look around on their own.

"Look," Phoebe said, pulling up the map she'd scanned onto the computer. "Some of the symbols are crosses."

"There could be religious significance," Miriam said.

"Yes, but look at this one when I enlarge it," Phoebe said, continuing to manipulate the map on the screen.

"They almost look like—" Miriam began.

"Hearts!" Phoebe finished with satisfaction. "I have a friend who uses little symbols like those instead of dotting her *i*'s. It was cute in grade school, but I've told her it looks kind of juvenile now."

"I'm sure it's just her way of trying to be distinctive," Miriam said. "Crosses and hearts. It would make sense if they were clustered in one area. They could have some significance in the cemetery, but they're scattered around what we now know was Suetville."

"You ladies are hard at work. How about a coffee break?"

Miriam was a bit startled but quickly realized Samuel had come into the shop when the bell rang.

"I can't get away now, but I learned something interesting," Miriam said. She told him about the cemetery as they walked to the front of the store.

"If your great-grandfather is buried there, it would go a long way toward understanding why he disappeared," Samuel said thoughtfully.

"That's what I think. At the least, there might be a date when he died. Unfortunately Phoebe hasn't found any cemetery records online."

"Maybe you should look for yourself," Samuel suggested. "I'd be happy to go with you."

"That's nice of you, but I can't ask you to take a day off from writing. The chance of finding a headstone for my great-grandfather is pretty slim."

"To tell you the truth," he said a bit sheepishly, "I'm hooked on the mystery of your disappearing ancestor. It's not often a person gets to help solve a puzzle like this. I'd really like to go with you."

Admitting to herself that she'd really like to have him, Miriam quickly agreed.

"How about tomorrow?" he suggested. "Or Saturday, if that's better for you."

"I promised Phoebe she could have Saturday off. Tomorrow would work best, but let me check with her first. I want to be sure she's okay with watching the shop."

After Samuel left, promising to call her later to firm up the details of their trip, Miriam returned to Phoebe in the office.

"Guess what, Mrs. Max. Those clocks you just bought are *petroliana*." She said the word a second time, letting the word roll off her tongue. "Who knew people collected stuff like old gas cans and signs?"

"I never gave it any thought until today," Miriam admitted.

At the rate Phoebe was learning the trade, she'd soon surpass Miriam in her knowledge of what was collectible. Miriam couldn't have been more pleased. *The Ugly Duckling* had been one of her favorite childhood stories, and now she had her own little duckling on the way to becoming a swan. Not even Bess had known what a knack Phoebe had for researching and selling antiques and collectibles.

Phoebe swiveled around on the computer chair and sent an empty coffee mug flying when she hit it with her elbow. Now if she could only be a bit more careful around breakables!

* * *

Samuel had gone to Ruthie's Antiques to ask Miriam to a fish fry Friday evening, but a day with her on the trail of her elusive ancestor was even more appealing. He didn't exaggerate when he told her how eager he was to solve the puzzle of the disappearance of Captain Thomas Davis.

Now that he had time and leisure to pursue interests other than his career, he wanted to clear the captain's name almost as much as Miriam did. If he'd been a brave and honorable soldier, he deserved to have the stain removed from his name. Even if they confirmed rumors about his desertion, they might find compelling reasons. Either way, Miriam's mind would be at ease, and that was becoming more and more important to him.

Samuel was confident about finding an answer to the historical mystery, but he was cautious about forging a new relationship with Miriam. If she was reluctant to take their friendship to a new level, he understood and respected her no less because of it. He especially didn't want to do anything that might seem he was pressuring her.

"Hey, Bentley!"

He turned and saw Mikey, red-faced and puffing as he trotted after him shortly after Samuel left the shop.

"Mikey, what are you up to?" Samuel asked.

"Just getting in a little run before it gets too hot," his friend panted, coming to a stop beside him. "My wife thinks I'm out of shape—well, she knows it."

He bent over, hands on knees, to catch his breath.

"Have you given any thought to the four of us getting together?" Mikey asked. "You know, Miriam and you with Millie and me. I thought we could make a big evening of it, a reunion for the three of us, and Millie wants to meet the famous admiral. She didn't grow up here, and she thinks all my old friends are losers."

"Hardly famous," Samuel said with dry humor. "I was just a good bean counter."

"Well, don't disillusion my wife, not that I believe you myself. Let me bask in your reflected glory for a few days. What are the two of you doing tomorrow night?"

"Hate to let you down, but Miriam and I aren't a couple. We've only seen each other a few times since I got back."

He was beginning to wish it were otherwise, but it had been a long time since he and Miriam had known each other. It wouldn't help if Mikey insisted on turning the clock back for them. In fact, it might make Miriam more reluctant to take their new friendship further.

Mikey was a great guy, but he didn't have good filters on what he said.

"Well, let me know when it would work for you," his friend said, straightening and checking a meter clipped on his waistband. "Another half mile to go. Millie checks my time. Nothing like a woman to keep a man on his toes."

Samuel watched his friend run off, smiling at Mikey's exuberance. Behind his comic exterior, he had a sharp mind and zest for life, but he was pretty sure Miriam wasn't ready for his friend's assumptions about their relationship. For now, he was ready to be patient and enjoy her company whenever possible.

Chapter Eighteen

Friday morning Miriam was ready to leave long before Samuel was due to pick her up. Although she was loath to admit it to herself, she'd chosen an outfit more appropriate for a date than prowling through an old cemetery. She'd taken time to iron her white linen slacks, the only ones she owned that weren't wash-and-wear. She felt almost nautical with a navy print tunic and a little white hat with a bill to shade her face from the sun in the cemetery.

Always practical, she wondered whether she was being foolish to enjoy Samuel's company as much as she did. Was it just lingering nostalgia for her youth, or was it possible to find happiness the second time around?

After filling her red-and-white-striped carryall with bottled water, sunscreen, a silk scarf in case Samuel had the top down on his convertible, and a pad and pencil in case she wanted to make notes about what they found, she was eager to go. Samuel didn't keep her waiting. As was his custom, he was ten minutes early.

"I thought we'd take some back roads just to enjoy the countryside," he said. "That is, if you don't mind a slightly longer trip."

"Not at all," she said, willing to spend as much time with him as possible. "Who knows? We might pass other old cemeteries on the way."

"Yes, the more isolated ones do tend to be close to a road," Samuel said.

"I hope I'm not keeping you from your book," she said, genuinely concerned about interfering with his work time.

"I seem to remember asking you," he teased. "Anyway, I can't wait to continue our search for a son of the South. If he was unjustly accused of desertion, it's our duty to clear his name."

"I would like to be able to tell my daughter and granddaughters their ancestor was an honorable soldier, someone they should be proud of."

"Then let's go," Samuel said. "I have a good feeling about the Stewartstown cemetery. Who knows? I may even find a naval veteran. I can chalk it up to research." He flashed her a mischievous grin.

Miriam was glad she'd brought the scarf to keep hair from whipping around her face, but it felt wonderful to ride through the countryside by Samuel's side. He stopped twice beside the narrow road to snap pictures of picturesque barns, commenting on tin roofs and weathered gray siding. She felt enriched as she saw them through his eyes.

"I thought of buying an old barn and converting it into a home," Samuel mused, "but the pull of the Chesapeake Bay was too strong."

Miriam marveled at the many interests of her old friend, enjoying his company more with each passing day.

Halfway to Stewartstown, Samuel pulled to a stop by a general store with two working but vintage gas pumps in front. Signs in the front windows advertised groceries, soft drinks, and antiques.

"I don't need gas," he said, "but let's stretch our legs and see what they have for sale here."

The town was so small, Miriam didn't know how they supported a store, but she loved exploring out-of-the-way places. Inside she found a jumble of grocery items and a wall devoted to taxidermy. Samuel picked out a bag of malted balls, a treat they both used to like. When he went to pay a bored young clerk behind a battered wooden counter, Miriam spotted something of interest. The postcards on a circular metal rack weren't the modern kind made for tourists. Instead they were much older, most dating back to the early 1900s.

Glancing through them, she saw several views of Maple Landing and, even more interesting, a faded photo postcard of Stewartstown.

"How much are your postcards?" she asked.

"Two bucks apiece or six for ten bucks." The long-haired youth slapped Samuel's change on the counter without bothering to count it out.

The postcards weren't easy to view, since each slot was full of cards in no particular order. She bypassed flowery greetings, knowing they weren't much in demand, but the small-town views fascinated her. Most were actual photographs with postcard backs, and a few had been used before 1910.

Without delaying their trip too much, she purchased half a dozen and slipped them into her carryall.

"Find some good ones?" Samuel asked when they settled down in the car.

"I'm not an expert, but I think the views of small Maryland towns might be valuable. More importantly, look at this view of Stewartstown."

After studying it for a minute, Samuel grinned broadly. "You have a great eye for details."

There, halfway down the main street of town, was a window with clear lettering: Undertakers, Fine Furniture.

"I've heard a carpenter might practice the two trades from one location, but this is the first time I've seen proof in print," Samuel said.

"I almost feel as though I should go back and pay more for this card," Miriam said.

"If you do, the clerk will think you have a hundred-dollar card and feel bad about selling it," Samuel said.

"You're probably right," Miriam agreed, although some aspects of the antiques trade were still hard to accept. At least she had no intention of reselling the Stewartstown postcard. It made her feel one step closer to discovering her great-grandfather's fate.

The old cemetery wasn't hard to find once they reached the town. Samuel followed the main street west until they spotted it, an austere burial ground with antiquated stone monuments, some tilting to the side.

"There doesn't seem to be a way to drive into it," Samuel said, pulling off the road to park on a grassy shoulder.

"I planned to walk," Miriam said, glad she'd been practical about footwear and chosen a pair of well-worn deck shoes.

Samuel took her hand and led her through the front section of the cemetery where most of the graves dated from the early 1900s. But they soon found older dates, and it wasn't hard to identify the section set aside for war veterans. Just as Miriam had expected, the site was still well tended. The caretakers had decorated the graves with small flags, patriotic plastic wreaths, and a scattering of flowering plants in the ground.

Even though she'd never known her great-grandfather, Miriam had a vision of a proud, handsome young captain ready to serve as so many on both sides of the war had been. Her eyes unexpectedly grew moist, and Samuel put his arm around her shoulders.

"Do you want to walk down the rows?" he asked in a soothing voice.

"Yes." She didn't know whether Thomas Davis was buried there, but she still felt for all the young men who'd sacrificed their lives. And for those who had reached old age still bearing the scars and trauma of war.

The first row meandered among a grove of trees, some markers tilted where roots had undermined them. The next three rows were spread out on flat land, the tombstones still close together. Some had wives' names too. One veteran had four spouses buried beside him, reminding Miriam of the perils of childbirth before modern medicine.

The lettering on some stones was badly weathered, but Samuel managed to decipher the names by running his finger over the remnants of writing.

The sun was getting hotter, and Miriam's little hat did nothing to keep her cool. When they reached the last of the gravesites, she was discouraged but unwilling to leave any stone unread.

"John Tyler, Abraham Lenoir, Charles Wilson, Austin Woolsey," he said, reciting the names on the last stones in the row. "No Davis, I'm sorry to say."

"And no naval veterans," Miriam said. "I guess it was a long shot at best. Whatever the map is trying to tell us, it has nothing to do with my great-grandfather's final resting place."

"I'm thirsty enough to drink a gallon of iced tea," Samuel said when they got back to the car. "How about finding a place for lunch before we head back?"

"That would be nice," Miriam said, trying to mask her disappointment.

* * *

The choice of restaurants seemed pretty limited to Samuel, at least in the area of Stewartstown where they were. They agreed to pass up a place that had once been an A&W Root Beer drive-in, but both liked the look of a historic home with a restaurant on the main floor. They walked into a cozy front parlor with small oilcloth-covered tables and walls hung with memorabilia from the 1860s and the next hundred years. A pair of crossed swords dominated one wall. Though he appreciated the artifacts on display, Samuel was glad to see a number of other diners occupying the tables. It was a good sign if local folks liked the food there.

"I like the way you've converted this," Samuel said to the waitress who turned out to be the co-owner with her husband.

"Thank you kindly," she said. "What can I get for you folks?"

Samuel knew immediately what he wanted: green tomato soup and a pulled pork sandwich, things he'd never make for himself even if his cooking skills were up to it. Miriam was undecided, looking peaked from their unsuccessful visit to the cemetery.

"I guess we need a minute," he said to Johanna, identified by a patch on her starchy pink cotton uniform.

"Take all the time you like," she said cheerfully.

"Sorry to be so indecisive," Miriam said, pale except for the bright pink of her cheeks.

"It doesn't matter. I'm just disappointed for your sake. This has been the best lead so far, and it didn't pan out." He wanted to hold her against him and comfort her, but this wasn't the time or place.

"I didn't have high hopes," Miriam said, but he wondered if that made it any easier to accept. "But I have decided what to order."

She pointed it out on the menu.

When Johanna returned to their table, most of the diners had left or were enjoying desserts such as key lime pie or Southern pecan pie.

"Can we get a pitcher of iced tea?" Samuel asked, though he appreciated the cold water she'd put on their table as soon as they were seated. "The lady would like pimiento-bacon spread on whole wheat toast. That comes with lettuce and tomato, right?"

"Yes, sir."

"I'll have green tomato soup with a pulled pork sandwich. And bring us an order of fried okra to share."

"You have a wonderful collection of artifacts," Miriam said, seeming to throw off her gloom.

"It all came with the house when we bought it a few years ago. I still intend to get everything better organized, but my husband and I have all we can do right now to keep our customers happy. He's a splendid cook, as you'll soon find out."

Samuel was quick to agree when she brought their meals to the table in heavy white ironware dishes.

Although Miriam first declined a share of the fried okra, he convinced her to try it. She enjoyed it so much that she shared the serving with him.

"I'm going to get as rotund as Mikey if I eat like this very often," Samuel joked. "By the way, I ran into him downtown. He was running, apparently his wife's idea. He suggested we get together with him and his wife for dinner sometime."

He was relieved when she agreed it might be fun. There was a fine line between pressuring her and enjoying time together. If they went, he'd have to coach Mikey to tell his wife not to assume he and Miriam were a couple yet.

"Can I get you folks some dessert?" Johanna asked when their plates were empty.

"Not for me," Miriam said. "I don't know when I've had such a delicious lunch, but I'm full."

"Me neither," Samuel said. "I've eaten far too much because everything was so good."

"I've just taken over an antiques business, so I have some idea of how hard you and your husband have worked here," Miriam said.

"It was a struggle, but now we see every customer as a friend. It's long been our fondest wish to have a place like this. I worked as a

doctor's receptionist, and my husband did drywall for a construction company. Both jobs got pretty stale, but once the kids were on
their own, we decided to make our dream come true."

"I'd love to buy a jar of the cheese spread," Miriam said. "Where
can I get it?"

"We sell it here—our own recipe. If you like, I'll get you one."
Johanna was a tall, plain woman, but when she smiled, her face lit up.

"Great!" Miriam said.

"While I think of it, we have tons of historical items, a lot more
than we'll ever be able to display. I haven't had time to do any sorting or selling, but if you'd like to look through some things, you'd
be more than welcome. I imagine most of what we have would sell
well in your antiques shop."

Samuel saw a flicker of interest on Miriam's face and hastened to
assure her he wasn't in any hurry.

"Thank you so much," Miriam said. "But maybe another day. I
don't have time to do justice to your artifacts today. To be truthful,
I just took over the shop from my deceased sister. I have a lot to
learn."

Muzzling his own curiosity, Samuel walked back to his car, rais-
ing the top because Miriam looked like she'd had enough sun and
wind for one day.

"Are you sure you don't want a peek at her antiques?" he asked
when they were ready to go.

"I was tempted, but I'm 'antiqued out' for now. I still feel sad
about all the young soldiers' graves. Some were old men when they
passed away, but a sadly high number were causalities of the war."

"Or victims of the diseases the war unleashed. Imagine, men who'd never left their own county were all scrambled together in horrible circumstances." He gave her a quizzical look. "Are you sorry we visited the cemetery?"

"Oh no, certainly not. I'm sorry we're not closer to finding what happened to my great-grandfather, but now we know he isn't buried near Stewartstown. It was worth coming here for that."

As much as Samuel was interested in her quest, he was more eager to spend time with her.

Her smile, a little wan but still radiant in his eyes, was all the thanks he needed for going to the cemetery with her.

"Something else will turn up," he assured her with more confidence than he felt. Record keeping was spotty in the turbulent times after the War Between the States, and one veteran could easily have gotten lost, deserter or patriot.

"You always were a cockeyed optimist," Miriam said, sounding more chipper.

He silently agreed. Although years of heavy responsibilities had eroded his optimism, he still had hope for the two of them.

Chapter Nineteen

Sunday morning's church service was especially crowded, but Miriam was happy to see all the visitors. It meant summer people were taking advantage of the opportunity to worship at Old Mariners.

The one person she didn't see was Samuel. He'd sent her a brief note the day before saying he was off to Rhode Island to talk to an old friend who shared his interest in naval history.

Miriam wanted him to make good progress on his book, but she felt vaguely lonely without him. The congregation was blessed with an inspirational preacher, but she had a hard time concentrating on his sermon this morning. She kept remembering Sundays when Lisa was little. Her daughter could be mischievous in those days, but she was good as could be sitting in a pew between her parents and scribbling on a Sunday school paper until the last trace of white was covered over.

In the past, Miriam had always been more than willing to participate in church activities, although cooking in the kitchen with a group of women did stress her. There was no question Ray had always been the better cook in her family. She'd signed up to help with the Old Mariners fall rummage sale, but it was too far away to concern her now.

As she gradually renewed old friendships and made new friends, she was also strengthening her faith by worshipping in a community of believers. All that was missing was one special person to share the experience with her. Would Samuel ever fill that role in her life? Was she mistaking his kindness for something deeper and more lasting?

As she walked out of the church, she was still distracted by thoughts of Samuel. She nearly walked past the one person she really didn't want to talk to.

"Miriam, do you have a minute?" Natalie Downs called out from the sidewalk. "We need to talk."

No doubt Natalie wanted to discuss buying Ruthie's Antiques again, but Miriam didn't at all like the idea of letting her expand her furniture and appliance store into the shop.

"Have you given more thought to selling Ruth's store?" Natalie asked without preamble.

"I think I'll try running it myself for now," Miriam said as patiently as she could.

"Poor thing, you must be exhausted trying to follow in your sister's footsteps," Natalie said, not quite managing to sound sincere.

"I'm enjoying it," Miriam said, realizing as she said it that she actually was.

It was hard to cope with her sister's disorganized ways—a job made even more difficult because she tended to be secretive. For example, a rather lovely woven splint basket was sitting on top of a file cabinet in the office, but Miriam had no idea how to price it. There was no record of its origin, and she had no idea what Ruth had paid for it. For whatever reason, Ruth hadn't left any clues about it.

There were other items Miriam couldn't find in the inventory, and she had no idea why Ruth bought some of the things she had. Fellow dealer Sally had given her one possibility when she saw her at Yester's auction. Sometimes dealers had to buy boxes of junk to get one desirable piece at a good price. By the looks of the basement at the store, her sister had done that again and again and again, but Miriam still hoped to sort it all out. Maybe there were things she could donate to the church rummage sale if she couldn't learn anything about them.

"A retail business can be fun, but it's also challenging," Natalie said. "Long hours, periods of time when no one wants to buy anything. Of course, there's the problem of hiring good help too. I'm fortunate to have my grandson working with us. I'd love to have him take over the store when we're too old."

"I'm very fortunate to have Phoebe Watkins working for me," Miriam said.

"Oh, the Watkins girl. She's working out well?"

"Yes, very well. I'm afraid I'm going to let you down on the store," Miriam said. "I have no plans to sell it now or in the near future."

"Well, I hope your run of bad luck doesn't last," Natalie said. "It's rather frightening to have a break-in, isn't it?"

Before Miriam could answer, Bess came hurrying over looking determined.

"I didn't see you leave," she said to Miriam, barely nodding at Natalie.

"I'll be going," Natalie said stiffly. "Perhaps we can talk again when you've had time to think over my offer."

"Vulture," Bess said under her breath when her least favorite classmate was out of hearing.

Miriam laughed, then felt a little guilty. Natalie's black silk suit with a red blouse under the jacket did remind her somewhat of the infamous bird, not that she'd actually seen one in the wild. And there was no doubt Natalie was ready to pounce on her inheritance if she gave up on it. One thing was sure: Miriam wasn't ready to call it quits, even though she sometimes had doubts about her ability to run the store.

"Forget her," Bess said. "I've waylaid you to invite you to a picnic lunch at the inn. You have to sample my special Maryland potato salad, and Charlie is doing chicken on the grill. It's family day, and even Phoebe will be there."

"You don't need me at a family cookout," Miriam demurred.

"Nonsense! You're honorary family. In fact, Randy and Janice gave me orders to bring you. I can't tell you how much they appreciate Phoebe working at your shop. It's the first job she's really shown an interest in."

"I'm fortunate to have her," Miriam said. "She works hard and brings good computer skills to the business. We've even talked about putting some slow sellers up for sale on Internet."

After allowing herself to be persuaded, Miriam went home to change into picnic clothes, a long crinkle-cloth skirt in shades of pink and purple and a simple white top. She covered an apple pie with foil to take along, an impulse buy the day before. She'd hoped Samuel might get back to Maple Landing to share his favorite pie and coffee with her that evening, but she had no idea whether he would.

The picnic was set up in the backyard of the inn, and the family had already congregated when Miriam arrived with her pie. Bess's family enjoyed talking almost as much their matriarch did, and Miriam soon found herself in a conversation with Charlie about the best way to marinate chicken for the grill.

"You know what I've been looking for?" Janice asked when her husband gave her a chance to talk. Randy was as tall and slender as his father but as talkative as Bess. .

"Something antique?" Miriam guessed, since Janice's in-laws had just agreed to disagree about cleaning out the attic before winter. Charlie was totally in favor of it, but Bess wanted to save certain things for future generations—when she decided what was worth keeping.

"I'd love to find a pie bird," Janice said, enthusiastic about everything kitchen-related.

She flipped aside an errant brown curl only slightly tinged with gray. Miriam's first impression of Bess's daughter-in-law was that she looked too young to be Phoebe's mother.

"We may have one at the shop," Miriam thoughtfully answered. "I don't recall one on the shelves, but there's no telling what my sister secreted away on the second floor or in the basement. I don't know what I'd do without Phoebe's help sorting through things— and yours too, Bess."

"It doesn't have to be antique or fancy," Janice said, "but I would like a bird-shaped one. It's so cute when steam rises out of a little china beak. And, of course, it keeps the filling from boiling over and the crust from sagging in the middle. My grandmother wouldn't make a pie with a top crust without using one."

"I'll keep my eye out for one," Miriam promised.

Although she hadn't felt especially hungry, Miriam enjoyed Charlie's delicious chicken with his "secret" barbeque sauce and potato salad with crisp celery, onions, eggs, green olives, and the Watkinses' mayo—which Bess confessed was only store-bought thinned with lemon juice and a few special herbs from her garden. After the big meal under a large patio umbrella, Miriam was so drowsy she could hardly keep her eyes open. When the men were excused to watch a baseball game on TV, she helped the women clean up but was more than ready for an afternoon nap.

"It was a lovely picnic," Miriam told Bess when they were alone in the inn's large kitchen with copper-bottomed pans hanging over their heads.

"I'm sorry Samuel wasn't here too," Bess said. "What is he doing that's more important than joining you at a picnic?"

"He's not obligated to go anywhere with me!" Miriam protested. "Anyway, he went to see a friend in Provincetown who's keen on naval history. Samuel wanted to exchange some ideas with him."

Miriam went home as soon as she politely could. Bess was a wonderful friend, but being with her family made Miriam nostalgic for her own. Would she have felt differently if Samuel had gone to the picnic with her? She wasn't ready to answer that question.

* * *

Monday morning was usually slow at the antiques shop, but this day in late June was an exception. The sky was leaden gray, and there were weather warnings out on the bay. Without outdoor activities, visitors and locals alike must have chosen a visit to her shop as entertainment for the day. The fact that Samuel was out of town and hadn't called her made the day seem even more gloomy.

"Is this all the Rockingham you have?" a woman with a pronounced New Jersey accent asked. She picked up a pitcher with a mottled dark-brown glaze and a handle molded in the shape of a hound dog.

"Yes, that's all we have right now." Miriam had learned to suggest the possibility of more to come. Given the huge hoard still untouched, it was a distinct possibility.

"Did you notice the hairline crack on the bottom?" the woman asked, making Miriam a little nervous when she returned it to the shelf with unnecessary force.

"Yes, it's a shame, isn't it? But the price has been adjusted accordingly." Miriam had confidence in her sister's pricing. In fact, it was always a little lower than shown in guides. She only wished she could find more documentation. Customers liked a story to go with their purchases, but Ruth had kept so much to herself.

Half an hour later the pitcher was still on the shelf, but the customer had purchased a Rookwood vase with red bellflowers on a cream-and-blue background at a price that made Miriam blink. It amazed her that someone would make a quick trip to the store and buy such an expensive object without trying to bargain for it. Her sister certainly knew values and had a handle on what would sell, but she kept much knowledge in her head, not in her records. For all Miriam knew, the woman could've walked off with the bargain of the year.

Phoebe finished selling a Hummel candleholder with the figure of a sweet-faced little angel. Miriam was surprised a single holder sold so well. She'd worried because there wasn't a second one to make up a pair, but apparently any object based on the wonderful creations by Berta Hummel had a place in the hearts of collectors.

Fortunately Miriam didn't have time to think about the dead-end lead in Stewartstown or about Samuel's silence. People didn't just disappear, not even in the aftermath of a terrible war, but she was too busy to think about other possible leads. She didn't want to dwell on the time spent with Samuel, but not because it hadn't been pleasant. In fact, she was only beginning to realize how much she appreciated his enthusiasm for the quest.

When would she hear from him again? Had something happened to dampen the enthusiasm he'd shown her earlier?

"Good morning!" Bess came into the store with a burst of energy, clutching a paper bag in both arms. "You won't believe what I found!"

"Oh, Gran!" Phoebe said walking over to greet her grandmother. "You've been poking around in the attic again."

"Exploring, not poking around, Phoebe," Bess said, taking an old lantern out of the sack and setting it on the counter. "Your grandfather said this is a railroad lantern. Look at the bottom part. It burned kerosene. The red globe is in perfect condition, and there's even the name of the railroad."

"That is nice," Miriam said, tapping the metal with her finger and finding it sound.

"I was hoping to trade it for a pie bird," Bess said. "Janice's birthday is coming up next week, and it would be a nice surprise for her."

"I'm sorry, but we haven't found one yet. We've been so busy I couldn't spare a minute of Phoebe's time to hunt for one," Miriam explained.

"Why don't you take this on consignment? Then when you find a pie bird, we can do some swapping if the lantern hasn't sold," Bess suggested.

"I'd be happy to," Miriam said. "Since I bought some clocks advertising petroleum products, I've realized the shop is geared mostly to the things women collect. I'd like to start a section of 'mantiques' when I can make room."

"I can work on that when we're not—"

"Busy," Miriam said, finishing her sentence as the front door opened.

"Morning, ladies," Jack Yester said. "I saw you at my auction, Mrs. Maxwell, but you didn't buy anything."

"I'm surprised you noticed," Miriam said.

"Didn't. I looked at the sales record when it was over. You missed a chance to bid on a nice country hutch and a brass headboard for a bed. They were still in the house when you left," Yester said.

It felt a bit creepy to have the auctioneer keeping track of what she did, but she tried to brush aside the feeling.

"I can see why you didn't buy anything," he said. "Your sister was a major player in the area. You probably have items tucked away you haven't even seen yet. My crew could sort through everything and give you the choice of what to keep and what to sell."

"She's already said she isn't ready to sell," Bess said, obviously not a fan of the auctioneer.

"Nice lantern," he said, ignoring Bess. "I could get a hundred for it any day."

"It's my lantern, and there's no way I'd consign it to auction," Bess said, in full defensive mode.

"Was there a hoard of old stuff when you bought the house for your B and B?" he asked, switching attention to Bess.

She sniffed and didn't answer.

"I'm sorry you wasted your time coming here this morning," Miriam said. "But I'm not anywhere near ready to sell anything at auction. I have a lot to sort and research before I even consider selling any part of the stock."

She shook her head. Although she understood people had to make a living, she felt badgered by Natalie Downs and the auctioneer. They seemed to think she wasn't competent to run her sister's business.

"When you change your mind, give me a call," Yester said on his way out.

"The nerve of—" Bess was interrupted by a large crash from the back of the display area.

"Oh no, Phoebe!" her grandmother cried out as she hurried to see the cause.

"It's okay," the young woman said holding up a metal peg. "I didn't know the shelves in this bookcase are held up by tiny little metal things. How can anyone expect them to support heavy shelves and the stuff on them?"

Miriam quickly realized the falling shelf hadn't held any expensive breakables. A stack of old board games was scattered on the floor with game pieces and cards mixed up, but they could be sorted into the right boxes. She took the metal peg from Phoebe and located the other three so she could replace the shelf.

While Bess and her granddaughter hurried to put the games back together, Miriam pushed the pegs into the holes made for them. They'd just have to remember the shelves in this bookcase weren't too reliable.

Picking up the fallen shelf, she was surprised to see an envelope held on the bottom side with brittle, yellowed tape.

"What on earth…"

"I'm really sorry, Mrs. Max," Phoebe said as she sat down on the floor to sort out the fallen game parts.

"You may have done me a favor," Miriam said as Bess looked over her shoulder.

The envelope contained a bill of sale from an auction house outside of Baltimore. The item was listed as a mechanical cast-iron clown bank, and the price Ruth had paid made Miriam whistle through her teeth.

"Wow!" Bess said.

That was about all that could be said about the receipt Ruth had hidden away nearly seven years ago. The big question was: Why?

"I haven't seen anything like that around here," Bess said.

"Neither have I. Ruth must have sold it. She had a lot invested in it."

Phoebe stood and brushed off her skirt. "I don't see any more pieces."

"You haven't seen a cast-iron clown bank anywhere, have you?" Miriam asked, not expecting a positive answer.

"No, I'd remember something like that," Phoebe assured her.

A couple dressed in matching yellow rain slickers came into the store, and Phoebe went to greet them. Miriam's first thought when she heard the bell was it might be Samuel dropping in to say he was back in town.

"I was hoping it was Samuel," she confessed to Bess.

"Oh, I'm sure you'll hear more from him," her friend said optimistically.

"I guess we can't avoid each other in a town the size of Maple Landing," Miriam said, hoping she didn't sound depressed about it.

She might as well try to hide a semitruck in the room as fool her friend. Bess picked up on her sad tone immediately.

"You'll hear from him," Bess assured her. "And not just to look for a missing ancestor."

"Am I being foolish, Bess? Maybe it's too late to have a second chance at love."

"You're the least foolish person I've ever known," Bess insisted with an emphatic shake of her head.

"Maybe I've been subconsciously keeping him at a distance while I figure out how I feel after so many years."

There was nothing like talking to her longtime friend to clarify her thoughts. In high school Miriam had been the one to get high grades, but Bess had skated through the cliques and ended up with everyone loving her.

"Things have a way of working out," Bess said, about as philosophical as she ever got.

"We'd better go help Phoebe," Miriam said. "That man in the rain slicker is trying to buy the railroad lantern, and we haven't priced it."

One thing Miriam knew for sure: the antiques business brought together fascinating people and fantastic objects. If somewhere along the line, she found a way to clear her great-grandfather's name, all her efforts would be worthwhile. She badly wanted Samuel to share in her quest, but she had to have faith in the future, whether with or without him.

Chapter Twenty

After the shelf fell, Miriam decided to work on some silver that needed polishing. She and Phoebe went to work on rows of silver spoons laid out in front of them on a plastic-covered table near the rear of the store.

"I hope the polishing cloths work as advertised," Miriam said. "It would be much too messy to use old-fashioned silver polish here at the store."

"I sort of like polishing silver," Phoebe said. "I'd rather do this than be my mother's gofer in the kitchen."

The inclement weather that morning had brought hordes of customers into the shop, but now the store was deserted except for the two of them. The rain was coming down in buckets, but the afternoon lull was welcome. Miriam hoped she and Phoebe could get all of the silver polishing done. Ruth had bought lovely old pieces and some more recent souvenir spoons. Unfortunately many were too tarnished to display in the glassed-fronted case at the front. Removing the tarnish was tedious work, but it needed to be done.

"Mrs. Max," Phoebe said, pushing aside a stray lock of strawberry-blonde hair, "I can polish them by myself if there's something else you need to do."

Miriam laughed. "Thank you, Phoebe, but it's been such a hectic day so far, removing tarnish seems relaxing."

It wasn't that Miriam had any complaints about the many sales they'd made so far that day. She was pleased to have so much traffic in the store. She still had a lot to learn about running a retail business, but she knew beyond a shadow of a doubt how important it was to be busy. Even when customers didn't buy anything, people filling the store was a good thing.

"I agree, Mrs. Max," Phoebe said, pulling up a chair to use while polishing.

Even though her shop assistant was willing to tackle the silver, she didn't sound like her usual enthusiastic self. In fact, she sounded unhappy.

"Is everything okay with you?" Miriam gently asked as she pushed a tiny bit of polishing cloth through an intricate cutout design on the handle of a Niagara Falls souvenir spoon.

Phoebe sighed as though she was carrying the weight of the world on her shoulders.

"Yes, fine," she said in a tone that told Miriam things were anything but.

"Is there anything you want to talk about?" Miriam asked, satisfied the spoon she polishing was as bright as it was going to get. Newer souvenir spoons were lacquered to keep their shine, but she much preferred the sheen of old silver, especially on Colonial pieces.

It wasn't likely they would find more historical pieces in Ruth's hoard, but she really appreciated the few early American spoons, picking up one to polish with an especially gentle touch.

"There's nothing I can say," Phoebe said dramatically, sighing once again. "My parents insist on monitoring my social life, and Gran is even worse. You'd think I wanted to go out with an ax murderer!"

Miriam hated to see the young woman so distressed. She knew the cause, but she couldn't give Phoebe advice that went counter to her family's. The last thing she wanted was to take sides against her dear friend Bess. Reconnecting with her was one of the best things about moving to Maple Landing. While she didn't agree with her friend's attitude toward Jason Downs, she hated to see her young shop assistant so sad.

"Hey there," Bess called out cheerily, coming into the shop and shaking her umbrella out.

"Hi, Gran," Phoebe said glumly.

Miriam looked at her old friend and shrugged her shoulders. Bess got the message and didn't press for reasons why her granddaughter seemed so dejected.

"How are you?" Miriam asked.

"Other than feeling like a drowned rat, I'm fine," Bess said, looking around for a spot to set her dripping umbrella.

"Just put it back in the office," Miriam said, seeing her friend's hesitation. "Nothing there will be harmed by a little moisture."

"A little!" Bess guffawed. "It's raining cats and dogs out there. I thought I'd need a rowboat to get here."

"You want to help us polish silver?" Miriam asked.

"You know," Bess said, "I said to myself this morning 'Gee, I wish someone would ask me to polish some spoons.' I guess the answer would be yes."

Miriam appreciated her friend's sense of humor, but she could tell by the look on Phoebe's face nothing was going to cheer her up, not even her grandmother's attempt at lightheartedness.

The bell on the door sounded, but instead of a customer, Jason Downs came into the store and rushed back to where they were working. When Miriam saw Phoebe light up like a Christmas tree, she couldn't help wondering if Samuel had the same effect on her. She suspected he did but still wondered why she hadn't heard from him since he'd left for Rhode Island.

The earnest, dark-haired young man looked like he was bursting with news, but the sight of Miriam and Bess seemed to rein him in.

"Jason!" Phoebe said, sounding more upbeat than she had all morning.

Miriam noticed the scowl on Bess's face but didn't say anything to her good friend. Jason Downs definitely had something on his mind. He seemed to be gathering up his courage to say—or do—something.

"I have a confession to make!" he blurted out.

"I knew it," Bess said, before the poor boy could say anything more.

"Knew what?" Miriam asked as the two young people moved away a short distance.

"I'm sure he broke into your store for his grandmother. It would be just like her to try scaring you into selling," Bess said in a triumphant stage whisper.

To Miriam's amazement, neither Phoebe or Jason seemed to have heard Bess's accusation. The young man, dripping wet without a raincoat or umbrella to keep him dry, took Phoebe's hand and led her toward the front counter. They stared at each other for several long moments before he seemingly made up his mind to tell her why he was there.

"Phoebe...," he said hesitatingly.

"Yes," she answered. Miriam could hear the pent-up tension in her assistant's voice. She felt like a snoop listening to their conversation and unsuccessfully prodded Bess to go into the office with her.

Bess was immovable, so Miriam reluctantly stayed where she was, pretending to polish a spoon from the 1969 World's Fair in New York. When she looked over at Bess, her friend was scrubbing at the bowl of an eighteenth-century spoon with so much vigor she might be removing layers of old silver.

"I've run out of excuses to give my grandmother for coming here when I should be working in the store," Jason said, apparently regaining his use of language. "I want us to go out on a real date instead of sneaking around."

Before Phoebe could answer, he turned toward Miriam and Bess, who were still pretending to be interested in polishing spoons.

"Mrs. Watkins," he earnestly said to Bess, "I know my grandmother was a thorn in your side in the old days."

Miriam suppressed a burst of laughter at Jason's use of the old-fashioned phrase. She knew Bess, who was staring open-mouthed at the grandson of her high school nemesis, would not take kindly to her friend dissolving into peals of laughter.

"But I'm my own person, and I want to court your granddaughter," he declared dramatically.

"Court?" Bess finally managed to sputter.

Miriam couldn't stop herself from laughing now. Jason Downs was so sincere and sweet and old-fashioned. How could Bess possibly object to him dating her granddaughter—even if his grandmother had been her high school rival?

"I found that word on the Internet," he admitted. "I wanted you to know how serious I am."

"Oh, Jason," Phoebe sighed with pleasure as he stood up to her grandmother.

"Oh, good grief," Bess said noisily exhaling.

Miriam could tell her opinion of Jason had gone up, but was she ready to accept the young man on his own merits?

Miriam smiled broadly as both Phoebe and Jason looked expectantly at Bess. Her old friend looked like she'd rather be anywhere but where she was.

"Oh, all right, you two," Bess said. "You have my blessing."

Miriam grinned at Bess as the two young people beamed at each other.

"Okay," Miriam said with an approving smile. "Why don't you two take a coffee break and plan your date."

"Really, Mrs. Max?" Phoebe earnestly asked.

"Really."

"Gran…?"

"Go on, I'll help Miriam polish this silver. What could be more fun on a rainy day?"

Excitedly Phoebe grabbed her umbrella from the office and joined Jason. They headed out into the downpour as though the sun was shining just for them.

"You're a good egg, you know," Miriam teased gently.

"I guess so," Bess grudgingly said, although her eyes were glistening.

"Young love—there's nothing like it," Miriam said sagely.

"Unless it's old love," Bess teased.

* * *

At his bayside home, Samuel stared out at the downpour as the rain darkened the boards of his wooden deck. On the drive home from Rhode Island, he'd only had one thing on his mind: spending time with Miriam. Now he could hardly ask her to get soaked for the sake of a coffee break with him.

But he was a navy man. Water never intimidated him. He had a better idea.

Half an hour later he sprinted to the door of Ruthie's Antiques with an insulated bag dangling from his arm. The shop was empty except for Miriam sitting at a table in the back.

"Samuel." She stood and smiled, making his trip to town more than worthwhile. "I was going to finish polishing one more spoon, then close the shop for the day. I gave Phoebe the rest of the day off because we've had zero customers since the storm hit."

"Let me do it for you," he said, putting his bag on the counter and pulling the shade over the door. He was pleased to see a new bolt lock, which he slid shut. "How is the new security system working?" he asked.

"So well I almost have to break in myself, but I'm glad I have it. Did you have a good trip?"

"I had a long one. I had to listen to my friend's family history until my eyes glazed over. I couldn't wait to get back here."

"I'm glad to see you're back," she said.

"Paul was helpful, and he has quite a library. I checked a few army sources too, hoping to get a new lead on your great-grandfather. Unfortunately, everything was a dead end. It almost seems as if Captain Thomas Davis deliberately disappeared, but he must have had children. You're living proof of that."

"So I am," Miriam said with smile in her voice.

He hoped it was because she was pleased to see him.

"It's too wet to go out for coffee, so I brought the fixings to you," he said, unzipping the bag and taking out a thermos of gourmet coffee—her favorite, not his. "They were glad to see me at the bakery. Business is so slow this afternoon, they insisted on giving me three rolls for the price of two."

"Are those bear claws?" she asked as he laid them out on napkins.

"*Raspberry* bear claws. Remember when we used to sneak off at lunchtime and eat them behind the school?"

"You'd pick them up on the way to school. They were a secret treat."

"Until the coach caught us and lectured me for breaking training rules. He was on a meat and vegetables kick for his football players. I tried his diet for a week and was too hungry to do well in the game."

"You always did well," Miriam said, biting into the bear claw with obvious pleasure.

"You were always my number-one supporter."

"I wasn't even on the cheerleading squad," she said.

"That's what made you so special. I was the only one you cheered for."

"We had fun," Miriam said, pouring out coffee in one of the two mugs he'd brought with him.

"We did. I spent my first year at the academy wishing I could see you."

"You didn't call."

"I wanted to, but I didn't think it was fair to lead you on when I knew what it took to have a career in the navy." He sipped the steaming-hot coffee, not sure he wanted to hear whether she would've waited for him.

She didn't respond.

"I'd like to show you my cottage. The Queen Anne desk is perfect for my office. I was lucky to find a cozy place that still has room for everything I want to do."

"I'd like to see it, but maybe on a day when it isn't raining so hard. I should go home and make sure the roof isn't leaking. I had it repaired, but I'm not convinced it won't need to be replaced sometime soon."

"Yes, I imagine older homes take a lot of upkeep, even when they look as sturdy as yours. I seem to remember it was an early example of a prefabricated home."

"Sort of," Miriam said. "Sears, Roebuck and Co. sold the plans and many of the components. Our model is a foursquare house. My grandparents bought it after their first house burned down."

"That was before my time," Samuel said, reaching out with his napkin to wipe a dab of pastry from her lip. "Has the shop been busy?"

"We could hardly keep up with the customers this morning, but when the weather got worse, no one came. Except for Phoebe's friend, Jason Downs. Bess finally seems resigned to having them date. He's really a very sweet boy, nothing like Natalie."

Samuel decided he hadn't felt so content in a long time. Miriam was more than just a good companion. She was understanding and interested in everyone around her. There was a sweetness in her nature that was hard to define but so soothing he hated to have this interlude end.

"Did you walk to work?" he asked when she was ready to go home.

"No, not today."

"A shame. I could spend more time with you if you needed a ride home."

"You're welcome to come for dinner," she said.

"Would that I could! I promised Mikey I'd have supper with him. His wife is out of town, and he wants to go out for the seafood special at Captain Bailey's Fish House. You're welcome to join us."

"I'll pass this time," Miriam said. "You probably have a lot of catching up to do with Mikey. Anyway, it looks like a good evening for a roaring fire and a book I've been meaning to start. Considering how many fireplaces there are in my old family home, I rarely think of using one."

"Not surprising in the summer," Samuel said, standing to gather the remains of their coffee break. "Can I convince you to take this bear claw home?"

"Oh, please, no," she said with a good-natured laugh. "I'll hardly need dinner after your lovely treat."

When the shop was locked down with all but the security lights extinguished, Samuel walked with her to her car parked in the back alley, even though it meant a rather long trek to his vehicle parked on the street in front. Soggy shoes and damp khaki pants were a small price to pay for spending time with Miriam. He only hoped she was beginning to see him as more than an old friend from high school.

Chapter Twenty-One

Tuesday the sun came out, but Samuel hardly noticed. He was up early working on his book, trying to incorporate into his notes what he'd learned in Rhode Island.

Oddly enough, his perfect working place wasn't as helpful as he'd expected. The cottage was too quiet, and he missed the hustle and bustle of his job before retirement. As dedicated as he was to completing his book on the Confederate navy, he wasn't focusing as well as he usually did. The reason was no mystery: Miriam was constantly on his mind.

He wasn't a teenage kid with a crush, and he was trying to be patient. He sensed Miriam wasn't ready for a serious relationship, and the last thing he wanted was to rush her into something she'd later regret. The sensible thing was to pull back and give her time to know her own feelings. It was easier said than done.

Halfheartedly pressing the print key on his computer, he went to the printer to retrieve a page. The words came out a dull gray, but the poor copy brought a broad smile to his face. He was out of ink and didn't have a new cartridge. His only option was a trip to town, and it just happened to be close to lunchtime. With any luck, Miriam might consent to join him. A casual noon meal hardly counted as a date.

Feeling like a kid again, he parked on the street near the office supply store and made his purchase. He was walking toward the antiques store when Bess nearly bumped into him going in the opposite direction.

"Samuel, imagine running into you," she said in her usual breath-less way.

"It's a small town," he teased.

"I've been wanting to talk to you," she said, standing in front of him with a serious expression. "I'm not at all happy about the break-in at Miriam's shop. The police haven't done a thing about it, and I doubt they will."

"She did have an up-to-date security system installed," Samuel said to reassure Bess, although the situation bothered him too.

"Yes, I guess that would discourage burglars, but nothing was stolen. It seemed to be a malicious prank, but who would want to harass Miriam? I can't believe she has an enemy in the world," Bess said.

"Me neither," Samuel said, biting his lower lip in frustration.

"Maybe it would help if both of us went to the police station," Bess suggested.

"That might make us feel proactive," Samuel said, "but I don't think Miriam would like it. She might think we're interfering in her business."

"I didn't think of that," Bess admitted. "It probably wouldn't do any good anyway. Nothing was stolen, so there's no way to find out where the loot was fenced."

Samuel suppressed a smile at Bess's observation. She must watch too many crime dramas on TV, but he did think she was right to be concerned.

"We need to figure out who would benefit if Miriam was scared into closing her business," he said.

"Easy!" Bess said with a triumphant look. "Natalie Downs wants to buy the building so she and her husband can expand their store. She has everything to gain if Miriam gives up."

"I never knew her in high school, but her family runs an established business now. I can't see her risking their reputation by hiring someone to break into Miriam's shop."

"I think she'd do anything to get what she wants," Bess said, sounding convinced of the woman's ruthlessness.

"Maybe, but I think she's more likely to hire lawyers or involve local politicians. And we don't even know if her husband is as eager to expand as she seemed to be," Samuel reasoned.

"I guess you're right," Bess admitted, "but I'm not taking her off my list of suspects—my very short list."

"The important thing is that Miriam doesn't get hurt. Vandalism can take much worse forms—smashed windows, arson…"

"We've never had had things like that in Maple Landing," Bess protested.

"And there's no reason to believe we will," Samuel assured her. "Why don't I sound Miriam out and see if she's apprehensive?"

"That's a good idea," Bess said. "She thinks I worry too much—well, maybe I do. But it's so nice to have her back in town. Since I've reconnected with her after so many years, the last thing I want to see is her give up and go back to Indiana."

"Do you think she's considering it?" Samuel couldn't hide the alarm in his voice.

"Not that she's said, but what would keep her here if she sells Ruthie's Antiques?"

What indeed? Samuel thought, rethinking his decision to give Miriam time and space to let their new relationship blossom slowly. At least he could sound her out on the break-in and see whether she was as disturbed as Bess.

"I'm glad we talked, Bess," he said before hurrying toward the antiques shop. He felt very protective of Miriam, regardless of how she felt about him now.

"Hi, Admiral Bentley," Phoebe said when he entered the shop.

The Downs boy was lounging against the counter, and two women were examining a corner cupboard near the rear of the store, opening and shutting the door as though they expected it to fall off. Samuel walked past them and looked into the office, but Miriam wasn't there.

Phoebe was deep in conversation with the Downs boy when he returned to the front. He was tempted to point out that she had potential customers in the furniture section, but he reminded himself not to interfere in Miriam's business. She seemed pleased with Phoebe's help, so it wasn't his place to tell the girl what to do.

"Where is Mrs. Maxwell?" he asked.

"She had some errands to do," Phoebe said.

"Is that the best you can do on the corner cupboard?" one of the customers asked before Samuel could question where Miriam might be.

His concern about Phoebe's seeming indifference vanished as she began to negotiate on the price of the cupboard. As he left, he felt confident Phoebe would make the sale on terms favorable to the shop.

* * *

It wasn't like Miriam to stay home on a potentially busy Tuesday morning, but her heart wasn't in the business today. Fortunately Phoebe seemed to relish being in charge, and she'd already called on Miriam's cell phone to tell her about a big sale at a really good price. She'd wanted to get rid of the bulky corner cupboard since taking over the shop. It took up too much room, and now she would have wall space to hang some nicely framed art.

Phoebe called a second time, excited because the buyers had paid cash and made their own arrangements to move the cupboard. It turned out they were dealers from Baltimore who expected to make a good profit themselves.

"That's your first commission," Miriam reminded Phoebe. She'd promised a small bonus on any sales her employee made over five hundred dollars. She was as pleased to be paying it as Phoebe was to receive it.

Her plan for today was to put some effort into organizing the house. It had been a struggle to find space for her own furnishings in the crowded rooms. Possibly she would find where Ruth had kept additional store records, although no obvious hiding place had turned up yet. As a young woman, her sister had secreted away coins and even dollar bills, saving them for emergencies. Miriam also remembered a diary, although it had been full of girlish observations from middle and high school. She'd found that and returned it to the dresser until she made decisions about all of her sister's personal possessions.

Before she could do more than a little cleaning in the kitchen, there was a knock at the front door. She saw a man peering through the screen door and hurried to see why he was there.

"Mrs. Maxwell?" he asked with the screen still between them.

"Yes." He looked respectable, dressed in a light summer suit with a pastel striped tie, but she wasn't ready to invite him into her house until he stated his business.

"I'm Grant Gillis of Maple Landing Realty. I was in school with your sister, Ruth." He pulled a business card out of his jacket pocket and held it in her direction.

She didn't have a reason for talking to a Realtor, but she didn't have the heart to turn away anyone who'd known Ruth.

"Come in," she said as cordially as possible. "Were you in my sister's high school class?"

"Two years behind," he said, taking out a snowy white handkerchief and blotting his moist forehead. The top of his head was totally bald, but little white ringlets curled around his ears. "But I was definitely one of her admirers. In fact, I sold her the building her store was in."

"*Is* in," Miriam said. "I've taken over. Would you like to sit?"

"Yes, please. I understand Ruthie's Antiques is open for business again, but as I'm sure you're aware, it's very difficult to make a success of a retail store in a town as small as Maple Landing."

He followed her to a beige suede couch she'd brought from Indiana and sank down with a sigh of relief. "It's going to be a hot one today."

"What can I do for you, Mr. Gillis?"

"Please, call me Grant. It's more what I can do for you."

She wasn't pleased by his patronizing tone, and she doubted he knew the first thing about her sister.

"Nothing, I'm afraid. I've settled in here and don't plan to sell the house."

"No, of course not. Your family has been in this location for a century or more. I'm quite a fan of historic homes. Actually I'm here representing Mrs. Natalie Downs—and her husband too, of course."

Miriam wanted to groan, but she forced herself to hear the Realtor out.

"My client is prepared to offer you an extremely generous price for the building where your late sister had her antiques shop. She has no interest in the contents, but I suspect you could realize quite a bit by selling them as a lot to another dealer or in a series of auctions."

"Mr. Gillis…"

"I understand this is a very big decision. You must have a sentimental attachment to Ruth's business. She had quite a reputation in Maple Landing. Her many friends were very saddened by her passing."

Miriam sat and let his spiel run down, but everything he said made her more determined to make a success of the shop on her own. What made him—and Natalie Downs—think she couldn't run a business? Obviously they were driven by what they wanted—her property for Natalie and a fat commission for Grant Gillis—but she didn't respond well to pressure. Even if she wanted to sell, she would look for another buyer.

"I have no interest in selling," she said as firmly as possible when he ran out of arguments.

"Of course, I understand. It's too soon after your sister's passing to make major decisions. But please keep my card and call me when you're ready to consider selling." He mopped his forehead with the handkerchief again and stood to leave.

"That's not going to happen," she said as he walked to the door. "I'm sorry you wasted your time, Mr. Gillis."

"It was a pleasure to meet you," he said. "And I'm sure you'll find that Maple Landing Realty would be sensitive to your every need. My grandfather started the business when he returned from World War II. We've always put the welfare of our clients and the community first."

Miriam had heard more than enough, but he turned and continued to talk through her screen after she showed him out.

Did people really respond to such a hard sell? She sighed with relief as he retreated to his car parked on the street.

The house seemed big and empty, and she was beginning to wish she'd gone to the shop. She thought life would be simple and pleasant if she returned to her childhood home, but the Realtor's visit only reminded her of the break-in. Someone had tried to send her a message. Would Natalie stoop low enough to hire an intruder? She could understand if valuable antiques had been taken, but who would break in and walk away with a bottle opener, and not a valuable one at that?

The phone rang, and her first thought was Samuel might be calling. But she certainly wasn't disappointed when a cheery voice said, "Hello, Mom."

"Lisa!"

"I tried to call you at the store, but the woman who answered the phone said you'd stayed home today. Are you all right?"

"Fine," Miriam assured her daughter. "I'm just trying to sort some things out at home. Your aunt was pretty disorganized in recent years, and I need to find more inventory records. How are my little sweethearts?"

"They both want to tell you about summer camp. We wouldn't call at work, but they're going to a friend's house and couldn't wait until tonight," Lisa said. "I don't have any news about when we're moving or where we'll live, but here's Abby."

Miriam forgot about the Realtor and everything else concerned with the shop as her beloved granddaughters regaled her about their summer adventures. She hung up feeling lonely for her family. Should she consider Natalie's offer?

Another knock on her front door erased that thought as she saw Samuel through the screen door.

Chapter Twenty-Two

After the unwelcome visit from the Realtor, Miriam was delighted to see Samuel on the other side of the screen mesh.

"Got time for a shore-bound sailor?" he teased.

"All the time in the world," she said enthusiastically. "Come on in."

"When I stopped at the shop and you weren't there, I was afraid you might be ill," he said.

"Oh, I'm fine, thank you," Miriam said, pleased by his show of concern. "I still think Ruth must have hidden some shop records somewhere in the house. This seemed like a good time to do some housecleaning and look for them."

"You don't think she used the false desk drawer as a hiding place, do you?" Samuel asked.

"Unlikely, since she put it in the store to be sold. Can I get you a nice cool drink? I have a pitcher of iced tea in the fridge."

"Sounds good," Samuel said, following her to the kitchen, the one room she felt was organized enough to use for company. Of course, she hadn't been a very good Southern hostess with the Realtor, but his visit was particularly unwelcome.

As Samuel sat across from her at the table, she told him about Natalie's latest attempt to buy the store.

"What was the Realtor's name?" he asked.

"Grant Gillis. I take it his family owns Maple Landing Realty."

"I met him when I first started looking for a home here," Samuel said. "I decided to work with his competition instead. Gillis was a little too pushy. When I checked around, his reputation isn't the greatest—although I can't say he actually does anything illegal."

Her glass of tea made a wet ring on the tablecloth, white with bright red and yellow apples. It was one Miriam remembered from her days growing up in the house. Samuel drank his quickly, but hers sat, untouched, as she expressed her own doubts about the Realtor.

"Bess thinks Natalie hired someone to mess up my shop. If she did, she doesn't know me at all. I won't be scared off," Miriam said.

"Nor should you be. But I don't buy that theory. Natalie has done exactly what I'd expect: get a Realtor to pressure you."

"Yes, I guess I should've expected that," Miriam said.

"Bess is worried about you," Samuel said. "I saw her on my way to your shop."

"Bless her," Miriam said. "Renewing our friendship was one of the best things about moving here—not the only one though." She smiled, and Samuel looked pleased.

"I wonder whether your sister had any family mementos going back to your great-grandfather," Samuel speculated.

"If she did, she might have hidden them away someplace safe," Miriam said. "She never mentioned it to me, but I have to confess: I never had much interest in history, our family's or anyone else's."

"The owner of an antiques shop who doesn't like old things," Samuel teased.

"Putting the store in order has given me a whole new appreciation of all things old. I'm starting to look at them through the eyes of the original owners. When I handle an artifact, I wonder what their lives were like. Maybe that's what Ruth wanted me to feel when she left her store to me."

"Do you have your great-grandfather's letter at home?" Samuel asked. "I've been thinking about it a lot. Maybe there's something we're missing."

"I put it in a book to preserve it temporarily. Let's look at it again, although I think I've managed to make out most of the words. I also picked up on an urgency in what he was saying, but not the reason behind it. He was concerned about the location of something, but I still haven't a clue what or where."

Leading the way to a glass-fronted bookcase in the back room that had served as a den and office, she quickly found the letter and laid it flat on an oak library table much like the ones in the high school library in her day. Or maybe it was one of the tables she remembered. If she'd learned one thing about Ruth's buying habits, it was that she went everywhere to find items for her store.

"I remember most of it," Samuel said. "In fact, I get distracted from my own research thinking about it. Guess I can't resist a mystery, especially a historical one that affects someone I care about."

This was as close as Samuel had come to telling her how he felt. Miriam didn't know how to react, so she said nothing.

"Here's one of the words that stuck in my mind," he said, pointing at faded text. "*Riches.*"

"He repeated it several times, but I don't understand why," Miriam said. "From everything I know about the Davis family, their finances were wiped out after the war. If my great-grandfather had any resources at all, they were lost to history. He certainly never produced any riches to help the family's struggle. The more I learned from the letter, the more confused I became. I would love to know more about him."

"This is just as I remembered it," Samuel said, pointing to the letter. "It raises more questions than it answers."

"Unless Ruth hid away more family papers, I don't see any way to learn more about my ancestor."

"Let's not give up yet," Samuel said, and Miriam found herself relishing the plural pronoun. "In fact, I did a little research about Confederate money, or 'Greybacks,' as some called them. In 1861 Greybacks were used throughout the South, but the longer the war lasted, the more they were devalued."

"That must have been so discouraging for people who depended on it to buy food and other necessities." Miriam felt sad just thinking about it.

"By the end of the war, it was practically worthless," Samuel said. "It was like the currency issued by the Continental Congress during the Revolutionary War. There was no gold or silver to back it up. It was a promise to pay, in the South's case two years after a peace treaty was signed with the United States."

"And the rest is history." Miriam said.

"Exactly. Any gold they had went to purchase goods they needed abroad. They never backed the currency with their most lucrative crops: cotton and tobacco. Now collectors are interested in buying Greybacks, sometimes at prices far exceeding face value."

"But that doesn't explain why my great-grandfather hid the money away."

"At the beginning of the war, his cache must have had the purchasing power of approximately one thousand of today's dollars. Maybe he expected to need cash at some point," Samuel speculated.

"But why?"

"That's the big question," he said.

Miriam leaned back in her chair, the iced tea forgotten. "I can't thank you enough for all the effort you've put into this."

"It's been a pleasure. I just wish I had answers."

"We've learned some things," Miriam said, trying to sound optimistic. "He must have had a family—as you pointed out, I'm living proof of that. He had a reason to hide a map, letter, and Confederate money. Somehow he was associated with Suetville, now Stewartstown, but no big battle or anything significant happened there."

"Although providing meat for the Confederate army was no small contribution to the war effort," Samuel said.

"But there's no family tradition that he was a butcher. In fact, his life before he joined the army is shrouded in mystery too. His son, my grandfather, was a schoolteacher in his youth. I guess you could call that the family occupation."

"Maybe there are school records in Stewartstown that would show that." Samuel looked thoughtful. "I have one suggestion if you're willing. We should make another trip to Stewartstown. The cemetery can't be the only way to trace a former resident, if that's what your great-grandfather was."

"Samuel," Miriam said, "I seem to keep taking up your time." Still, even if they learned absolutely nothing—which she strongly suspected would be the case—the prospect of another day with Samuel was appealing.

"You're not taking up my time," he said with a gentle smile. "You're enhancing it. I can't think of anything I'd rather be doing."

"That's so kind of you," she said.

"It's settled then. We'll play detective one more time. Who knows? We may have some success. When is the best time for you to take time off from the store?"

"Phoebe has really proved herself lately. Unless there's some reason why she can't work, I'd love to go tomorrow. I'll have my cell phone with me if she needs anything, and besides, I won't be able to concentrate on anything else until I know we've done everything possible to clear my great-grandfather's name."

"If he was innocent of any wrongdoing, we'll find out," Samuel said in a serious tone. "I promise."

Distracted as she had been by her two visitors, Miriam decided to go to the shop after Samuel left. If Ruth had hidden anything in the house, she wasn't going to find it in an obvious place. And she had better check with Phoebe about tomorrow.

Excited as she was about returning to Stewartstown, she didn't know whether it was the quest to clear her ancestor's name or the prospect of a day with Samuel that pleased her most.

Chapter Twenty-Three

Heavy rains overnight brought the temperature down, so Miriam put on a lightweight yellow windbreaker over her white knit shirt. Although they wouldn't be walking through any cemeteries this visit—at least as far as she knew—she'd opted for tan cotton slacks and sensible walking shoes. Her only concession to fashion was a shimmering silk scarf in shades of bronze and green. If Samuel had the top down, she would be ready for it.

She was dressed early, but Samuel was late—something she could never remember happening before. As the minutes crawled by, she was almost ready to call and see if he was all right. When he did pull up in front of her house, she was sitting on the front stoop with her cell phone out.

"Sorry I'm late," he called out as he walked toward her.

Although the sky was still partly overcast, his hair picked up the feeble rays of sun and seemed as snowy white as clouds. He was wearing a blue sweater with long sleeves and khaki slacks, but on him the casual attire looked überneat.

"I was getting a little worried," she admitted. "You're never late."

"I made a few contacts and called in some favors," he explained. "Turns out one of my buddies from my academy days is superintendent of schools in Stewartstown. He's going to give us access to the old records, those that haven't been put online yet."

"Wonderful!" Miriam said. "If my great-grandfather ever taught there, we might be able to trace him."

"It's only a possibility," Samuel warned. "As backup, I called a friend who knows the mayor. We played his football team back in high school, and the current mayor was the quarterback. After some back-and-forth online, he agreed to give us access to town records too. If Captain Davis ever owned property in Stewartstown, there might be a record of the deed."

"You're a marvel," Miriam said. "After all your time away, you still know people all over the state."

"It's a small world," Samuel said, smiling at her praise. "Of course, the Internet has made the whole world smaller. Unfortunately I drew a blank when I researched your great-grandfather's name. I found seven soldiers named Thomas Davis who enlisted or were mustered out of the Confederate army in Maryland, and none fit his profile. In fact, there were four in one family, all cousins, but only one came home. He lost a leg in the war and spent his remaining years as a postmaster."

"I can't wait to read your book," Miriam said with broad grin. "I'm sure it will be a fresh, exciting take on the Confederate navy."

"I'll reserve the first copy off the press for you," he said. "Assuming, that is, it gets printed."

"Just so you're sure I'm not taking up time you need to work on it."

"Mrs. Max, I deem it a pleasure to pursue your elusive ancestor," he said.

"Mrs. Max! You've been around Phoebe," she teased.

"She's a breath of fresh air. Is she doing any better on the breakage?"

"She's trying," Miriam said. "She's not allowed to dust the breakable items."

"Well, shall we go?" Samuel offered his arm, and they walked to his car together. She was pleased to see the top was up, although she loved a ride in the open air when it was a little warmer.

The miles flew by as they talked nonstop. Miriam was amazed by how much they had to say to each other after so many years apart. During the time it took to get to Stewartstown, they never once ran out of conversation.

Driving into the town was a sobering experience. When Samuel turned off onto a street of antebellum homes with huge maple trees shading lawns with cast-iron fences, Miriam could imagine life as it had been in her great-grandfather's day. As far as they'd been able to discover, this was the older part of town, the area that had once been called Suetville. Did Captain Davis find refuge in one of the well-weathered homes after the war? Today most had been converted to apartments or condos, judging by the multiple entrances, some with baby buggies or strollers parked by the doors.

"Let's try the school's administrative offices first," Samuel suggested.

Miriam brought her mind back to the present, seeing a part of Stewartstown they'd missed on their first trip. Some Redbrick storefronts had suffered modernizing fifty or more years ago with bland signs and tired-looking window displays. She much preferred the ones untouched by time: a shoe repair shop, a used books store, a pharmacy with a mortar and pestle hanging over the sidewalk to identify it.

Samuel found the school's administrative building without any difficulty and parked in the area designated for visitors.

As happy as she was to stretch her legs, Miriam felt a knot of apprehension in her stomach. Would she learn anything to vindicate her ancestor? Even though she'd never even seen a picture, she carried an image of him in her mind. When he returned from the war, he must have been thin and battle-hardened. Most likely he had sandy hair like her own grandfather, perhaps with a sprinkling of gray after the ordeals he'd faced. His face must have been lean and bearded, and his dark eyes shadowed from fatigue and grief over lost comrades.

"A penny for your thoughts," Samuel said when she stood beside the car without moving.

"Oh, I was just imagining how my great-grandfather must have looked. Of course, I only have stories my grandfather told as a guide, but Thomas Davis has become very real to me in the last few weeks."

"I understand," Samuel said. "Let's go see if we can find another piece of the puzzle."

The Stewartstown schools were run from a building that had once been a factory, a three-story Redbrick structure. The restoration had captured the stark utilitarian nature of the original, but inside the first floor had a pleasing pattern of green and beige tiles.

Offices lined both sides of a corridor that divided the building in half. The first door had a pebbled glass window and a small sign inviting visitors to enter.

"Good morning," a tiny gray-haired woman said when they opened the door. "I'm Amelia. What can I do for you folks?"

After Samuel explained their purpose, she escorted them to a small elevator near the end of the corridor.

"Ah yes. Dr. Cochran told me to be on the lookout for you," she said, her heels clicking on the tiles.

"The superintendent of schools," Samuel said for Miriam's benefit.

The elevator was small enough to induce claustrophobia, but it chugged up to the second floor without incident.

"I'm sorry, but we have to use the stairs to get to the records on the third floor," the efficient little woman said.

The stairs were steep, and Samuel kept his hand protectively on the small of Miriam's back as she followed Amelia. They entered a large open space lined with metal shelves. The high, flat ceiling and bare board floors attested to its use as a factory.

"What was the original purpose of the building?" Samuel asked.

"At one time it was a corset factory, but during the war they made boots for the Confederate army. It sat empty until the 1880s, when a patent medicine company set up shop on the first floor." Her recitation sounded well-rehearsed. "Dr. Hennessey's Tonic was a big seller until the Pure Food and Drug Act of 1906."

"That was the law that required labeling of patent medicines, wasn't it?" Samuel asked, showing a polite interest in what she was saying although he was as eager as Miriam to get into the records.

"Yes, can you imagine all the ladies who suddenly learned their beloved tonic contained enough opium to make them drug addicts?" Amelia lowered her voice. "My own dear great-granny swore by it until she learned what was in it. Of course, it was still legal to sell opiates, but once respectable woman knew they were taking it, Dr. Hennessey was lucky to get out of town without being tarred and feathered. After that the factory went downhill. They tried making umbrellas, then plastic raincoats and down-filled sleeping bags, but the factory closed for good in the 1950s. The school board bought it for practically nothing, and I can tell you, the town was glad to see an eyesore put to good use."

"About the records…" Samuel must have sensed Miriam's impatience as he tried to hurry their guide along.

"I must apologize for the dust," Amelia said. "We rarely have anyone interested in the old records. Can I help you find what you need?"

"Please," Miriam said. "We're looking for lists of teachers who taught just before and after the war."

"The years 1866 and 1867 might be good starting points," Samuel said.

Miriam's knees felt shaky as Amelia pointed to a long row of boxes on the far wall. What they found could change her whole understanding of family history—or it could help prove her ancestor deserved his bad reputation.

"Can I help?" Amelia asked. "School board policy insists I stay in the room when anyone uses the records."

"We're looking for a teacher named Thomas Davis," Miriam said, too tense to explain her reason.

"There might be an account book with his name in it. Teachers were paid in scrip right after the war. Everyone was broke, including the town. They could exchange the scrip for food and necessities. It was a hard time."

"Yes," Samuel agreed as Miriam located a wooden crate with no top. The date 1866 was on the front in faded letters.

The contents had been exposed to dust, heat, cold, and parasites, and the first notebook Miriam touched was so brittle she was afraid it would fall apart.

"Would you like some plastic gloves?" their helpful guide asked.

The gloves made her fingers clumsy, but with Samuel's help, she managed to extract a sheath of age-darkened papers.

"If these were made of today's newsprint, they'd be dust," Samuel commented. "Fortunately there was a large rag content in old paper."

"Look, this is a journal of some kind from an elementary school. It lists the teachers and their students." She carefully turned the pages, but all the teachers were women.

"Here's the high school," Samuel said. "Sadly, not many children got that far in school. One instructor taught all the classes."

"Not Thomas Davis?" Miriam asked without much hope.

"Afraid not."

Miriam searched as quickly as she could between sneezes as dust whirled up around them. When Samuel suggested they quit, she insisted on checking one more year. At last she had mercy on

Amelia and gave up the search. They hadn't found a scrap of evidence that Thomas Davis ever taught school there.

After profusely thanking Amelia, they went to the car.

"Historical research isn't for the faint of heart," Samuel said trying to cheer her.

"As much as I sneezed," Miriam said, "I must be allergic to it."

Samuel laughed, then asked, "Do you still want to check the town's archives? The records may be more accessible since they involve buying and selling property."

She was tempted to say no, but they'd come this far. She brushed flakes of dried paper and dust from her jacket and decided to leave it on even though the sun was warm now. At least she had a clean layer under it for the ride home.

"I think we can get there before noon," she said, remembering that town offices tended to close down for lunch. "If they let us in, we'll check their records. If not, we can start for home. I don't have a good feeling about finding anything. If my great-grandfather hid his valuables in a desk in Maple Landing, he probably didn't own property here."

Although the receptionist at the town hall couldn't have been more helpful, Miriam was proved right. The modern brick building had well-organized records in a spacious, well-lit basement. A computer search turned up nothing, and the boxes of deeds weren't helpful either.

Their guide offered to let Miriam wash up in the public restroom, a courtesy she greatly appreciated as she scrubbed her face and hands with liquid hand soap and dried them on paper towels.

With her hair combed free of dust and her jacket bundled to take home and launder, she felt more like herself.

"You're amazing," Samuel said as they returned to his car. "Five minutes ago you looked like you'd been Dumpster diving, but now you're as fresh and pretty as you were this morning."

"Fresh on the outside," Miriam said with a smile, noticing that he still looked clean after peeling off his sweater to reveal the blue-and-white polo shirt under it. "On the inside I'm feeling bedraggled—and a little guilty. I've taken up your whole morning, and we didn't discover a thing."

"I've enjoyed it. Would you like to look around for the public library?" he asked. "Maybe they have some records not online. Or we could grab some lunch."

"I vote for food," Miriam said.

"Would you like to go back to the same restaurant? We had a tasty lunch there."

"Great idea." Miriam smiled at him, realizing that any day spent with Samuel was a good day.

Chapter Twenty-Four

After the discouraging morning sorting through aged records, Miriam was glad to return to the restaurant where they'd enjoyed such a lovely lunch. When they stepped into the cozy dining area, it was obvious a lot of other people had the same idea. Every table was full, and a couple was waiting to be seated.

"Glad to see you folks again," Johanna said as she dashed by with a full tray. "It shouldn't be more than a ten-minute wait."

"We're in no hurry," Samuel said.

It was immediately obvious that the owners had added a lot of items to their wall display in the short time since Miriam and Samuel had last been there. Miriam was looking around the room when her heart started pounding with excitement.

"Look, Samuel!" He turned his gaze from a Confederate sword and immediately spotted the source of her excitement.

"It's the other half of our map!" Miriam breathlessly exclaimed. "I'm sure of it."

Samuel stepped as close as he could without hovering over a table of diners. "You're right! There's the rough edge where it was torn."

"And those little hearts and crosses look exactly the same. Oh, Samuel," she whispered, "I hope I can buy it."

"Play it cool," he advised. "I seem to remember Johanna saying some things were for sale. Maybe this is one of them."

The owner's wife was clearing a table for the couple who were ahead of them, but it wasn't long before several customers drifted out.

"Can we use this table?" Miriam asked, pointing at the one directly under the map in an oak frame.

"You surely can. Just let me clear it. Our busboy took the week off for a youth retreat at church. Have to admit I miss him."

Feeling so impatient she was ready to bus the table herself, Miriam managed to contain herself until they were seated. She scarcely saw the little bouquet of daisies or the crystal water glasses.

"We were admiring your map," Samuel said, managing to sound much more casual than she felt.

"I'm pretty sure it dates back to the War Between the States or shortly afterward," Johanna said, handing them menus in leather folders. "Our special today is tomato pie—my husband makes the crust himself, and it will melt in your mouth. It comes with Waldorf salad."

"That sounds wonderful," Miriam said, so entranced by the map she scarcely knew what she was ordering.

"I'll take a crabcake-and-cheese po'boy," Samuel said after briefly scanning the menu. "And a cup of gumbo."

"And what would you folks like to drink?"

"You know, I haven't had a frosty mug of root beer since I was a kid. How does that sound to you, Miriam?"

"Lovely," she said, ready to agree to anything. "Johanna, is there any possibility you'd sell that map?"

"It's only half a map, and I can't tell you what location it shows. I just hung it because it had a nice, aged look. It might fall apart if you take it out of the frame."

"But would you sell it? I'd be happy to pay for the frame too."

"Let me check with my husband. He's the one who appreciates artifacts, although what you see here is only the tip of the iceberg."

"Please do," Miriam said, trying to disguise how eager she was.

When their server walked away, Samuel grinned broadly. He was better at hiding his feelings than she was, but she could tell he was as excited as she was to find the missing half of the map. Now the only question was whether the owners would sell it.

Today's lunch was every bit as delicious as the first ones they'd had there. The crust on Miriam's tomato pie was so flaky and light it practically melted in her mouth, and she appreciated the subtle flavors of sweet onions and cheese even though she was focused on the map.

"I haven't had Waldorf salad since I was a kid," she said, offering Samuel a taste of the apple-walnut side dish.

Johanna was scooting in and out of the dining room, but she didn't come to their table to put them out of their suspense.

Samuel finished his crabcake po'boy but was obviously keeping his eye on Johanna. The luncheon crowd was thinning out, but their server was busy taking desert orders and putting leftovers in Styrofoam containers.

"Dessert for you folks?" she asked, at last coming to their table.

Samuel politely declined, praising his sandwich and the gumbo, but Miriam was too excited about the map to do more than shake her head.

"About the map," he said.

"Oh dear, I've been so rushed I forgot to ask my husband. I'll go do that now," Johanna said.

When she returned there was a big smile on her face. She named a price that was reasonable, actually less than Miriam was prepared to pay.

Johanna took down the frame and led the way to a small counter at the front.

"I'll just wrap this so it the glass won't break," she said, pulling a large sheath of newsprint from under the counter.

While she waited, Miriam saw a small grouping of photographs on the wall behind the counter. She recognized them as cartes de visite like the ones a woman had offered to sell her in the shop. She was pretty sure they hadn't been there on their first visit, and Johanna was quick to confirm it.

"Aren't they the sweetest young ones," Johanna said. "We don't know whether they're the children of the original owners. I just hung them because some of them look so sad. Of course, getting your picture taken back then was a tedious process. I heard the photographer sometimes used a device to keep his subjects from moving their heads."

"Did you find them in the house?" Miriam asked.

"Yes, up in the attic. Folks in those days never threw anything away. Can you believe, I found an artificial leg worn by some poor Confederate soldier. It sort of creeped me out, but my husband is adamant about keeping it. I drew the line at displaying it in the dining room though."

"Are the photographs for sale?" Miriam asked, hoping she had enough cash to buy them all.

"Yes, I could let those go." She stated a price that might have seemed high if Miriam hadn't been so eager to purchase them.

Samuel didn't say anything until they were in the car.

"They don't look like one family to me," he said. "One little girl has black hair, and the two who look like brothers are towheads."

"Yes," Miriam said, taking them out of the plastic sack. "And look how many photos I have. Even in the days when people had large families, seventeen children would be excessive."

"What are you going to do with them?" Samuel asked.

"They look so much like the ones a woman offered to sell me in Maple Landing, I'm going to try to buy hers too. Maybe there's something to be learned from comparing them."

"The map is what intrigues me," Samuel said. "I'd like to take it out of the frame and see it anything's on the back, but it looks pretty fragile."

"I was so excited when I saw it, I started trembling," Miriam admitted. "I don't have a clue what we can learn from it, but it can't be coincidence that it was in that house."

"That reminds me," Samuel said. "Didn't the letter mention a map?"

"Yes. In fact, I finally managed to decipher all of the old writing. I typed a copy of it that would be easier to read to share with you and forgot about it with everything else going on. Let me read it to you," she said, taking it out of her handbag. "It says:

Honorable Sir,

I write this with some haste, as our mutual concern allows me little leisure to fulfill our common goal. Please know that I endeavor to carry out my promise concerning our riches to the utmost of my ability. To this end, I have sketched a rough map as a guide and encouragement in the dark days that are upon us.

"He signs it: *Yours with great respect, Capt. T. Davis.*" Miriam folded the paper and put it back in her bag.

"So the map is the real key to understanding the captain," Samuel said thoughtfully.

"Yes, that's the main thing I've gotten from the letter."

* * *

On the ride home, Miriam was unusually quiet, but Samuel respected her need for silence. Their search for records had been a failure, but finding the other half of the map hanging on the wall of a house dating back to the 1860s was intriguing. In his own way, he was excited as Miriam.

"I didn't pay enough attention to the cartes de visite a woman offered to sell me," Miriam said with self-reproach. "If they're just like the ones I have, they could be a valuable clue. I didn't even look for writing on the backs. I hope she hasn't sold them to someone else."

"Don't be so hard on yourself," Samuel said. "There's no way of knowing whether they had anything to do with your great-grandfather."

"I don't know that for sure. Isn't it strange to find them in the same place as the map? It's all such a muddle, but there has to be a reason behind it."

Samuel couldn't remember when he'd seen her so agitated.

"The map is probably a better clue," he said, trying to calm her. "I have an idea. I'll remove it from the frame, then you can come over for an old-fashioned clambake on the beach. I've been wanting to show you what I've done with the cottage I bought."

For a moment he thought she hadn't heard him.

She shook herself from her reverie. "I can't seem to focus on anything but my great-grandfather's reputation. Think what it would mean to my children and future generations if I could clear his name."

"Miriam, I don't want to discourage you, but you may not like what you find. Maybe the rumors had some truth behind them. They were chaotic times, but sometimes a man deserved the reputation he had."

"I can't let myself believe that. I'm not going to give up. Maybe it would be best if I take the frame home myself. I won't be able to rest until I have a look at both sides."

"If you like," he said, a little hurt. So far they'd been in this together. He was only trying to prepare her for disappointment, but he felt let down when she rejected his offer to take the map out of the frame.

"My invitation to a clambake is still open," he said.

"I appreciate it," she said tiredly, "but I'm afraid I won't be very good company until I understand what all this means. Can you imagine what a burden it is to believe an ancestor was guilty of wrongdoing? The more I learn, the more determined I am to clear his name."

"I understand," he said, not altogether truthfully.

Their search for her ancestor had started out as a historical quest. She was making it a personal crusade, one that could end badly. Where would they stand if she learned some terrible truth about her great-grandfather? He'd only wanted to help, but he might end up looking bad in her eyes if Thomas Davis deserved his bad reputation. He didn't want it to be that way, but she was obsessed with clearing his name.

"I really appreciate the time you've spent helping me," she said in the voice of a polite stranger.

"It's been my pleasure." What he'd enjoyed most was getting reacquainted with her, but she didn't seem in the mood to hear that. "Don't worry about the clambake. We can do it some other time."

Maybe she only needed some space. Her life had changed dramatically in a very short time. He wasn't a man to give up easily, but he couldn't see any good coming if he pressured her now. Time would tell whether her ancestor's disappearance was a puzzle that could be solved.

"Would you mind dropping me off at the store?" she asked when they were close to Maple Landing. "There are a few things I need to do, and I should check on Phoebe too."

"No problem," he said, wondering where they would go from here. He was beginning to believe it would be better if they didn't see each other for a while, but he didn't want to close the door on a relationship by saying so.

"I'll let you know if I learn anything from the map," she said. "It's not that I don't trust you to remove it from the frame. I'm just so eager I want to get at it right away."

Was she only seeing him because he was helpful in her quest? It was a sobering thought, and one he didn't at all like.

"Have a nice day," he said when she hopped out of the car on the street in front of Ruthie's Antiques. Was there a more inane thing he could say? A day that had started with promise turned out to be a big letdown.

He drove home, wondering when or if he should call Miriam. He hated the thought of not seeing her again, so he willed himself not to think the worst.

Chapter Twenty-Five

When she entered her shop after saying good-bye to Samuel, Miriam was surprised to see Bess behind the counter. There was no sign of Phoebe.

"I hope you don't mind," Bess said, hurrying out to meet Miriam. Her cheeks were flushed, and she'd replaced a button on her pink-striped blouse with a safety pin. "Phoebe totally forgot she had a dentist's appointment this afternoon. I offered to cover for her until you got back. I had no idea how busy I'd be. I don't know how Phoebe handles it all by herself. I'm frazzled."

"I'm glad you're here, but sorry you were overworked," Miriam said. "I have lots to tell you."

"You found out more about your great-grandfather?" Bess asked.

"Not exactly, but look at this." She laid the framed map on the counter and removed the layers of newspaper. "It's the other half of the map we found in the secret drawer."

"Where was it?" Bess leaned over for a close look.

"Hanging in the restaurant where we had lunch on our first trip to Stewartstown. Their food was so good we went back, and there it was on the wall. Not only that, I bought these too." She took the package of cartes de visite and spread them out on the counter.

"What adorable children!" Bess exclaimed. "Oh, look at this little girl. She looks as if she'd been crying. I just want to hug her. But what do they have to do with your ancestor?"

"Maybe nothing," Miriam admitted. "But oddly enough, a woman came into the shop wanting to sell some similar ones. I really regret not buying them, but I do have her number. I'm hoping she still has them."

"What does Samuel think about the map?" Bess asked.

"He wanted to take it home and remove it from the frame, but I was so eager I insisted on doing it myself. I hope I haven't hurt his feelings."

Before Bess could respond, the door flew inward. Phoebe came in looking distraught.

"I have to have an impacted wisdom tooth out! Mom will have to drive me to Baltimore because there's no oral surgeon here."

"Dear, that's a shame," her grandmother said, "but I'm sure it must be necessary if Dr. Gordon recommends it. Do you have an appointment?"

"Yes, unfortunately. The oral surgeon had a cancelation, so I get to have it done tomorrow. How can I have a tooth out when you need me here, Mrs. Max? My dentist said I might not feel like working for a few days, and we've been so busy. I don't want to let you down."

"You're not letting me down," Miriam was quick to assure her. "I don't know how I would've managed without you, but you should take time off until you feel like coming in."

"If it eases your mind, dear, I'll help out here," Bess said. "It's fun to see what people buy. In fact, today I sold the cutest planter in the shape of a blue elephant. The woman who bought it said an up-raised trunk was supposed to bring good luck. I'd never heard that. I learn something every day I'm here."

"You're the best, Gran," Phoebe said, giving her a quick hug.

"If you're up to watching for customers now, I'm terribly eager to take this map out of the frame," Miriam said.

"It looks like the other one you have," Phoebe said, leaning over for a closer look.

"I'm going to match the torn edges, but I'm almost certain it's the other half of the one Samuel found in the desk," Miriam explained.

"It was hanging on the wall in a restaurant," Bess said.

"Not an ordinary restaurant. The owners converted a house built in the mid-1800s," Miriam explained.

"How did the map get there?" Phoebe asked, studying it with interest.

"They don't know. It was in the attic of the house along with a lot of other artifacts," Miriam said.

"Look at the sweet children in these photos," Bess said, pointing at the cartes de visite.

"Aren't they adorable!" Phoebe exclaimed. "And look at the clothes they're wearing. Some look almost threadbare. They couldn't have had rich parents."

"You're really observant," Miriam said. "None of them look as if they came from affluent families. The biggest thing they have in common is that they appear to have been taken around the same time by the same photographer."

"A long time ago," Bess added.

"Can I watch you take the map out of the frame?" Phoebe asked. "I'll listen for the bell in case a customer comes."

"Yes, we can use your sharp eyes," Miriam said.

"There has to be a reason why you found all these at a house in Stewartstown," Bess said as the three of them went back to the office carrying the frame and cartes de visite.

Miriam felt the same way. She carefully laid the map facedown on the office desk. The backing of unfinished but aged wood was held in place by small straight-edged bits of metal that were more pegs than nails.

"We have needle-nosed pliers here somewhere," Miriam said. "Do you remember seeing them, Phoebe?"

"I used them to cut the wire around an old box upstairs," Phoebe said. "I put them back in the plastic work box on that shelf."

When Miriam tried pulling out the small nails, they proved to be surprisingly hard to remove. If Johanna's husband had framed the map, he'd used an old frame made of stout wood.

"Let me try," Phoebe said when Miriam stepped back after removing only two of the eight stubborn pegs.

By taking turns, the three of them finally freed the backing, and Miriam gingerly lifted out the map. The paper felt brittle with age, but it was in as good condition as the other half of the map, which she removed from the office safe.

"A perfect fit," Bess said when Miriam matched the torn edges.

"Look," Phoebe said. "There's some kind of legend on that corner."

Miriam stared at the faint hand-drawn legend on the newly purchased half of the map with growing excitement. "It explains the little symbols. The crosses stand for *B*, and the hearts represent the initial *G*."

"But we don't know what *B* and *G* stand for. Whoever made this map liked to keep secrets," Bess said.

"Maybe, but I don't think it was ever meant to be more than a reminder of something the maker wanted to keep track of," Miriam said.

"Your great-grandfather's letter talked about 'riches,'" Bess reminded her.

"Yes, but that could've been a code word too. I'm afraid the map doesn't tell us as much as I'd hoped." After the initial euphoria of discovery, Miriam felt some of her enthusiasm draining away. She'd had high hopes for the second half of the map.

"It's only a guess," Phoebe said, "but the mapmaker may have drawn it to indicate some hidden caches."

"But what was he hiding?" Bess asked. "Maybe the *G* stands for gold."

"What riches would start with the letter *B*?" Miriam asked.

"Bullion?" Phoebe suggested.

"Gold or silver bullion and gold coins," Bess said. "It makes sense."

"It would if my great-grandfather had been rich. But like most Confederate soldiers, he lost everything in the war. At least that's what family tradition told us. I know his son, my grandfather, married late in life—my grandmother was much younger. I always believed it was because he wanted to restore the family's finances before starting a family. It wasn't easy to do in those days. I think he went prospecting the West, but there was never any suggestion he struck it rich."

"The second half of the map only makes your ancestor's fate more mysterious," Bess said.

"I suppose it's possible my grandfather made the map instead of Captain Thomas Davis, but that doesn't make good sense either. After teaching, my grandfather started a business and bought a house with whatever money he had. He wouldn't have hidden it. The more clues I find, the more complicated things seem."

"I'm sorry you didn't find what you need to clear Captain Davis's name," Bess said. "Hopefully you had a nice time with Samuel so the day wasn't wasted."

Miriam felt a twinge of conscience but didn't say anything to her friend in front of Phoebe. Samuel had been wonderful, but she'd been too excited about the map to give him his due. She hoped he wasn't hurt because she'd declined his invitation to a clambake.

"The day wasn't wasted," Miriam conceded.

"You still have the pictures," Bess said. "Even if they don't have anything to do with your ancestor, they're charming and poignant."

"And there's a chance I can buy the other ones I saw. I have to call the woman who brought them to the shop."

The bell on the door sounded, and Phoebe hurried out to greet a customer.

"I'm going to call her now," Miriam said as Bess studied the images of young people.

"Yes, that's a good idea," her friend agreed, still studying the children's photographs as Miriam found the number and made the call.

"Is this Dora Henderson?" Miriam asked when the owner of the cartes de visite answered her call.

"Yes, who's calling, please?"

"This is Miriam Maxwell at Ruthie's Antiques. I wonder if you still have the cartes de visite for sale."

"I do."

"I'd be happy to come to your house to buy them," Miriam said, hoping to conclude the sale as quickly as possible.

"I'm afraid that won't be convenient," Mrs. Henderson said. "I'll come by your shop as soon as I get a chance—maybe tomorrow."

Miriam contained her impatience with difficulty and courteously thanked the owner of the vintage photographs.

"She still has them?" Bess asked.

"Yes. I hope I didn't sound so eager she changes her mind about selling them to me. Sometimes people only appreciate what they have when someone else wants it. Ruth told me that some time ago."

Several customers were in the store now, and Miriam was pleased to see the courteous but efficient way Phoebe managed to sell a Westmoreland glass basket. It wasn't an expensive piece, but she wrapped it with exaggerated care, obviously eager to demonstrate she could handle breakables without incident.

When Miriam got home after closing the store, her first thought was to call Samuel. She wanted to share what she'd learned from the second half of the map, although it wasn't the breakthrough she'd hoped for.

He didn't answer, so she left a brief message asking him to call. After a very light dinner, she did her laundry and prepared for bed early, disappointed that Samuel hadn't returned her call. Of course, she couldn't expect him to stay home just in case she phoned, but he did take his cell phone with him when he went out.

In spite of her intention to catch up on sleep, she couldn't settle down. She tried reading in bed, but her gaze kept going to the cell phone on the nightstand. It was well past midnight when she finally felt sleepy enough to turn out the light.

* * *

Thursday was a day of disappointments. The woman with the cartes de visite to sell didn't come to the store, and Miriam was reluctant to pressure her by calling again.

Even more discouraging, she didn't hear from Samuel. She debated whether to leave another message on his phone, but it seemed a pushy thing to do. Maybe he was wrapped up in his own research and writing. Or he could be out of town. He wasn't under any obligation to let her know where he went.

Bess called and asked if Miriam could get along without her until early afternoon. Her son, Randy, and his wife had both decided to go to the oral surgeon with Phoebe, and Charlie couldn't watch the inn until after lunch.

"Wouldn't you know," Bess said. "Charlie has to take the van to the dealer in Summit City. He expects to be back by noon, but sometimes it takes longer. I'll rush right over as soon as he's back."

"Please don't rush," Miriam said. "You're a sweetheart to help me out, but have lunch with your husband first. I'm sure we won't be so busy I can't handle it."

It was true Miriam could get along without her friend's help, but she missed having her there. She was closer to Bess than to any of the new friends she'd met at church, and so far she hadn't had the leisure to meet many potential friends. No doubt that would change when she'd lived in Maple Landing longer, but right now Bess and Samuel were her closest companions.

A young woman pushing a baby stroller came to the door and tried to wheel it through the opening. Miriam hurried to hold it for her and spent the next ten minutes chatting with the customer and showing her the shop's small collection of cookbooks.

"It's for my mother-in-law's birthday," she explained. "I know she has the *White House Cook Book*, but I'm not sure about this one." She looked through a 1930s book devoted to baking, but her little son was trying to escape from the belt that held him in the stroller.

"I'm afraid I'd better come back without Benjamin," she said apologetically. "He isn't big on shopping."

"That's perfectly all right," Miriam said, meaning it. She wouldn't dream of putting a No Children sign in her shop, but sometimes it was a trial to sell antiques around unhappy little ones. So far she hadn't had any breakage by customers or their young, and she hoped she wouldn't have to post one of the off-putting signs warning customers they were responsible if they broke anything.

Benjamin was wheeled out happily waving at her. She wondered whether she should stock some lollipops for children but wasn't sure their parents would appreciate it.

There was still no word from Samuel, and Mrs. Henderson didn't come to the store with her cartes de visite.

Bess came sooner than expected, bringing with her chicken salad sandwiches on croissants and a plastic container of fresh strawberries with the stems left on.

"I know you," she said when Miriam started to tell her she didn't need to provide lunch. "You always were a great one for skipping meals. Fortunately Charlie got home early, and he'd already had a fast-food burger. If I didn't watch that man, he'd live on saturated fat and drive-in malts."

"Come into the office, and we can chat between customers," Miriam said, pleased to have her friend's companionship.

"Have you heard from Samuel?" Bess asked before they could begin eating.

"Not a word," Miriam admitted. "I really would like to tell him what we found on the map, but he hasn't answered my message."

"You sound down," Bess said. "This isn't just about tracking down your ancestor, is it? You do like him."

"Of course I like him."

"I mean, you really like him," Bess said. The meaning in her emphasis was unmistakable. "You two had a good thing going in high school. I've never seen two people more compatible."

"Bess," Miriam said, unable to hide her discouragement, "that was a long time ago. I'm just worried he thinks I brushed him off. I was too tired and too excited about the map to be interested in a clambake, but I really didn't intend to hurt his feelings."

"Men aren't that sensitive as a rule," Bess said, unwrapping a croissant and putting in it in front of her friend. "Give him another call. Maybe he wasn't close enough to his phone to hear it. He might have forgotten to check his messages."

Miriam sadly shook her head. "I thought of it, but I don't want him to feel obligated to keep in touch with me."

"You know the old adage," Bess said between bites of the delicious croissant stuffed with her own recipe of chicken, celery, onions, and doctored-up mayonnaise. "Chase your man until he catches you."

"Bess Watkins! That sounds like something you would've said in high school."

"Yes, but that doesn't mean it isn't true. Every widow and divorcee under eighty will be sizing him up, but I have a hunch he only has eyes for you."

"He's a widower. I've lost my husband. Neither of us is ready for the kind of romance you're talking about," Miriam chided her friend.

"No?" Bess raised one eyebrow and wiped a smidgen of mayonnaise from her lip. "I'd rather see you sell out to Natalie than be unhappy living alone."

"There's nothing I can do," Miriam said, nibbling at a strawberry. "Samuel has helped me a lot, but I don't want him to feel obligated to do more. If he wants to talk to me, I'm sure he'll call."

"We'll see," Bess said with a knowing look.

"Have you heard anything about Phoebe?" Miriam asked.

"Not yet. Her mother promised to call as soon as her surgery is over. Whatever did we do without cell phones?" Bess asked. "They certainly cut down on a lot of worry—when people use them." She gave Miriam a pointed look.

"I hope she's okay," Miriam said, refusing to reopen the conversation about calling Samuel.

She would be terribly sad to lose him as a friend, and she had to admit to herself how important he'd become in her new life.

"Thanks for the lunch," she told Bess, feeling saved by the bell as a customer came into the shop.

Chapter Twenty-Six

Friday morning was sunny and pleasant with blossoming bushes and flowers in every yard as Miriam walked to work. The cool, wet spell had left everything sparkling clean, and the breeze off the Chesapeake Bay was so refreshing she wanted to go to the waterfront and bask in the perfect day.

It wasn't to be. Phoebe had too much pain from her oral surgery to think of coming to work that day, and Miriam had assured Bess she could manage alone. Since her friend refused to be put on the payroll, Miriam didn't think it was fair to rely on her even when her granddaughter couldn't be there.

Opening the front door for business, Miriam realized how much she enjoyed being in the shop surrounded by artifacts of the past. There was much she'd still like to do to make it a better setting for the many fine antiques in stock, but she couldn't deny that Ruth had created a homey—if cluttered—ambiance.

In spite of the perfect day and her pleasure in the business her dear sister had left her, Miriam couldn't shake her melancholy mood. Samuel hadn't returned her call, not even last night after she'd left a second message using the map as an excuse.

Her first customers were a young couple, and at the time they were taking to look at every piece of furniture in her inventory, they might be there until closing.

"Is there something I can help you with?" Miriam asked, not to hurry them along but to answer any questions they might have.

"We just got married, and we're furnishing our home with antiques, just buying a piece at a time when we can afford it," the willowy young brunette woman said.

"This is a great Pembroke table," her husband said, brushing a strand of sun-bleached hair out of his eyes. "We looked at it the other day when you weren't here, then went home and researched it. If I'm right, it's federal period, around the 1790s."

"We're pretty sure it's cherry," his wife said.

"You've certainly done your homework," Miriam said.

"I don't suppose you could come down a little on the price," he said, sounding hesitant.

Miriam studied the price tag tied to the drawer handle, grateful she'd memorized her sister's code. Ruth had given the table a substantial markup over what she'd paid, which told Miriam she could lower the price. She offered a ten percent discount, and the couple beamed with pleasure as they agreed to buy it.

"We're going to enjoy this forever," the young bride enthused.

"Antiques are the best investment in the world," he said. "We'll enjoy this as it increases in value."

As much as Miriam appreciated the sale, she watched the young newlyweds carry out the table with a touch of sadness. She wanted to tell them that financial investments weren't the basis for happiness. She'd been blessed with faith, love, friendships, and opportunities to serve others. She counted herself among the most fortunate of women, and she was just a little put out with herself for her glum mood.

Her spirits rose when a familiar face came through the door of the shop. Dora Henderson had been true to her word and brought the cartes de visite.

"Well, here they are," Dora said in a matter-of-fact voice. "My nephew did look them up on his computer, but I'll stick by my price since there's not a famous face in the bunch."

"I appreciate that," Miriam said. "They're lovely photos of children. In fact, I don't plan to sell them anytime soon."

Apparently that pleased Mrs. Henderson. She smiled and agreed that they were nice pictures.

Miriam quickly paid cash for the whole lot. From her experience with the man with the signs, he'd learned that sellers were distrustful of checks, even though Ruthie's Antiques was a long-established business.

"Before you go, I'd like to show you some photos. I bought them this week in Stewartstown from a woman who'd converted an old house into a restaurant," Miriam said, curious to see what Dora's reaction would be.

After spreading them out on the counter next to the ones she'd just bought, Miriam waited for a reaction. There wasn't one.

"The person who sold them to me thought they might be the children of the house's original owners," she explained. "Of course, that seems unlikely since there are so many. Maybe these are the nineteenth-century version of school pictures."

"No, they're orphan kids, just like the ones in my photos," Dora said decisively.

"Orphans? How do you know?"

"What else could they be? Look here." She turned over one of her photos to reveal faint pencil markings. "*This is Lucinda Grady, found with two small brothers in a farmhouse four miles south of Stewartstown.* I think this word is *pneumonia*, but I can't read it for sure. That would be what took the mother."

"Oh my," Miriam said as the purpose of the cartes de visite became clear. "The house in Stewartstown must have served as an orphanage. The people who ran it made a record of the children in case any relatives came to claim them."

"I imagine some returning soldiers came looking for their young ones. Some were gone so long they might not recognize their own babies, especially if they were born after they left for the war," Dora Henderson said.

"No wonder I felt so drawn to the children in the pictures," Miriam said. "I haven't been able to get them out of my mind."

"Well, I'm not much on history, but they do tell a sad story," Dora said. "Hope you enjoy them. I'll keep you in mind if I find anything else you might be interested in."

"Yes, please do," Miriam said. "And thank you so much for parting with them and for pointing out who the children were. Knowing their story makes me even more determined to keep them myself, at least for now."

With a few minutes to herself, she took the cartes de visite back to her office and carefully looked at the reverse sides. Several others she'd just purchased had faint pencil markings, but none of the ones she'd bought in Stewartstown did. Perhaps the people who ran the orphanage simply didn't know anything about many of the children. They could have been abandoned on their doorstep by neighbors or people who found them wandering the roads or trying to find shelter in towns.

Sorting them out by separating the very young from older children, Miriam soon determined that each carte de visite showed a different young person. Now she understood why their clothes often seemed shabby and their expressions sad. People in very old photographs rarely smiled, because of the time necessary to take their pictures, but these children looked genuinely distressed. Were any reclaimed by family? What was their fate if no one came to take them home?

The bell interrupted her musings, and she looked up expectantly, still hoping it would be Samuel. She had so much to tell him, but she wasn't sure he was still interested.

Instead of her friend, two older women came into the store. One had elaborate white curls lacquered in place and the other was skinny as a rail with henna hair and a bright flowered tunic that practically labeled her as a tourist. They spent the next half hour examining everything in the shop and pointing out items their grandmothers had once owned.

"My nana filled a garbage pail with Depression glass," the white-haired woman said. "Can you imagine what it would be worth today? But she was tired of it."

"I bought my mother one of those glass apples," the other said. "She kept cinnamon sugar for our toast in it."

The women had as many questions as comments, but both left without making a purchase. Miriam didn't mind people using the shop for entertainment because people often returned later to purchase something that had caught their eye, but she was eager to share her findings with a friend, either Bess or Samuel. Knowing the children had been orphans was news too helpful to keep to herself, even though they didn't seem to have anything to do with her quest to clear her great-grandfather's name.

She closed the shop at noon to run out for a sandwich but found she had almost no appetite. The afternoon went even more slowly than the morning with just enough customers to keep her from studying the cartes de visite spread out in the office.

When she finally locked the door for the day, she hurried to look through her collection of orphan children another time. Everything Dora Henderson had said about them seemed true. These weren't happy family pictures. They were a record of abandoned young ones, perhaps the only images that rescued them from obscurity. Miriam thought of her photograph album stuffed full of pictures of Lisa and her grandchildren and felt even more sorrowful about the orphans. She could only imagine how frightened they must have been, caught in the aftermath of a lost war and on their own in the world.

"Thank the Lord for the good souls who took them in," she said out loud, still wishing Samuel was there to share their story.

* * *

The sailboat was a big disappointment. Samuel was sorry he'd hurried off to Baltimore to see it based on a glowing advertisement online. It had sounded exactly like what he wanted: a thirty-footer in good refurbished condition. He hadn't been put off by the age. Nineteen seventy-seven had been a good year for the builder, but the owner had greatly overrated the condition. The motor needed a complete overhaul, and the sails would have to be replaced. Added to that, the boat had to have new wiring and plumbing, not to mention a lot of work on the interior and exterior teak. As a naval officer, he'd been disgusted with the shoddy maintenance.

He'd planned to stay overnight if he wanted to buy the boat, but now he was eager to get back to Maple Landing. No, not to the town, he mentally corrected himself, but to Miriam.

When she dismissed his idea of a clambake and insisted on taking the map out of the frame herself, he couldn't help but feel miffed. He'd been with her every step in the search for her ancestor's fate and wanted to see it through. But he understood it was a personal quest for her, and she was excited by their find in Stewartstown.

The bottom line was he missed her. In the short time since they'd rediscovered each other, she'd come to be important to him. He'd thought she needed some space, but he hadn't reckoned on how hard it would be on him.

Several times he'd taken out his phone to answer one of her two messages, but some things needed to be said in person.

When he got to town, he stopped first at her house because it was past time for her store to be closed. She didn't answer the doorbell, so he decided to check the shop in case she was working late.

The front door was locked with the shade pulled down, but he knocked anyway, waited, and knocked again. His patience was rewarded when she peeked around the edge of the shade and opened the door for him.

"Samuel, I was getting worried about you," she said without scolding.

He had an apology ready for not answering her messages, but instead he took her in his arms for big hug.

"Well...," she said slowly.

Was she surprised or pleased? Either way, her smile was certainly welcoming.

"I had a lead on a sailboat in Baltimore. I should've let you know I was leaving town," he said.

"I don't expect you to tell me everything you do. Did you buy the boat?"

"No, it didn't live up to the description in the ad. About your phone calls..." He wasn't sure himself why he hadn't answered her messages, only that he wanted to talk to her in person.

"It doesn't matter. Now that you're here, I can share my news in person."

"Did you find something interesting on the other half of the map?" he asked.

"Yes and no. Come back to the office," she said, relocking the front door.

Her excitement was contagious as she explained the legend on the second half of the map.

"It's only a guess, but maybe the Gs stand for gold and the Bs for bullion. Phoebe is really good at puzzles, so she was a big help. The poor dear had to have an impacted wisdom tooth out. I really missed her in the store today."

"Wonder why the mapmaker used the hearts and crosses instead of putting the initials on the map," Samuel said.

"I think it has something to do with the 'riches' he mentioned in his letter," she said. "And there's more. I bought the cartes de visite a woman offered me."

He listened with growing interest as she explained about the orphan children.

"You have been learned a lot," he said, fascinated by the children's pictures.

"Yes, but there's no connection between the map and the cartes de visite as far as I can tell. And we still don't know when or where my great-grandfather died. Or whether he owned property in any-place shown on the map."

Samuel liked that she'd said we. He very much wanted to be part of her search, especially if it meant spending more time with her.

"We still have loose ends to follow. Your great-grandfather must have had some connection to the house in Stewartstown since half of his map showed up there. We really haven't investigated from that angle." He enjoyed saying *we* almost as much as he liked hearing it from her.

"Maybe I should let him rest in peace and forget this," she said thoughtfully. "I was a little upset when you said I might not like what I learn, but you were right. What if he was a deserter and deserves his bad reputation?"

"The Miriam I know wouldn't be afraid of the truth," he said to soothe her doubts. "We need to make a trip to the county courthouse and learn more about the house where the restaurant is."

"I can't possibly ask you to take more time off from your book," she said.

"You're not asking. I'm volunteering. They'll be closed over the weekend, but first thing Monday morning we should go on another road trip. Since Johanna and her husband recently bought the house, the deed should be up to date."

"I'll have to see if Phoebe is up to watching the store," Miriam said, still sounding hesitant.

"That girl has spunk. She probably can't wait to get back to work," he said optimistically. "If not, you can close up for as long as the trip takes."

"I can, can't I?" she said, sounding enthusiastic about the trip.

"Meanwhile, this old sailor is hungry enough to eat a whale. Can I take you to dinner?"

"Looking like this?" She spread her arms to demonstrate how grubby she felt in tan walking shorts and a light green tunic, but to him she was beautiful.

"Even beautiful antiques dealers need to eat," he said.

"Flattery will get you nowhere," she said, although he could tell she was pleased by the compliment. "Why don't we go to the market and pick out something you'd like? We can go to my house, and I'll cook."

"You'll cook?" He raised on eyebrow. "Like you fixed hot dogs for the pep rally before homecoming?"

"You're still holding a little charcoal against me?" She laughed, and everything felt right in his world.

"No, but how about Thai takeout? I understand there's a new restaurant in town."

"I'm up for that," she said, linking her arm in his as they started to leave.

He impulsively leaned over and planted a soft kiss on her cheek. Whether Captain Thomas Davis was a rogue or a hero, Samuel was going to owe him a debt of gratitude for bringing Miriam close again. He was more determined than ever to clear the soldier's reputation if it could be done.

Chapter Twenty-Seven

Everything seemed right in Miriam's world when Samuel arrived at her house Sunday morning to accompany her to church. He was wearing a beautifully tailored suit in a silky fabric that hinted of sea-green and gold without being either color. His tie and shirt were shades of gold that picked up the shimmering tones of his jacket, and he'd trimmed his snowy beard to a sharp-edged triangle. All in all, he looked beautiful, although she picked more masculine words to compliment him.

For the first time since moving back to Maple Landing, Miriam really wanted to look her best. She took a special dress out of a plastic garment bag, a silky peach creation originally worn to a wedding. She'd almost given it away because it seemed too young for her, but this morning it seemed exactly right.

"My goodness, you two look spiffy," Bess said when she caught up with them after the service.

"Spiffy?" Miriam giggled at her friend's use of her favorite word from high school. "I've been wondering how Phoebe is."

"She's doing well. There's still a little swelling, but she's home with an ice pack and determined to go to work tomorrow."

"That's good news," Miriam said. "Tell her the store is all hers if she's up to it tomorrow."

Bess gave her a quizzical look but another friend called out to her before she could ask any questions. Samuel captured Miriam's hand, and they walked away lost in a world of their own.

Later that day, after a lovely Sunday dinner at a country inn an hour away from Maple Landing, Samuel gave her a tour of his cottage. It looked quaint, even rustic from the outside, but he had the inside arranged as efficiently as the bridge of a ship.

"The Queen Anne desk looks as if it were designed for your office," she said.

"It's the best purchase I've ever made," he said. "After all, it brought you to me."

"I can't remember when I've had a nicer day," she said.

It felt wonderful to be with Samuel, but she also needed a day of rest from concerns about the store and her quest to clear her ancestor's name. When her daughter called her that evening and she talked to her granddaughters, the day seemed complete.

Monday morning she went to the store. She and Samuel had decided not to leave for the courthouse until noon so she could see if Phoebe really was up to running the store alone. Her shop assistant regaled her with the horror story of her tooth, but she seemed cheerful and very much herself.

"How's it going, ladies?" Bess asked, coming to the shop in mid-morning.

"I'm doing just fine, Gran," Phoebe said a bit indignantly. "You don't have to check on me."

"I came to tell my dear friend Miriam something she needs to know," Bess said just as a customer walked through the door.

"What are you up to?" Miriam asked as she led her friend to the office.

"This is serious," Bess said, closing the door behind them. "I didn't want to spoil your nice day with Samuel yesterday, but Charlie heard something when he went to the barbershop Saturday afternoon. He was just coming out, heading toward the pharmacy to pick up a few things, when he noticed two guys arguing beside an old pickup. They were talking about doing a job for Yester."

"Jack Yester, the auctioneer?"

"The same," Bess said, lowering her voice although no one was within hearing distance. "Apparently they did a 'job' for him, and he only paid them half what he'd promised. One guy wanted to quit working for him, but the other said Yester would come through because they knew too much about him."

"They must work at his auctions," Miriam said, not sure where her friend's story was going.

Bess shook her head. "There's more," she said. "Charlie knows all about your break-in, of course, so he decided to play detective, bless him. He's usually as subtle as a hurricane. But he pretended to tie his boot—he was wearing the awful boots he uses for yard work. He sort of ducked down out of sight, not that the men were paying any attention."

"What did he learn?" Miriam asked.

"Apparently Yester is overextended. His auction business isn't doing very well—I suspect his reputation has something to do with that. He badly needs ready cash and is on the lookout for good quality items that will sell well in his auction."

"My stock?" Miriam had a sinking feeling she knew what was coming.

"He sent his goons…"

"Goons?" Miriam almost giggled at the term, but she didn't want to hurt Bess's feelings.

"You know what I mean," her friend said. "Anyway, those two obviously broke into your store. Yester wanted to scare you into going out of business. He seemed to think you'd have no choice but to let him liquidate your stock in an auction. Or maybe he thought you'd be so eager to close that you'd sell everything to him super cheap."

"Charlie learned all that tying his shoe?"

"His boot. They have lots of laces. Anyway, he followed when they strolled down the street. Charlie is a man of many talents, but a vivid imagination is not one of them. If he believes Yester sent those two to break into your store, you can be sure it's true."

"But what can I do about it?" Miriam asked. "There's no proof."

"Just what Charlie overheard," Bess admitted. "I can see where you'd hate to go to the police with hearsay evidence. My hubby says I watch too many detective shows, but I know you don't have a case. I just wanted to warn you about Yester."

"I appreciate it," Miriam said. "If that man thinks I'll ever let him sell a single one of my sister's antiques, he's very much mistaken— not that I would have anyway."

"Charlie thinks we should keep it to ourselves and see if anything else happens. Usually I don't pay much attention when he tells me not to gossip—I call it being informed—but this time I think he's right."

"Yes," Miriam agreed, "but I am going to mention it to Samuel."

"Do that," Bess said. "You two made a lovely couple in church yesterday, by the way."

"We're just good friends," Miriam said.

The knowing look Bess gave her didn't hide what her friend thought about that statement.

After Bess left, Miriam was eager for Samuel to arrive. She very much wanted to share Charlie's information about Yester, but she also wanted to see him just because… Sunday had been a perfectly lovely day, the kind she'd never expected to have again. She'd been content before Samuel came back into her life, but what she felt now was something special. She couldn't help wondering once again if this was her second chance at true happiness.

* * *

Samuel's habit of being early had sometimes put his subordinates off balance when he was on active duty, but that wasn't his motive today. He arrived at the antiques shop half an hour before Miriam expected him, but only because he was impatient to see her.

"Is it noon already?" Miriam asked when he walked into the store. Her smile told him how glad she was to see him.

"I thought we could have lunch before we go to the courthouse— if it's not too early for you."

"It's just right," Miriam said. "I didn't take time for much breakfast."

"Hi, Admiral Bentley," Phoebe said as the customer she was helping left without buying anything.

"How's the tooth, Phoebe?" he asked with genuine concern.

"The tooth is history, but my jaw is still a little tender."

"Are you all right watching the store this afternoon?" Samuel asked.

"It sure beats watching daytime TV," she said with a little grin. "Anyway, my mom is bringing me a thermos of soup for lunch, and a special friend promised to check on me this afternoon."

"It sounds like you've got all the bases covered," Samuel said, winking his approval of the Downs boy.

He and Miriam drove off with the top down and a warm wind whipping her silvery locks around her lovely face. The woman sitting beside him was infinitely more beautiful in his eyes than the girl who had been his teenage crush.

"I have a suspect in the break-in," she said when they were under way. "Charlie Watkins overhead two of Jack Yester's men talking downtown."

Samuel listened intently while she told him what Bess's husband had learned.

"I think Charlie has it right," he said. "I don't know whether to be relieved or more worried he might try something else."

"Do you think I should let him know?" Miriam asked. "Maybe if I convince him there's absolutely no chance I'll let him sell anything for me, he'll forget about me."

"Let me take care of it," Samuel said, weighing the alternatives in his mind. "I'll see he doesn't bother you anymore."

He wasn't sure what the best course of action was, but their old classmate, the police chief, would have to pay attention now. Maybe a warning from him would be enough to ensure Miriam's peace of mind. If it wasn't, Samuel would have a talk with the auctioneer himself.

He'd found a wayside inn twenty miles from Maple Landing that specialized in fresh seafood. The dining room was nearly full, but he'd had the foresight to make reservations.

"I didn't expect anything so fancy for lunch," Miriam said, trying to pat her hair into place as they waited for their table.

"You look gorgeous. In fact, I like the casual way your hair looks."

"Windblown, you mean," she said with a light laugh.

They shared a seafood platter featuring all the inn's specialties, including a tender lobster claw with drawn butter and the best scallops he'd tasted in ages. Better still, her lively conversation was the best sauce any meal could have.

Although he was tempted to linger over lunch until the staff asked them to leave, he knew Miriam was still eager to learn more about the orphan home. He didn't know what connection the Stewartstown house had to her ancestor, but he was curious too.

"Are you ready to play Sherlock Holmes?" he asked as they resumed their trip.

"Only if you're my Watson," she teased.

At the county seat where the Stewartstown deeds were registered, Samuel parked in the visitor's lot, hoping the call he'd made earlier to a lawyer friend would give them easy access to the information they needed.

The county building was Georgian architecture with imposing white columns that seemed a little large for the size of the Redbrick building behind them, but it sat in dignified splendor surrounded by a well-manicured lawn and ancient oaks with a sparse number of leaves on twisted branches.

"If we don't learn anything here, I'm afraid I'll never clear my great-grandfather's name," Miriam said, sounding a little nervous. "This may be our last chance."

"He didn't just disappear," Samuel assured her. "Somewhere there's a record of what happened to him."

"I hope you're right," Miriam said, squeezing his hand when he took hers.

The first person they met was a middle-aged woman with blonde hair piled high on her head. She was courteous but reserved until Samuel mentioned the attorney he'd contacted.

"Oh, you're Mr. Zimmerman's friend," she said enthusiastically. "I'm sure we can accommodate you, Admiral Bentley."

That was twice today someone had called him Admiral. He wasn't sure whether he preferred to be Mr. Bentley instead, but he was glad old friends like Silas Zimmerman remembered him.

"Is there anyone in this state you don't know?" Miriam teased as they followed the receptionist to an elevator that had seen service for a century or more. It creaked its way downward into a dimly lit storage area, but their guide flicked a switch and neon lights overhead brightened the space.

"I love reading old deeds," Samuel admitted when they were comfortably seated at an old oak library table. "You can trace a property back to the colonist who first got the land grant. You'd be surprised how complicated land ownership can be. One of the owners of the land where my cottage is may have been hanged as a pirate."

"Really?" Miriam sounded mildly skeptical, but that was one of the things he loved about her. She weighed everything she heard and couldn't easily be fooled.

The earliest records of the property were written in ink faded to light brown, and they had to sit with their heads close to read it together.

"Originally it was part of a farm," Miriam said. "I guess that's not surprising."

"It stayed with the original family for more than a hundred years," Samuel said. "The town sort of grew up around it. The house that's still there wasn't built until 1856."

"Maybe it replaced the original farmhouse. Imagine the history under the basement floor if that's what happened," she said.

"Now we're getting to the important part," Samuel said, carefully going on to the next page bound at the top. "The house was in the town of Suetville until it merged and became Stewartstown. The family that owned the house must have been well off. They sold it to a minister for one dollar for 'the generous protection of our riches.' That was the same as donating it for his work."

"There's that word again," Miriam said, saying just what he was thinking.

"*Riches*," Samuel said. "Your great-grandfather mentioned 'riches' in his letter."

"For some reason, I don't think he was talking about gold or anything else of monetary value," she said thoughtfully.

"I agree," he said. "Apparently the minister was the one who turned the house into an orphanage. We might know more if we knew the church he was affiliated with, but there's no indication in the deed."

"The important thing is the orphanage. Now we know how the house was used, but we still don't know how my great-grandfather was tied to it."

"He never owned the house," Samuel said. "We have confirmed that."

"But obviously he had a home and a family."

Samuel took a small notebook out of the pocket of his blue striped polo shirt. "I'm going to make a few notes just in case we want them."

"I should've thought of that," Miriam said.

"Nonsense, my dear Holmes. Watson is always the one who does the writing," Samuel teased.

"Is he also the one who finds wonderful places for lunch?"

"Watson was unfortunate in being a man of the nineteenth century. He didn't have a computer."

"You certainly know how to make good use of yours," Miriam said. "I can't thank you enough for helping me track down my great-grandfather."

"There's still mischief afoot," Samuel said in his best imitation of a British accent.

"Isn't that what Sherlock used to say?" Miriam asked.

"Something akin to that," he said grinning.

When they returned to the ground floor level, Miriam profusely thanked the woman who had taken them to the storage area.

"It means a lot to us," Samuel added.

Miriam gave him a quizzical look but didn't say anything until they returned to the car.

"Did you mean that?" she asked as she fastened her seat buckle.

"Mean what?" He started the vehicle but was in no hurry for their expedition to end.

"That clearing my great-grandfather's name means a lot to you too?"

"Yes, because I know it will make you happy." He reached over and brushed her cheek with the backs of his fingers.

"You're an exceedingly nice man," Miriam said with a sweet smile.

Even though they were almost sure now that Captain Thomas Davis had a link to an orphanage that took in children left parentless by the War Between the States, they still didn't know why his map had been found in the attic of the house.

"Do you think there's anything to be gained by going back to the house and talking with Johanna and her husband?" Samuel asked.

"Maybe another time. I think they told us all they know when I bought the second half of the map and the cartes de visite. They didn't seem to know the children in the photographs were orphans."

"It was a lucky coincidence a woman had more cartes de visite and wanted to sell them," he said.

"Yes," Miriam agreed. "And there was no reason why she saved them for me when I failed to buy them on her first trip to the store. Speaking of the shop, I wonder if I should call Phoebe and see how she's doing."

"I think she enjoys being in charge of the store," Samuel said. "You don't want her to think you don't trust her."

"How did you get so smart, Samuel Bentley?"

He glanced around the parking area and saw they were alone before leaning toward her and gently kissing her.

"If I'm smart, I'll keep you on my radar for a long, long time," he said.

She laughed, but there was no mockery in it.

Samuel cautioned himself to proceed with caution until he was sure there was nothing but smooth sailing ahead.

Chapter Twenty-Eight

I can't wait to share what we've learned with Bess and Phoebe," Miriam said as Samuel pulled to a stop in a parking spot on the street.

"Bess is a good friend," he said. "I always liked her, and Phoebe is a great kid."

As soon as they walked through the door of the shop, Phoebe rushed forward to greet them.

"You'll never guess what I sold, Mrs. Max," she said. "All three memory jugs. Does that count as one sale since I got five hundred dollars for them?"

"All three? It certainly does," Miriam said with a broad smile, assuring Phoebe she would get a commission.

"What are memory jugs?" Samuel asked.

"Folk art," Miriam said.

"People use plaster or clay or something like that and stick on all sorts of things like buttons or costume jewelry or shells or just about anything small," Phoebe said in one breathless sentence. "Ours sold for a lot because they had some old political buttons."

"There was one for Grover Cleveland," Miriam told Samuel.

"Wow, I learn something new every day in your shop," Samuel said.

"Can you believe Phoebe sold all three of those odd jugs?" Bess asked, coming to the front of the store with a feather duster in her hand.

"I'm proud of her," Miriam said, "but you didn't need to dust for me."

"I love being here almost as much as Phoebe does," Bess admitted. "Anyway, I'm curious to know what you learned this trip."

"It's nearly time to close. Let's lock up, and we can tell you the latest," Miriam said, moving to the front door and pulling down the shade.

When all four were gathered around her desk in the office, Miriam brought out the two separate pieces of the map.

"We were all wrong thinking this map had anything to do with treasure, at least not the monetary kind," Miriam said.

"The house where the restaurant is was once an orphanage," Samuel said.

"Yes, the owners donated it to a minister who must have been the founder of the orphanage," Miriam added, carefully moving the two halves of the map closer together. "We have to rethink what the symbols mean."

"B and G," Bess said thoughtfully. "Are you thinking what I am?"

"Boys and girls," the other three said in unison.

"The hearts and crosses must show the places where orphan boys and girls were found," Miriam said.

"It would be a way to trace possible relatives," Phoebe said.

"Yes, and with soldiers coming home from the war, there was always the possibility that a father, brother, or uncle might be alive to take responsibility for a child or children," Samuel said.

"That's where the pictures come in," Miriam speculated. "Some men had been gone for four years. A child can change a lot in that time, especially the babies. Some of the cartes de visite look like they've been handled a lot, especially the ones I bought from Mrs. Henderson."

"Possibly they were taken to the child's home area and passed around to see whether anyone could identify them. This is so sad," Bess said.

"The ones you bought at the restaurant are in better condition. They don't look as though they've been handled as much," Samuel said.

"Perhaps they're the children who didn't have any hope of finding relatives. If there weren't any leads to living relatives, the cartes de visite wouldn't have been circulated," Miriam said. "Isn't it amazing what a story old photographs can tell?"

"The 'riches' must have been the children," Bess said. "What a touching way to refer to them. Nothing is more valuable than young people. They were the hope for the future. They're still our greatest asset." She gave Phoebe a hug, and her granddaughter reciprocated with an embarrassed grin.

"There's one thing we don't know yet," Samuel pointed out.

"Exactly. We don't know how my great-grandfather came to have half of the map." Miriam leaned over the map with a puzzled expression. "Or why he wrote the letter he did."

"Or why family tradition branded him a deserter," Samuel said. "It's a serious charge, and one those close to him would take to heart."

"Okay, so I guess there's more than one thing we don't know," Miriam conceded. "But this is the best lead we've had so far. We know the house was donated to a minister, and we are almost certain he established an orphanage there. The owners must have had a lot of faith in him to sign away their home. Now we have to learn how my great-grandfather was connected to it."

"What puzzles me most is the way he disappeared. A captain in the Confederate army should have left some trace of his eventual end," Samuel said. "We don't even know where he was mustered out."

"What does that mean?" Phoebe asked.

"Released from service in the army," Samuel said. "I can search more records on the Internet, but I have a feeling nothing will turn up."

"What else do you know about your family?" Bess asked.

"My great-grandmother had to raise her children alone. It was a source of pride in our family that she carried on without her husband. She managed to eke out a living on a small farm for a while, but eventually she moved to Baltimore to live with a distant relative. I guess she took in sewing and watched other people's children until her son, my grandfather, was able to provide for her. That's part of the reason why he didn't marry until he was quite old."

"Your grandfather must have been a good man," Bess said.

"Yes, he took responsibility for his mother and siblings as soon as he was old enough to find work. He was only ten when he got a job working at a livery stable. You can imagine how hard it must have been to spend his days doing menial labor when he should've been in school. His mother taught him to read and do numbers. When he was older, he was an avid reader, trying to learn all the things he missed as a child."

"That's so sad," Phoebe said. "I guess I shouldn't have complained when I had to help around the inn."

Bess patted her arm as if to say she understood.

"Yes, and the saddest thing is, his family believed Thomas was a deserter. Apparently he just disappeared from their lives. They had to live with his disgrace," Miriam said. "I can't do anything for them, but I still hope to restore his reputation with my own family."

"Maybe he headed west," Samuel said. "A lot of veterans found they couldn't fit into society after years of bloody strife."

He reached over and patted Miriam's hand. His touch was comforting, but she knew her mind wouldn't be at ease until she knew the truth, one way or another.

A sudden knock on the front door caught her attention, and she started toward the front.

"You'd think people would see the shop is closed," Bess said.

"That's all right. I'll get it," Phoebe said, sprinting ahead of Miriam.

"Oh dear," Bess said. "That will be the boyfriend."

"You know you like him," Miriam teased.

"Well, considering who his grandmother is, he's turned out remarkably well," Bess conceded.

"Can I leave now, Mrs. Max?" Phoebe called out.

"Yes, and thanks for all you did today," Miriam said with a smile. "I never thought we'd sell those memory jugs."

"You know," Bess said, "it might be fun to make one of those. I could clean out all the bits and pieces I've hidden away over the years. Remember the little medals we got when our seventh-grade team won the basketball intramurals? Do you think windowpane putty would hold something like that on an old chipped pitcher I have?"

"Bess, if you need a hobby," Samuel teased, "you can help with the rock garden I'm planning."

"In your dreams, Admiral," Bess said in mock protest.

Miriam smiled at her two dear friends and silently thanked the Lord for bringing her back to Maple Landing. Right now she felt as though she'd never left.

Bess located her purse and got ready to join her family for dinner. "I guess we can put Phoebe's plate back in the cupboard. She's always on the go. Sometimes that girl reminds me of someone."

"You!" Miriam said, echoed by Samuel.

The three of them laughed together, and it felt wonderful to Miriam.

* * *

Although Samuel had enjoyed his day with Miriam, he had one more task that day. As soon as he dropped her at home, politely declining her invitation to stay for dinner, he hurried to his cottage and his computer. He had a major issue to settle, and the sooner it was done, the better.

By the time all his ducks were in a row, it was too late to act on what he'd learned. First thing tomorrow he would make sure Miriam wasn't harassed again.

Samuel woke up the next morning more determined than ever to ensure Miriam's peace of mind. According to a small notice in the shopping news, Jack Yester had an auction scheduled that evening. He operated out of a prefabricated metal building that had once been a small factory, and the odds were he would be there early in the day to prepare for the sale.

Samuel arrived there in midmorning, not at all impressed by Yester's setup. The parking area was dirt with patches of weeds, unpaved with deep ruts. He hadn't even gone to the trouble and expense of putting down some gravel to keep vehicles from getting stuck in the mud in wet weather.

The door wasn't locked, and Samuel didn't hesitate to enter. Inside, the large room had seating for a hundred or so bidders on an eclectic collection of chairs, everything from folding chairs with peeling plastic seats to lawn chairs and a couple of couches with threadbare upholstery. It looked like Yester had raided the city dump to get seating for his sales. The front and either side of the room were lined with tables, most with a sparse arrangement of the goods to be sold.

At the front, a raised platform held a podium and a table to keep track of bids. Samuel had been to a few auctions and knew this was a low-end operation. An area behind the platform held an assortment of larger items: a few sad pieces of furniture and what looked like the contents of a barn. If anything valuable or collectible was hidden in the untidy stacks and piles of junk, he didn't see it.

"What can I do for you?" Jack Yester came in through the double doors at the rear carrying a wooden box of rusty parts.

"Mr. Yester?" Samuel asked, although he recognized the auctioneer from his farm auction. "I'm Samuel Bentley."

"Yeah, you're the admiral. Guess everyone in town knows the hometown boy who made good. Looking for something special today?" He put the box down with a sign of relief. "My boys don't come in until after lunch. I'm getting old for this heavy lifting."

If he was looking for sympathy, Samuel was the last person to give it.

"I'm here about the ring," he said.

"We don't have any jewelry in tonight's sale," Yester said. "At least not yet. Never know what someone might bring in at the last minute."

"Not that kind of ring," Samuel said. "The auction ring you ran in Pennsylvania, the one that got you arrested."

"I never went to jail," Yester protested, his face an angry mask. "Anyone who says I did is lying through his teeth."

"You did six months under house arrest and lost your sales license in that state. You were an antiques dealer then, and you had the clever idea of organizing a ring to defraud auction houses and the people who consign things to them."

"You got the wrong guy." Yester turned his back and pretended to sort through the rusty objects in the wooden box.

"You and five other dealers used an old ploy. One person would bid without any competition from the others. On a good day you'd virtually steal antiques without a qualm. Then you'd meet in secret and hold another auction among the six of you."

"There's no law says a person can't resell." He sounded even more belligerent.

"Auction rings are illegal. You got caught, and it put you out of business in Pennsylvania."

"I'm legit here. You got nothing on me." He tossed a rusty garden tool back into the box.

Samuel wasn't easily intimidated.

"How about breaking and entering?"

Yester narrowed his eyes suspiciously. "I'm no burglar. You can't prove a thing."

"You didn't use your men to rob Ruthie's Antiques—although I imagine the police could find a corkscrew in your collection that one of them stole for you—a dachshund, if I remember correctly. Instead, you had them break in to intimidate her. You hoped she'd panic and want to sell out in a hurry—and there you'd be, willing to help her out with a quick sale at auction."

"You can't prove a thing."

"If you're going to hire men to break the law, you really should pay them what you promised," Samuel said. "Then they might not complain in town where they can be overheard."

"Why are you here? If you know so much, why not go to the police?" For the first time, Yester's voice betrayed his anxiety.

Samuel wasn't going to admit he didn't have any evidence that would hold up in court. "I want to make one thing absolutely clear. Mrs. Maxwell is not going to close her sister's business, and she certainly will not trust you to sell any stock for her. None. Ever."

"I'm only trying to make a go of my business," Yester whined, all the fight gone from his voice.

"Do we understand each other?" Samuel asked. "Threaten Mrs. Maxwell or her business in any way, and the police will know exactly where to look."

"Hey, I don't want to see her at any of my auctions. I won't give her a bidding number. No way. You can tell her that for me."

"Somehow I think she can live with that," Samuel said, stifling a smile.

Outside the unsavory auction room, he took a deep breath, clearing his lungs with the fresh air. He didn't like using intimidation, but the alternative was much worse. There was every sign Jack Yester's business was in trouble, and Samuel couldn't allow Miriam to be a target in the auctioneer's desperate attempt to save it.

He fervently hoped Miriam would keep her antiques business and make Maple Landing her permanent home. It was her decision, but at least he could give her peace of mind about Jack Yester and the break-in.

Before he drove away, he called her on his cell phone.

"How does tomorrow sound for another trip to Stewartstown?" he asked.

"Great. I'll check with Phoebe, but if she can't work, I'll close the store. I can't wait to go back to the orphanage—I can't stop thinking of the house as an orphanage. Johanna was so nice on our other visits. I hope she won't mind if we do some investigating—especially when we share what we've learned with her."

"One more thing," Samuel said, carefully thinking of how to put her mind at ease about the break-in. "I paid a visit to Yester's Auction House. We had a talk, and I'm almost certain he won't bother you anymore."

"Did he admit being responsible for the break-in?"

"More or less," Samuel said. "And don't be surprised if the missing corkscrew turns up sometime soon."

Chapter Twenty-Nine

Anxiously pacing her front room, Miriam could hardly wait for Samuel to arrive Wednesday morning. She was afraid of what they might learn about her great-grandfather, but she wouldn't have peace of mind until the truth came out.

When he drove up—only ten minutes early—she hurried out to the car before he could come to the front door.

"I can't tell you how eager I am to go back to the orphans' house," she said, tying on a pale blue scarf as she hurried down the walk.

"I can put the top up if you like," he offered. "It's going to be a hot day."

"It's fine now, as pleasant as we can expect in early July." She opened the car door on the passenger side before Samuel could do it for her and slid in.

"I hope you won't be disappointed," Samuel said, his forehead wrinkled in concern.

"One way or the other, I want to know the truth," she said.

As much as she enjoyed Samuel's company, the trip to Stewartstown seemed to take twice as long this time. Miriam was tempted to ask the question on the mind of every child who has ridden in a car: Are we there yet?

When they arrived at the house, it was still midmorning. The restaurant hadn't opened yet since they specialized in the lunch trade.

Miriam sat in the car for a few moments looking up at the freshly painted white facade of the antebellum house. She could imagine the faces of little orphans peering out the long shuttered windows of the second floor. Did they stand there hoping to see a familiar face coming to take them home? Her eyes grew moist just thinking of the sorrow they had to endure.

Stepping out of the car, she noticed part of a garden patch in the rear of the house. Were the orphans set to work weeding and harvesting produce to keep their numbers fed? Even though the house had been donated, it must have been difficult to feed, clothe, and care for the number of children shown on the cartes de visite.

Did any of them have happy lives after the trauma of losing their parents? Or did the tragedies that brought them to the Stewartstown orphanage blight their adult lives?

"Ready?" Samuel asked coming up beside her and taking her hand in his.

"I hope Johanna doesn't think we're intruding," Miriam said, although she knew nothing would stop her from pursuing her ancestor's connection to the house.

282 | CHESAPEAKE ANTIQUES MYSTERIES

"She seemed like a very nice woman," Samuel said. "Let's tell her what we've learned."

At first Miriam wasn't sure anyone would answer Samuel's soft knock on the front door, but after what seemed like several minutes, Johanna opened it.

"You're the folks who bought the photographs," she said in a welcoming tone. "I'm sorry, but we won't be open for lunch for another hour."

"Actually, we're not here to eat, delicious as your lunches are," Samuel said. "We've learned something interesting about the children on the cartes de visite, and we thought you might like to know."

"Come on in," Johanna said. "I have my niece helping today, so I have a few minutes to spare. I'm teaching her how to set up the tables and wait on people. We've been so busy, I really need the help."

"We'll try not to take up too much of your time," Miriam said, stepping inside with Samuel. "I don't know whether you knew, but this house was an orphanage after the War Between the States. The children in the photographs were orphans."

"We think their pictures were taken to help in trying to find relatives who might care for them," Samuel added.

"Orphans," Johanna said. "That would explain why there were so many."

"I bought some very similar ones from a woman in Maple Landing," Miriam explained. "She knew the background of the photos. Some even had markings on the back."

"Wow!" Johanna said. "Let me call my husband. He'll love knowing this. Gus, come out here!"

"What's up?" A lean balding man with a drooping mustache came into the room drying his hands on a dish towel. "I've gotta keep an eye on the gumbo."

"These people found out the kids in the photographs were orphans," Johanna excitedly told him.

"We checked the background of the house, and apparently it was donated to a minister who used it as an orphanage," Samuel said.

"So that's why someone gave it away. We knew about that but thought maybe it served as a temporary church."

"Or maybe a hospital for wounded soldiers," Johanna said. "I like the idea of children living here much better than the thought of men dying."

"How did you folks get interested in this?" Gus asked, running the towel through his hands in a way that showed his excitement.

"My great-grandfather had the other half of the map we bought from you. We think the little hearts and crosses on it marked places where the orphans came from." Miriam was encouraged by the couple's interest. "We're trying to figure out what he had to do with the children."

"More than that," Samuel said, looking to her for approval before he told them more. When she nodded, he explained her family's belief that her ancestor had been an army deserter.

"This seems to be the one chance I have of clearing his name. Right now, we don't even know where he died or is buried. It would mean a lot to my family to learn the truth, whether it clears his name or not."

"I don't know that we can be much help," Gus said. "You seem to know more about the house than we do. I've been meaning to do some digging into the history of it, but right now running the restaurant takes all our time. In fact, I'll let Johanna show you what we have. I have lobster rolls on the menu today, and my prep work isn't done."

"We don't want to hold you up," Samuel said. "Thank you for your time. And by the way, we've had lunch here twice and each time was well worth the drive from Maple Landing."

"Yes, the food was delicious," Miriam said.

Gus left the dining room smiling, but Johanna looked preoccupied.

"There is a Bible I can show you," she said thoughtfully. "Some letter sheets filled with writing were slipped into the back, but the words are kind of spidery and faint. I've never taken the time to try to read them. I think it belonged to the minister who was given the house. Would you like to see it?"

"Oh, could we?" Miriam asked.

"Come back to the room we use as an office," Johanna said. "I'll bring the Bible down from the attic for you. We haven't known what to do with it. I wanted to donate it to the library, but Gus didn't want to part with it yet. He's always hoped to have time to decipher the writing."

In the crowded office Samuel sat on an old oak chair by a roll-top desk, the cubbyholes stuffed with papers, but Miriam was too nervous to sit in the swivel chair with a leather seat. She paced the small space until Johanna returned with the Bible.

"We put it in a box and stuffed tissue around it," Johanna said, taking it out of the nest of wadded paper. "It was pretty beat up when we found it, but we didn't want it to get any worse."

"Good idea," Samuel said as she put it on a small table in one corner of the office. He pulled his chair close, then moved the second one beside it so Miriam could look at it with him.

"I sent my niece down to the cellar for a jar of the corn relish I canned," Johanna said. "I'd better see if she found it. We'll be opening up for lunch pretty soon. Are you folks okay if I leave you to look through the Bible here?"

"That would be great," Samuel said as Miriam sat and slid the chair close to the large leather-bound Bible.

When Johanna left, they both moved as close as they could to the aged book. The spine was chipped and the cover discolored by age, but the pages inside seemed to have survived the ravages of time.

"It's so much larger than any Bibles we use today," Miriam said. "I guess it's a sign of how important Scripture was to people in those days."

Samuel very carefully turned the front pages, impressed by a series of engravings showing familiar scenes from the Bible.

"Here's a special place for the owner's name," he said. "The Reverend Josiah Daniel Crofton."

"He had lovely penmanship," Miriam said. "That's the name on the house deed, isn't it?"

She was trembling with excitement. Would they finally learn her great-grandfather's connection to the orphanage? She was almost afraid to hope.

"It's a wonderful Bible," Samuel said, "but I suspect what we want to see is at the back."

Being as careful as possible, he turned the book so he could extract a handful of loose sheets.

"Johanna is right. They're not going to be easy to read," he said.

"We have to try while we have the chance. I can't believe they would let us take the pages away from the house. They belong here as part of the history of the orphanage."

With her head close to Samuel's, Miriam struggled to make out the words in ink faded to a light brown. Johanna opened the door after a bit, asking if they needed anything. She thoughtfully brought them tall glasses of iced tea.

"It looks like thirsty work to me," she said. "Is there anything else you need? We'll be opening up soon."

"Thank you so much," Miriam said. "We'll just work on trying to read these pages if it's all right with you."

"I can't wait to find out what you learn," Johanna said. "Take as long as you like."

When she left, Samuel carefully turned to a second page of writing.

"So far it's mostly a list of children and the locations where they were found," Miriam said.

Samuel studied the next page, a whole sheet of paper filled with dense writing. "It's not going to be easy reading."

Between them they read the first few pages, a diary of the founding of the orphanage.

"It wasn't an easy undertaking," Samuel commented.

"He mostly talks about shortages of food and other necessities. Look at the date. Is that January 5, 1866?" Miriam asked.

"That's how I read it."

"Oh my." Miriam was too stunned to speak for a moment.

"Yes, this could be what we're looking for," Samuel said with excitement.

"He talks about a Confederate soldier who gathered up lost and destitute children whose parents were known to be dead," Miriam said. "He calls him Captain Tom."

"Apparently this benefactor managed to bring things to help support the orphanage too. Look, the Reverend Crofton thanks the Lord for the captain's donation of ten pounds of potatoes, a slab of bacon, and three dollars in Yankee coinage. He mentions Confederate money wouldn't buy anything anymore."

Samuel skipped ahead a few pages, and they both scanned the pages for further mention of Captain Tom.

"His support of the orphanage continued," Miriam said, finding it hard to hold back tears.

"This sentence is telling, if I'm reading it right," Samuel said. *"The captain hopes for vindication. His nearest and dearest have fallen prey to the lies of his enemies and no longer receive him in the home that was once his. He fears it is a ploy to steal his land and prays his wife can keep it for the survival of their young ones."*

"That sounds like his own family believed he was a deserter," Miriam said in a troubled tone.

"It also tells us he was innocent. What better way to get possession of his farm than to turn his family and neighbors against him? Whoever was behind it must have thought your great-grandmother wouldn't be able to run the farm herself," Samuel said.

"She did for a while, but it did prove to be too hard for her. Her children were too young to be much help, and so many men didn't return from the war even if she had had the money to hire help." Miriam continued reading, frustrated when words were too faint to decipher.

"Look, this entry is dated August 14, or maybe the 17. Captain Tom brought a sack of apples which were much appreciated, as the orphanage was running low on food and had no surplus to save for the winter."

Samuel paused, afraid the next sentence would distress Miriam.

"What is it?" she asked.

"I think this tells us what happened to your great-grandfather," he said, reading out loud as best he could the hasty scrawl that was unlike the earlier ornate penmanship. "*Our good Samaritan has taken a fever, and I fear for his life.*"

"Is there more?" Miriam asked.

"The next entry is dated about a week later: *On the 24th of August in the year of our Lord 1866, our noble benefactor succumbed to the fever that ravaged his body. His last request was to be buried among the valiant soldiers of the Confederacy, his name to remain forever lost should the stain on his honor cause the removal of his remains from that honorable resting place.*"

"Oh my." Miriam trembled with emotion as the reason for his disappearance struck home.

"He wanted to be buried with an anonymous headstone so his family would never suffer disgrace if he was denied burial in the military cemetery. This doesn't sound like a man who ever betrayed his cause or his fellow soldiers," Samuel concluded.

"That must mean he's buried here in Stewartstown," Miriam said. "We may have walked right past his tombstone. How can we tell which one is his?"

"*It is the great regret of my life that I cannot offer comfort to the family of our Good Samaritan, for I never knew his true name*, the reverend writes." Samuel paused and put his arm around Miriam. "It seems your great-grandfather was a hero after all."

"He spent the remainder of his life caring for abandoned children when everyone believed him to be guilty of desertion." There was a catch in Miriam's voice.

"There's no way we can prove he wasn't a deserter, but the reverend obviously believed he was innocent of the charges," Samuel reasoned.

"And there was a motive for smearing his reputation," Miriam said. "He had valuable farmland. If the community and even his own family believed him to be a dishonorable soldier, it would have been easy to force his wife from the land and buy it for almost nothing."

"I think he found a cause to give meaning to the rest of his life," Samuel said. "He deserves all the honor we can give him today."

"I need to find his grave," Miriam said, standing to leave.

"We'll go back to the cemetery. This time we have the date of his death. It may lead us to his tombstone even if his name isn't on it." Samuel led her out to the dining room where Johanna and a young girl were busily serving platters of food to a crowd.

"Thank you so much!" Miriam said, waylaying Johanna for a brief word. "We have to leave, but we'll come back to the restaurant sometime very soon and tell you everything we've learned."

"I'd like that," Johanna said as she rushed back to the kitchen. "So would Gus."

"You don't want lunch now, do you?" Samuel asked in a tone that told her he knew the answer.

"No, I have to pay my respects on behalf of his family to Captain Thomas Davis. They're much too long overdue. I only hope we can find his final resting place."

Chapter Thirty

I'm still puzzled about the map," Miriam said as they rode the short distance to the cemetery. "Why do you think he tore it in half and hid part of it in the old desk?"

"My guess is he hoped for vindication sometime in the future. The map tied him to the orphanage and the good work he'd done for the children," Samuel said.

"But how did he manage to hide anything in the desk when his wife denied him access to the house?"

"He was a soldier with skills we can only imagine. He wouldn't have had any trouble living rough and keeping an eye on his family from a place of concealment. He probably knew about the secret drawer and used it as a hiding place while his family was away from the house, possibly at church."

"But what about the Confederate money? Surely he knew it was worthless," Miriam said.

"It was all he had to give his family as a sign that he still wanted to help them."

"Yes, that makes sense," Miriam said. "It was a symbolic gesture since he didn't have any other way of helping them. The miracle is that my great-grandmother took the desk with her to Baltimore when she moved."

"It may have been the most valuable piece of furniture she owned," Samuel speculated. "She didn't want to part with everything from her past, so she kept the things that meant the most to her."

"It's so sad she never found the secret drawer. I wonder what she would have made of the things her husband left there," Miriam said.

Samuel parked the car and took her hand as they followed the meandering dirt-and-gravel path that led to the military burials. The sun was a searing orb high in the sky, and there wasn't a whisper of wind to cool them, but Miriam hardly noticed the heat. A solitary woman was watering plants by a tombstone on the far side of the civilian cemetery, but she scarcely noticed her.

"Watch your step," Samuel warned, taking her arm as they left the path and started walking on the uneven grass separating rows of grave markers.

"We looked at all the tombstones the last time we were here," Miriam said. "I wonder how we overlooked an unmarked grave."

"They're all hard to read," Samuel pointed out. "We were looking for the name Davis."

"Now at least we have the date of his death. We'll have to check each one carefully." She bent down to read the markings on a weathered slab, pleased to see a small Confederate flag marking the spot. "Someone still cares enough to honor the fallen soldiers."

She hadn't remembered that so many were buried in the military section, yet they carefully scrutinized every one they passed. Samuel found a small twig and used it to scrape away moss and dirt when the inscriptions were too hard to read.

Time stood still as Miriam anxiously studied each marker, afraid they might not find the one they wanted. The heat was making her feel light-headed, and Samuel commented on how flushed she looked.

"Wouldn't you like to wait in the car? I can put the air-conditioning on and come get you when I find the right stone," he offered.

"No, thank you. I have to look myself."

"I understand," he murmured, taking her hand in his as they continued their search.

Knowing the date of her great-grandfather's death helped them eliminate all the wrong sites, but it was still a tedious process to make out the marking on the stones. Samuel looked as red-faced as she felt by the time they reached the furthermost row.

"If he's not here, we'll never find him," Miriam said. "Maybe someone learned a deserter had been buried with the honorable dead. His body could've been moved ages ago."

"I don't think the reverend would've let that happen, not after all he did for the orphans," Samuel assured her.

The next two markers they checked clearly belonged to others, one a Smithson and one a Grover. The third in the row was mossy and difficult to make out, but Samuel carefully scraped until the date was revealed.

Miriam held her breath in anticipation as he read the inscription out loud: 24 August 1866.

"It's a match," she said.

"There's a name above the date. Let me see if I can make it legible." He stooped beside the stone and carefully cleaned the incised lettering.

"It's not unmarked," he said with awe.

Miriam knelt down beside him and read out loud: "*The Good Samaritan.*"

"The reverend kept his word and didn't reveal his identity," Samuel said.

"But he honored him just the same." Tears welled up in her eyes.

Samuel put his arm around her shoulders. "What do you want to do? Add his name to the inscription?"

"No, I think I'll respect his own wish to remain an unknown soldier. What greater tribute is there than to credit him for the goodness he did for helpless orphans? The important thing is that my family will know he was unjustly accused, and that he spent the little remaining time he had helping children. I think they'll be very pleased. Thank you so much for helping me find him, Samuel. I can't tell you how much it means to me."

"The time I've spent with you has been the happiest I've known in years," he said, helping her to stand.

"I feel the same way. It wasn't just about my ancestor, was it? Captain Tom has a second chance at vindication, and we have a second chance ourselves."

"Those are the sweetest words I've ever heard," Samuel said, cupping her chin and lightly kissing her. "We do make good partners, don't we, Holmes?"

"We certainly do, Watson." She smiled up at him and touched his cheek. "You're as hot as I am in this sun. I think I'm ready to leave, but I would like to find a flower shop and buy a wreath. It's never too late to leave a token of love and respect."

"It certainly isn't too late for love," he said, taking her hand and leading her away from the venerable gravestones.

"No, it certainly isn't," she agreed, bringing his hand to her lips and gently kissing his fingers.

About the Authors

Pam Hanson and Barbara Andrews are a daughter-mother writing team. They have had more than forty books published together, including many for Guideposts. Pam's background is in journalism, and she previously taught at the university level. She and her husband, also a college professor, have two sons. Pam writes about family and faith at http://pamshanson.blogspot.com. Prior to their partnership, Barbara had more than twenty of her own novels published. She began her career by writing Sunday school stories and was a longtime contributor to antiques publications. She makes her home with Pam and her family in Nebraska.

A Note from the Editors

We hope you enjoy *Chesapeake Antiques Mysteries*, created by the Books and Inspirational Media Division of Guideposts, a nonprofit organization that touches millions of lives every day through products and services that inspire, encourage, help you grow in your faith, and celebrate God's love in every aspect of your daily life.

Thank you for making a difference with your purchase of this book, which helps fund our many outreach programs to military personnel, prisons, hospitals, nursing homes, and educational institutions. To learn more, visit GuidepostsFoundation.org.

We also maintain many useful and uplifting online resources. Visit Guideposts.org to read true stories of hope and inspiration, access OurPrayer network, sign up for free newsletters, download free e-books, join our Facebook community, and follow our stimulating blogs.

To learn about other Guideposts publications, including the best-selling devotional *Daily Guideposts*, go to ShopGuideposts.org, call (800) 932-2145, or write to Guideposts, PO Box 5815, Harlan, Iowa 51593.